Rising Son
Reflections of a Chinese Gentleman Warrior

Author: Janita Lo
Collaborating Writer: Randy Schultz

Copyright © 2009 by Janita Lo
Registration with US Library of Congress Copyright No.: TXU00158787178 / 2008-09-15
Registration with US Library of Congress Control No.: 2011904464

ISBN-10: No. 0615426042
ISBN-13: No. 978-0615426044

Book Cover Design by Helen H. Harrison

Printed in the United States of America
Distributed by Amazon.com and Kindle E books

This story is dedicated to my courageous father, Khan Ling, and my gracious mother, Chow Che Yu

Theirs was the life for which they were destined to live. Together, they experienced nearly unparalleled danger, adversity, passion and betrayal during war and peace times. Blessed at birth with wealth and all of its advantages, my parents faced a point in their lives when they were grateful to just have clothes on their backs. As extraordinary people do, they endured, facing adversity with courage and tenacity.

My parents were the rock and foundation of our rearing. As children, we were influenced by how they nobly coped with their unique daily circumstances, so often tense and dangerous. Their ideals, high moral and ethics standards, and compassion for others seeped into our very souls. We never forgot and feel blessed to be the receivers of such important life lessons…work hard, be forgiving and greet the day with cheerful thoughts, no matter what.

Thank you papa and mama. What you taught me was "my" inspiration to tell "your" story.

Your loving daughter,

Four Treasures,
Khan Ching (Janita Lo)

Acknowledgments

To Irene Tang: Thank you for your assistance on my first draft.

To my best friend, Nita Richards: Thank you for your advice and encouragement to write this manuscript. The wine and food stains on the pages remind me of your endless labor of love in editing my second draft.

To Helen Harrison: Thank you for your exquisite book cover design, you have expressed the essence of my story telling. Brilliant!

Janita.

Table of Contents

Rising Son

Reflections of a Chinese Gentleman Warrior

Prologue

Momentous change, through the eyes of history, often sweeps across the landscape on the wings of epic battles and dramatic episodes of heroism or treachery. We etch in perpetuity the names of business titans, wartime generals and shrewd political manipulators who literally willed themselves to succeed or to at least persevere against prohibitive challenges. Many times, however, the paths to historical transition are conjoined by the scattered debris of events unfolding on a more modest level and by individuals whose only choice is to react at a propitious time to dire circumstances or unintended opportunities.

So it was with 20th century China – especially the years between 1909 and 1949 – when the tumultuousness of the times opened the way for a sleeping giant to yawn and stretch its extraordinary limbs. A combination of events, some visceral and chaotic, most of them subtle and methodical, set the arduous process of reshaping in motion. To this day, this colossal Asian power continues to evolve in multiple ways that resonate the world over. China has always been, however, a land steeped in ancient traditions. Consequently, change has come in measured, sometimes painful steps.

Keeping pace with these transformations, the Khan family felt the country's pull of colliding cultures, competing values and ambivalent dreams as acutely as any of its billion citizens. The family's aristocratic background and life of privilege were closely intertwined with the upheavals of the period. China's turmoil became the Khans' turmoil, specifically as seen through the looking glass that was Khan Ling…gentleman, adventurer, husband, father and provocateur.

Though he had come shaking and bawling out of his mother's womb only two years earlier, Khan Ling was as much shaped by the events of 1912 as those who were much older and incontestably more jaded. It was then that the Republic of China, led by Sun

Yat-sen's Chinese Nationalist Party army, overturned the Ch'ing Dynasty, which traced its beginnings to 1644. Puyi, the last Emperor, had fled to the Northern China border under the protective guidance of Imperial Japan's authority.

In atmospheres of this nature, children are forced to grow up quickly. For all practical purposes, though, Ling was like most other infants of his time…or any other time. He cried when he was hungry or when he soiled his pants. He jerked and formed a toothless smile if a finger prodded him or moved hypnotically across his sight line. But it was conjectured, even then, that he possessed an intensity that could light up a room. Most might write this off to the hyperbolic ramblings of proud parents, but for his uncanny ability to sense the significance of any given moment. It was that trait, and his sheer daring, that set him apart in ways that even outsiders could acknowledge.

It was quite common, for instance, for Ling's parents or even their ancient housekeeper to observe Ling trying to extricate himself from the confines of his crib at an extremely early age. And in late summer of 1911, on the very day of the railway uprising in Szechwan that presaged the revolution, Ling actually wandered off for several hours. The family joke at the time was that little Ling had left momentarily to summon the revolutionary forces. How prophetic it seemed years later. Even the stoic Buddhist monks allowed themselves a heightened sense of joy during those times of his youth when he frequented the temple grounds. And the night of his birth there in the temple at the Purple Golden Mountain – well, suffice to say that it was peculiar in a most profound way.

To fully understand Khan Ling, or at least to understand him as best one could, some knowledge of the Sino-Japanese relationship might prove enlightening. Japan had been China's ally for years while the Ch'ing Dynasty was a flourishing empire. During this civil war, Japan seized the opportunity to aid the Ch'ing's dethroned emperor as a guise for conquering several of China's strategic northern cities. This was to be the first of many incursions by the Japanese in their thirst for China's vast resources, a powerful enticement that would influence Japan's foreign policy and master plan of empire building for years to come. In some ways, it was both China's death knell and its seed for dramatic rebirth.

As the son of a Chinese father and a Japanese mother, Khan Ling must have somehow known, even as a young child, that a powerful role in this conflict would be thrust upon him. It was not so much his birthright, but a calling card of sorts…to a complex game in which his dynamic persona would help gain entrance, and the art of nuance would prove to be his most formidable weapon.

-------- O -------

Chapter One
My political destiny began

I am Khan Ling, son of Khan Bei, a descendent of Genghis Khan; the only heir of my grandfather, Khan Gong Shun, a Royal Army Commander of the Ch'ing Dynasty, and my grandmother Princess May Szee, granddaughter of Emperor Xianfeng, whose wife was empress CIXi; Princess May Szee was the niece of Emperor Quangxu who ruled the great China from 1875 through 1908. But these are merely the particulars of my lineage. It is not so much the people, but rather the circumstances and my critical choices that made me who I am today

The simple facts are these: after I graduated from Waseda University in Tokyo, Japan, I returned to China and married my fiancée, Chow Che Yu. It was 1932, and I was 22 years of age with a degree in electrical engineering. More importantly, I felt that I was wise beyond my years. My upbringing was, by many measures, a comfortable existence, but one tempered by many family upheavals and twists of fortune. What I soon learned, however, was that wisdom was not merely measured by experience and circumstances, but by innate curiosity and, yes, an utter sense of desperation. And that is why I am who I am today.

This wasn't a truth visited upon me with hubris or fanfare. Rather it was a slowly evolving realization acknowledged by way of a long, circuitous journey. There's really no one place to begin…no defining moment from which to draw strength or enlightenment. The threads of my character and my belief system took shape from my ancestors and, like a rock smoothed and polished over time by the rippling brook, these traits were honed through every period of my life.

That's why, when my father-in-law, Mr. Chow, insisted that my new bride and I stay in his family estate until the civil war in China calmed down, we made our first home together there in Nanjing. Located along the scenic waterfront of the Yangtze River in southeast Jiangsu Province, Nanjing was just the type of prosperous city that could nicely enhance a professional business career. My considerable connections and my degree in electrical engineering helped me to land a position as Chief of Staff of a local radio broadcasting station. Though it was quite rare for the local Chinese of the area to attend college, I'm sure that my connections held the more influence of these two job attributes.

Within two years, I used that influence and a portion of an inheritance left by my late father to purchase the broadcasting station. I somehow knew that the smoothing and polishing was to take on a new, mysterious sheen.

I loved to design and improve the radio equipment at the station, which reported the local and national news for our listeners. We had hired several program coordinators to schedule interesting programs in addition to the news, and we had developed an eclectic mix of Chinese folk songs, popular music, Chinese opera, Western tunes and singers as well as storytellers, poetry readings and music recitals. The station was very successful and seemed to please the listening audience. On occasion, we would even receive a complimentary letter, so I felt that, if nothing else, we were noticed.

My father-in-law, whom I called Chow Papa, was a wealthy and influential man. Besides his many other endeavors, he served as chairman of the Nanjing Chamber of Commerce. It was he who introduced me to Chiang Kai-shek, commander of the Kuomintang (KMT), the National Revolutionary Army.

Several weeks before that initial meeting, my father-in-law met with me at my office one night. He quietly locked the door, then pulled a wooden chair next to my desk and spoke to me in a serious manner.

"Ling, your grandfather was a commander serving the Ch'ing emperor Quangxu, your father was a crusader and involved with Sun Yat-sen in the overthrow of the corrupt dynasty and the forming of the new Republic of China. It is in your blood that you are destined to be a leader in the military and political arena."

He paused ever so briefly to gauge my interest, then continued.

"With your electrical engineering background, you could be an asset to Chiang Kai-shek's army. I have been meeting secretly with Chiang for months and I know he could use a man like you in his organization. Though I know you are probably aware of the situation in general terms, let me bring you up to date."

Chow Papa proceeded to touch upon the Revolution's history, from Sun Yat-sen's early leadership role, to the abdication of the five-year-old emperor Puyi in 1911, through the establishment of the Kuomintang National People's Party by Sun Yat-sen and Chiang Kai-shek. They were facts that I already knew quite well, but I politely allowed Chow Papa to elaborate.

"You know," he said, moving in closer, "that Sun Yat-sen hoped for a political solution that would ultimately culminate with a transition to democracy. But he also invited Mao Tse-tung to join a united front against the belligerent warlords, with help from Soviet Russia. When Chiang succeeded Sun, he became increasingly concerned about Mao's growing Marxist leanings. They went their separate ways and Mao started to recruit farmers and peasants for his Communist party. Many, it was rumored, were forced into allegiance. Others were willingly swayed by Mao's dogmatic preaching."

"And it is quite impressive rhetoric, coming from a man who was an assistant librarian at Beijing University and never earned a college degree," I interjected, hoping to demonstrate my knowledge of Mao and of the circumstances surrounding his rise to prominence. "He is still, in many ways, a peasant…though a very influential one. And with the base he has built in Jiangxi, along with his modest but effective army, I can see where he might be a concern for Chiang Kai-shek."

"Yes, Chiang now finds himself opposing Mao's guerilla warfare and the many soviet areas he has been creating under Communist control. At the same time, Chiang is also fighting a battle to curb the voracious expansionist policies of the Japanese. Now fighting two enemies of equal will and persistence, he is spread dangerously thin.

"Ling, this is your opportunity to serve your country, especially with your Japanese background, your command of the Japanese language and your many contacts there. We could set up a meeting for you with Chiang Kai-shek. At least listen to him. See what he has in mind for a patriotic contribution."

That night I went home and pored through numerous volumes of Chinese history, from books that had been gathering dust on the shelves for longer than I cared to admit. Clearly, Chiang Kai-shek was a man of consequence. When Sun had died in 1925, Chiang had ably replaced him with boldness and a singular determination. His bid to unify the country with his Northern Expedition in 1928 had certainly showcased his leadership skills. And now he was in need of a person such as me?

One week later, I met Chiang Kai-shek for the first time at his headquarters. He was slightly built, much smaller in physical stature than his reputation. He invited me to sit down while he sipped hot tea from a blue and white porcelain teacup. I declined his gracious offer to share the tea since I feared a shaky cup would betray my sudden case of nerves.

As I watched him curiously, it was difficult to reconcile this man as the same one who had shot and killed Tao Chengzhang, leader of the Restoration Society, at point-blank range as Tao lay dying in a Shanghai French Concession hospital. But that was more than 20 years ago, and the slaying had actually been one of the many steps leading to Chiang's ascension to power and the emergence of the Kuomintang.

Chiang could be an engaging man and he also showed a keen interest in my own life experiences. Clearly, he viewed them as assets for his own strategic plans. He gave me a hint as to what those plans were.

"After Japan invaded Manchuria in 1931 and I resigned as chairman of the national government, I adopted a slogan," he told me. "First internal pacification, then external resistance. It means that first we will attempt to defeat the Communists before engaging the Japanese. But the advance on Shanghai and the chaos in Nanjing several years ago have disrupted my plans and changed some of the timing."

Chiang subtly changed his posture and exuded an almost avuncular warmth.

"Your father-in-law speaks so highly of you. And I have done my own review of your considerable talents and your distinguished family. There is a place within our group for someone of your caliber."

I met several times with Chiang over the next few months. When we spoke, Chiang often led the conversation to my own ambitions, as well as to his plans for the future of China. One particular evening, he came to dine with Chow Papa and me. Dinner was served in Chow Papa's study after one of my father-in-law's trusted bodyguards led Chiang and his two aides secretly through the back door that faced the Yangtze River. Steaming dishes were passed discreetly through a small window between the study and the large courtyard of the elegant walled compound, while inside we discussed matters of state that left me numb with exhilaration as well as a keen sense of apprehension. When the conversation turned to my possible involvement, I mentioned my commitments as a newlywed, but Chiang's flattery had clearly made an impression.

Finally, he offered me special training at the esteemed Whampoa Military Academy on the outskirts of Nanjing. I could attend for certain periods of time during the week, and still maintain my business at the broadcast station. In fact, that was vital to the success of the mission for which they would train me...to become Chiang's eyes and ears for the growing threat of the Japanese movement. On weekends, I would be entirely free to spend time with my family.

After finishing the red bean rice cake for dessert and taking his final sip of tea, Chiang rose with his aides and bowed to Chow Papa. When Chiang turned to me, I saluted him for the first time, crisply and purposefully, and he returned the same. The three men left through the back entrance and vanished behind the wooden gate.

Soon I joined Chiang Kai-shek's party and my radio station became a cover-up business, enabling radio operators from Chiang's party to eavesdrop on the Japanese. Learning to decode the messages between the Japanese Navy and Army, I became a double agent, spying on the Japanese movement. For outward appearances, I became friends of the most influential Japanese officials and businessmen with whom I ostensibly shared many confidentialities. At the same time, I became highly adept in my artillery training. I found that it was something quite suitable to my physical traits and personality.

Some nights I would spend at home with my wife, while at other times I shared quarters in a military barracks constructed of concrete blocks and devoid of adequate heating. The academy was built into the side of a small hill, with concrete walls and barbed wire fences surrounding the compound.

Clearly, my use to Chiang Kai-shek was in the area of communications. We utilized German-made Telefunken portable radio transceivers to talk to pilots flying overhead. Many German officers served as advisors for our training and, in addition to the vacuum tubes, transmitters and radio relay systems, most of the guns and artillery also came from Germany.

My task was to assist the German advisors with the maintenance of the transceivers. With my engineering knowledge, I could take apart the equipment and test the components with considerable skill. Often within several hours, I was able to locate the problem and put the equipment back into working order. Though the transceivers were large and heavy, they were the most highly developed communications equipment of their kind for military use. So all of the officers, including General Chiang Kai-shek and his assistant, General Lee, were astonished at my ability to maintain and repair these complex electronics systems. Soon after, the Germans left and I was entrusted to work with the transceivers on my own.

General Lee, a hard-crusted military man with a funny lisp, but a war record that commanded respect, gave me my first assignment...to design a transceiver similar to that of the Germans. My new transceiver design proceeded at a surprisingly rapid pace, especially with the help of parts purchased from the United States. I used a small, unobtrusive assembly building near my radio station in Nanjing to secretly develop the unit. Multiple tests proved successful, and Chiang's headquarters approved the prototype and entrusted me from then on to travel to Hong Kong to purchase the necessary U.S. parts.

Sixty people were put under my command, and we upgraded the research lab with the proper machine shop tools. By the time I had selected trained technicians to build the metal casing for the transceivers, I felt like we had some semblance of a legitimate research facility. Though small in size, its mission was enormous.

The broadcasting company was flourishing at this point. I had added Japanese staff for programs such as Japanese popular music, comedy shows and national news. I wined and dined the Japanese high officials and became their good friend, laughing at their jokes and regaling them with stories of my own, often wildly exaggerated or even manufactured out of whole cloth. Even though, on the surface, Japan claimed to be China's beneficent ally, we all knew there would be war between our countries soon. During this period, the Japanese never suspected my mission of providing crucial military information to Chiang's headquarters.

Chapter Two
Rendezvous with Japanese Admiral

My first official assignment came in late spring, 1937. Japanese Admiral Hiro Saka had requested my presence at a meeting between Japanese and Republic of China envoys. The Admiral had been a university professor of mine. Chiang Kai-shek selected Mr. Dao Chang, the Minister of Foreign Affairs and a graduate of Yale University in America, to accompany me. I would serve in the role as his interpreter.

As the first-born of the Chow brood, Che Yu helped her father to manage the family estate. Often, she also assisted him with his many business holdings, including several blocks of prime real estate, a bank, hotel, jewelry shop and other investment interests. So when I received out-of-town assignments, I never had to worry about her becoming the lonely, pining wife. Not only was she completely capable and self-sufficient, but at the time we lived in her father's estate, so she would have her parents, siblings and many other relatives to keep her company.

I broke the news about my first assignment to Che Yu the day I received the order from headquarters.

"Will you be gone long? Are you going to Tianjin City?" she asked. "I heard that the dethroned Emperor is hiding out with the Japanese government somewhere around the northern city."

I tried to be as candid as possible with her.

"Che Yu, this is top secret. You are not to tell anyone, not even your parents. I am leaving first thing in the morning. I can't tell you where we are going to meet. If anyone asks about me, just say that I have some important meetings in a nearby city for a couple of days. Be sure to pray to our goddess of mercy, Quan Yin, to protect me. I shall return as soon as the mission is completed. And remember…not a word!"

I had difficulty sleeping the night before I left. My mind wandered back to Admiral Saka and our time at the university together. There was also no containing my curiosity about the former emperor and my excitement at the possibility of seeing him. Though Puyi had only been a child when he relinquished his throne, much had been written and discussed about him. Though he now was disparaged for his lavish, hedonistic ways, he still tweaked the imagination of Chinese citizens.

As the grand-nephew of the Empress Dowager Cixi, the de facto ruler of China for many years, he had unwittingly played a key role in Cixi's palace connivances. In fact, his ascension to power at three years of age had been orchestrated by Cixi in order to keep her overly ambitious son from taking power.

Cixi's chaotic, manipulative rule actually had opened the door to Japanese adventurism. While she held power, the second Opium War and the Taiping rebellion helped to grind away at the Ch'ing Empire, bit by bit. Internal palace squabbles at the time kept her from taking an effective stand against encroachment from the West as well as from the Japanese. In fact, as the Chinese navy battled the Japanese in the Sino-Japanese War, she appropriated much of the military fund to restore the Summer Palace where she held lavish parties in which 150 different food dishes were served. And with so much rampant corruption at the regional levels, there were plenty of opportunities for clandestine deals to be brokered and spoils to be divided without concern for provincial boundaries or protocol. When Cixi died amid her 3,000 ebony boxes of personal jewels and other trappings of luxury, the inexorable Japanese influence had already become too ensconced to be turned back with a simple change of leaders.

Finally, sometime after 2 a.m., I fell asleep. It would be the only satisfying sleep I would have for awhile.

Minister Dao Chang and I took five bodyguards with us on the journey, along with the two pilots. I wasn't sure if the bodyguards made me feel safer or gave me a greater sense of dread. It took nearly eight hours to fly to our destination, and it seemed as if our pilot looked relentlessly for every cloud pocket he could find. By the time we landed just in time for our late afternoon meeting, I had lost much of my apprehension and nearly all of my enthusiasm. As our small plane landed on the makeshift runway on a remote mountainside along the border between Russia and China, several Jeeps with blindingly bright headlights approached us at full beam, even though it was still late afternoon.

Our entourage was escorted over the road's rough terrain, the strong desert wind blowing coarse sand into our faces. I tried to close my eyes and lips tightly, but still felt the gritty taste of the granules in my mouth. They dried my gums and made me long for a simple glass of water.

Absolute darkness surrounded us when we finally arrived at the camp, about two hours late for our meeting. We could see silhouettes of tents set up in the distance, and what seemed like hundreds of Japanese soldiers with weapons on their shoulders lined each side to create a path for us to pass. At the end of the walkway stood a glowing tent with additional guards standing watch around the entrance.

The Japanese captain leading us stopped, then exclaimed loudly, "Only the Minister and Mr. Khan are permitted to go into the Admiral's quarters. The rest of you, stay out here!"

Kerosene lamps lighted the inside of the tent, where a white cotton tablecloth draped a table in the middle of the room. Nearby, Japanese flags and their Imperial Emperor's photographs hung on the canvas wall. Standing at attention around the room, at least 20 bodyguards all carried pistols and guns with sharp metal blade tips.

Admiral Hiro Saka sat ramrod straight in a camp chair. He was an unusually tall man with sharp, black eyes that almost seemed to pierce one's soul. He reached out his hand, and the minister and I both bowed lowly toward him.

"I hope your journey was not too uncomfortable. Thank you for coming, Minister," he said.

Then he looked at me.

"Ling, it is good to see you again! I see that you have changed your business name to Khan Chi Yuen. This shows your ambition to be a great man. Major Khan, I like the name; it fits you. I noticed the change in the telegraph from your headquarters."

Minister Dao Chang and I both responded with a smile. I answered the Admiral in Japanese.

"Oaidekite Kouei desu, Admiral Hiro Saka san. It is good to see you after all these years."

The Admiral offered us sake in a small tin cup. I took a sip; it tasted sweet and refreshing after the long journey. At that very moment, Puyi, the puppet Emperor of the Ch'ing Dynasty, entered the room. Attired in a white western suit with an open shirt, he wore a straw hat that shadowed part of his face. Wire-framed spectacles seemed to emphasize his thin, frail appearance. A cigarette dangled from his stained, yellow fingers, and he blew the cigarette smoke right in front of us without any respect or courtesy, enveloping our faces with its strong odor and permeating the small tent. We were invited to sit across the table.

"Let me share with you why I called this meeting," began the Admiral.

"As you know, since the fall of the Ch'ing Dynasty in Beijing, Puyi has been under our protection. China has been an empire for thousands of years. Without your Emperor, China would lose its identity.

"As for now, Japan has already secured a few major cities and a few provinces in the North. We recognize that Chiang Kai-shek controls the majority of southern China. Puyi and our Imperial Emperor of Japan have agreed that we would be amenable to dividing China into two parts. Japan would control and administer the northern part with Beijing as the capital, and Puyi would still serve as Emperor of northern China under Japan's authority. Chiang Kai-shek could take over the full administration of southern China, which would become The Republic of China.

"I know this is all a bit broad in its terms, but you are a smart man. I am sure you understand the full implications. We hope you will bring this proposal to your chief commander. Of course, with his interest, we will develop a more detailed proposal outlining the division points, establishing mutual security measures and creating a plan that is satisfactory to all."

I translated what the Admiral had said, to Minister Dao Chang in Chinese, ending with my own opinion that this proposal was not acceptable and we should reject his offer. This was far from normal procedure for a translator, but I felt emboldened by my relationship with Admiral Saka.

My belief, made clear to the Minister, was that Chiang Kai-shek was in no mood for compromise of this sort. He already felt betrayed by two of his own…not only Mao, but also Wang Jingwei, a former ally who had been making overtures to the Japanese. It was suspected that Wang was positioning himself to lead one of several puppet governments that might be set up by Japan as they grabbed more Chinese territory. Like Mao, Wang was a leftist who could not be trusted.

In addition, Chiang's capture and arrest by forces loyal to Mao in December of the previous year had created even more complexities. Though Chiang's release was negotiated two weeks later, he had been coaxed to enter into an agreement establishing a united front against Japan. While no one doubted the enmity still felt by Chiang toward Mao, his mission was not so clear-cut anymore. At least publicly, Chiang had now made defeat of the Japanese, rather than suppression of the Communist movement, his main priority. Apparently Chiang's mantra of, "The Japanese are a disease of the skin; the Communists are a disease of the heart," had been trumped by political expediency.

The Admiral drank more sake while I continued translating his message and offering my unsolicited opinion. When I finished, the Minister and I both stood up at the same time. Mr. Dao declared, "This is preposterous! We will never agree to such a proposal! China is ours! This meeting is over!"

A deadening silence filled the room. Even I was surprised by the Minister's directness. Sensing the tenor of the conversation without the need for translation, the admiral slammed his hand on the table so violently that the flower vase tumbled over, spilling the water and soaking the white tablecloth. The clanking of the tin cups and porcelain teacups made a frightening sound.

The Admiral's blood rushed into his face. I could see the veins straining in his neck.

"I am sorry. This offer is not an acceptable starting point," I said as evenly and calmly as possible.

Admiral Saka sent the table flying across the room. He seemed like a roaring lion ready to devour his prey. The bodyguards immediately pointed their guns at the Minister and me.

The admiral yelled, "Get out, you pigs! Everyone get out of my sight! Puyi, you need to leave also!"

His face turning to the side, without looking at me, he added, "Ling, (he still called me by my family given name), you stay. You alone stay here!"

Everyone left quietly, one by one. The room suddenly was empty, filled with a chilling air. The Admiral composed himself and picked up one of the fallen chairs. He placed it next to his own chair.

"Sit down, Ling. What has happened to you? You were one of my best students with a promising future at the university. I know your grandfather was an Imperial Commander, and your grandmother was a Princess and close relative of Emperor Quangxu. You have the royal bloodline from the Ch'ing Dynasty and are half Japanese from your mother's side. Why are you siding with the Republic of China? Their leaders are commoners…not like you."

The admiral's eyes turned soft and gentle, with a caring expression on his face.

"Between you and me, you are also much brighter and stronger than Puyi, who is merely a weak puppet looking for someone to take care of him so that he can be a playboy."

He picked up his sake bottle and emptied the few drops that were left from the spillage into his mouth. He paused a moment, then continued.

"Ling, you share our Japanese blood. I encourage you to join us in building an empire in the North, and you may one day yourself be enthroned in the Palace with our support."

I pondered my next words carefully, then looked the admiral straight in the eyes and said, "Thank you for your confidence in me, Honorable Admiral Hiro Saka. But I am Chinese. I will never betray my country. I know this means I may not be leaving here alive today, but I beseech your understanding. My life and that of my companion, Minister Dao Chang, are in your hands tonight."

"Is that all you have to say to me?" blurted out the exasperated Admiral. "That is the only residue of our time together?"

I knew what I had just told him could jeopardize our lives, but speaking the truth brought a strange, soothing peace to my heart. And I recognized that, even though Japan was my enemy, Admiral Hiro Saka was different. We had a special relationship during my years in his country. A friendship that could perhaps still save me.

I spoke out, "No sir, your honor. Can I please tell you the truth? China is going to win the war. Japan eventually has to surrender. It would be my humble advice, if I may, to suggest that your country retreat from

China now before more blood is shed and the elixirs of power begin to taint even those with good intent. I know you. You do not believe in this Puyi any more than I do. Let him know that Japan no longer supports the decayed and corrupted dynasty."

The admiral sighed a deep breath, then spoke quietly.

"Ling, I admire your courage; that's why I like you so much. To tell you the truth, between you and me, I agree with some aspects of what you are saying. I think Japan's war with the Republic of China will be long and drawn out, with losers on both sides. But, I am under the orders of our Imperial Emperor. I cannot dishonor his proposal and must stay here until further orders arrive."

He studied me closely, without saying a word for 10 or 15 seconds. I never blinked.

"All right, you and the Minister may go in peace. Some day we will meet again, hopefully in better circumstances."

After we shook hands, Admiral Saka took a ring off his finger and slipped it into my hand. Bright gold, it featured an Imperial Navy seal with his name engraved on it.

"This is going to be a bloody war," Saka said. "If our Japanese troops ever capture you, send this ring and a note by messenger to the Navy headquarters. Be assured that I will try my best to help you. But as you know, our Navy and Army are not on the best of terms these days. Now here, I bid you farewell. Fate will determine our future, and I hope that you still have your head on your neck the next time I see you."

I walked out of the tent, and the Admiral commanded the soldiers to let us go. The Minister and I walked through the same path with soldiers standing on each side, only this time their weapons were thankfully at rest.

Without looking back, we hopped into the Jeeps and wasted no time departing. There was complete silence except for the hum of the Jeeps' engines and the crackling sound of the gravel under the tires.

I could still feel the after-taste of the sake. It reminded me of the summers I spent in Professor Hiro Saka's home. Since he and his wife had no children, I was like their son and they taught me many Japanese customs.

My mother, a medical doctor working in Kyoto, was Japanese and her father was a good friend of Professor Saka's. She would ride the train to visit me and stay as a guest in Professor Saka's house. We would drink sake and sing folk songs in their small, pristine Bonsai garden. Mrs. Saka taught me the rituals of the tea ceremony and the Japanese protocol when attending important events.

I remembered how self-important I felt when I related to the Sakas a story once told to me by my father about Chinese tea drinking customs. It involved an emperor who long ago wanted to disguise himself as a wood artisan to see how the commoners lived. One time, in a teahouse, he poured himself a cup of tea, then poured another for his bodyguard. It was, of course, the highest honor if the emperor served tea to someone. The bodyguard couldn't reveal his master's identity, so he subtly bent his finger on the table to signify his gratitude to the emperor. Thus, I told the Sakas, it became a Chinese custom to bend the finger and knock on the table as a way of paying thanks to the person pouring the tea.

The Sakas smiled genuinely when I had completed my story. It felt good to be treated as a person with something interesting to say.

Admiral Saka had his own engaging tales about the nuances of the tea ceremony and, on several occasions, took me to formal teahouses. Whenever my mother came to visit, he would offer stories of even greater depth and keep us spellbound for hours with his knowledge of peculiar local customs and his well-formulated theories on current events.

Those were happy days, which seemed just like yesterday.

Yet today it had nearly been necessary to ask clemency for my life, from this man who had shown me the many things that make life worth living.

For the next few hours, I was lost in thought. While Minister Tao still appeared slightly panicked, I was immunized from any feeling at all.

"Here we are. I am glad the plane is still here waiting for us!" said Minister Dao much later, breaking the silence after the journey back to the airstrip following the dramatic confrontation at the meeting site. The pilot saw the Jeeps approaching and started the engine. The Minister and I, followed by our entourage, quickly climbed into the plane and took off down the runway. It would be good to lift back into the sky, away from the quarrelsome day that had taken some frightening turns.

As we settled into our seats in the small plane, Minister Tao gave a sigh of relief and took out a small bottle of whisky. We celebrated with a modest toast and drank up once we were airborne. Hot towels were handed to us to wipe off our dust. As Minister Tao rubbed his face with the steaming towel, he turned to me.

"Major Khan Chi Yuen, how did you do it? I thought we were all going to be shot and never see our families again. Can you imagine how I felt in those excruciating moments waiting outside the tent?"

I briefed him on what had happened inside with Admiral Hiro Saka, telling him about everything except the ring he had given to me.

"Yes, we are very lucky to be alive," the Minister said, already feeling the effects of the whisky. "Our commander would not have agreed to such a proposal. We did the right thing. You were very brave, Major Khan Chi Yuen."

Perhaps. Perhaps not. I didn't feel particularly brave at that time. Only very lucky.

The plane flew through the ebony clouds of the night. The engine's deep rumbling sound lulled the minister to sleep after awhile. I also closed my eyes, but my mind drifted back to the past, to the treasured moments and to a critical time that made me who I am today.

Chapter Three
Wedding

Upon my return from Japan after graduating from Waseda University in 1932, I eagerly entered into my marriage with Chow Che Yu, who had been my childhood sweetheart.

The wedding was one of the biggest events in Nanjing. At least 600 guests were invited to the wedding feast held in an ornate hotel ballroom. Mr. Chow agreed to our request for a western-style wedding ceremony, but it would be followed by a traditional Chinese wedding feast.

Che Yu's wedding gown was intricately designed with French lace and white silk organza, studded with pearls around the bodice and waistline. She changed her hairstyle to reflect the latest western hair perm featuring dramatic curly waves. Her veil was a soft silk organza sprinkled with tiny pearls, and fresh white gardenia blossoms circled her head.

I wore a formal black tuxedo with tails, highlighted with a gray and white striped bow tie and a gray silk vest. Everyone said we were a stunning couple.

Gifts towered on the tables in the reception hall foyer. Setting the tone for the magnificent banquet were the serving pieces for the bride and groom at the head table. Gifts from the Ch'ing Emperor to my grandparents, this exquisite pair of solid jade chopsticks had delicate silver tips and rich carvings of a dragon on one and a phoenix on the other. The groom's rice bowl was carved from rose quartz, the bride's from elegant jade. Silver embellishments laced the outside of both bowls. The chopsticks and rice bowls had been used for my grandfather's wedding at the Royal Palace when he married Princess May Szee.

The royal family believed that the silver tips on the chopsticks could test for poison in the food. If the silver turned dark, poison was present. In the Royal Palace, food tasters digested the food before it was served to the Emperor and the Empress, so the silver tips were more decorative than functional. That was fine with me because I didn't anticipate anything more harmful than perhaps an overcooked chicken.

Even those fears were unfounded as guests raved for months about the scrumptious feast. The first course offered six appetizers: thinly sliced white jade pork rings and five-spice roast beef, thousand-year-old eggs with threaded ginger, honey-coated fried walnuts with crispy Shanghai egg rolls, thin threads of jellyfish marinated with rice vinegar, sesame oil and cilantro, and lastly, the drunken chicken.

The hot dishes began with sautéed Shanghai crystal river shrimp, Portobello mushrooms and bamboo heart linings, followed by abalone in oyster sauce with asparagus tips, seared scallops with garlic sauce, roast pork, pork ribs and sautéed lamb strips accented with green scallions.

During the serving of the shark's fin soup, my bride and I circulated among the tables and greeted guests. Champagne was served at this point for toasting. The two chambermaids carried two silver trays, on which the guests placed red envelopes containing cash with wishes for our prosperity. As we celebrated with our guests, Che Yu barely touched her lips to the champagne, only making a gesture of toasting. I, on the other hand, was on my third glass of champagne when we finished this time-honored tradition.

Next came the main course: Beijing duck, crispy chicken, roast whole baby pig, steamed fish with ginger and scallions, sizzling beef with hot peppers and onion, sautéed frog legs with rice wine and greens, Nanjing salty pressed duck and a variety of fresh green vegetables. Young Chow fried rice was served last, topped with bird's nest sweet soup with lotus seed, a Chinese tradition signifying the blessings of many sons to be born in the family.

As the orchestra played the strains of Strauss' Blue Danube, Che Yu and I waltzed around the elegant ballroom, gliding with graceful footwork. All eyes were affixed on us, or so it seemed, for at that moment we felt like a couple from a fairy tale, a prince dancing with his beautiful princess.

Silver plates and fancy glassware sparkled from the light of Austrian crystal chandeliers and wall sconces. Arrangements of pink roses and peonies centered the tables draped in red, signifying happiness. The festive evening lasted until well after midnight.

After the feast, Che Yu and I changed into Chinese ceremonial gowns. I wore a blue tone-on-tone silk gown with the woven dragon beside the Chinese characters symbolizing longevity, power and good luck. My bride dressed in a red Chinese Che Pou, featuring a mandarin collar and slits on each side from the ankle to the knee. Her red Chinese wedding coat was adorned with gold and silver embroidery over the phoenix and embellished with pearl studs. Che Yu's beauty outshone her family heirloom jewelry… three tiers of diamond earrings, bracelets and a ring of gold with Imperial jade.

Clusters of pearls decorated her red silk embroidered slippers, and for this ceremony her hair was pulled back into a braided bun with pure gold and jade hairpins. The crowning touch in her hair was a special ornament, a gold hairpin with a brilliant, turquoise-colored kingfisher bird feather inlay, a royal heirloom from my grandmother, Princess May Szee.

Mr. and Mrs. Chow sat on the redwood chairs and awaited the tea ceremony. Two chambermaids carried trays with teacups of steaming hot rare green tea simmered with lotus seeds and red dates to ensure a generous number of grandchildren, and Mr. Chow made a speech to the appreciative guests, to much applause. Che Yu and I both knelt and bowed our heads to the floor three times in front of her parents.

When the chambermaids handed the tea to Che Yu and me, with our outstretched hands we presented it to Mr. Chow. Silently, we bowed our heads and waited for his acceptance of the tea. After the same ceremonial ritual was repeated with Mrs. Chow, Che Yu's parents handed each of us a red envelope filled with a large sum of money.

The tea ceremony continued for an hour and the chambermaids collected red envelopes from all of the elders. It was one of my favorite events of the evening…the tradition, the sincere wishes…and the fact that we received quite a bundle of prosperity that night!

Since my new father-in-law had insisted that we stay at the Chow estate until I settled into my new job, Che Yu and I retired to her chambers – rooms I had never before been permitted to enter. A silver cast dragon and an Art Deco-style phoenix decorated each side of the custom-made double doors, enhanced by a marble doorknob carved in the shape of a lion's head. I ceremoniously gathered my bride up in my arms… she was actually heavier than I had remembered…and crossed the 10-inch wide door threshold to enter our honeymoon suite.

In the dimly lit room two chambermaids lighted red scented candles encircled with pink rose petals in the center of a round table. They bowed and addressed us with congratulatory greetings.

Ming Ming, a young, pixie-faced chambermaid with braided pigtails, said softly to Che Yu, "Mrs. Khan, would you like for me to help you undress?"

Immediately, I replied for my bride, "That is my job from now on! You two are free to leave."

The two chambermaids covered their mouths and giggled on their way out.

Locking the door behind them, I surveyed the room and saw the elegant Quan Yin statue and the incense sticks burning in the urn on top of Che Yu's dresser.

"Ah, there is my Quan Yin I left in your keeping while I was in Japan," I mused. "I see you have been faithfully burning incense on my behalf."

Che Yu followed my eyes as they shifted around the ornate room and stopped at the engraved poster bed, delicately paired with matching bed cover and pillows. Two sets of silk pajamas were carefully laid out on the bed.

"The one with pink embroidery is for me, and the light blue with the dark navy binding is for you," Che Yu said shyly. "My parents had this room redecorated for our special union, so everything is new."

She was obviously nervous, but excitement also flickered in her eyes, which appeared dark amber in the low light. Che Yu continued.

"The custom bed frame came in this afternoon, and the servants assembled it just a few hours ago."

Before she could utter another word, I pulled her close to me.

"Let me take a good look at my charming bride. The wine has made your face blush in a delicious way. Or is it the candlelight or the champagne, perhaps?"

We embraced and I kissed her for the first time on her lips. She was trembling and almost appeared to be feint and light-headed. But I wrapped her in my arms and pressed her against my eager body. I could feel her hands, at first gripping tight with a rigid tenseness, then relaxing, her fingers beginning to explore the muscles and curves of my back. I bent my head to her face and kissed her eyelids, then again met her eager lips. With desire pulsating in every part of our bodies, the fireworks ignited.

We quickly undressed without regard to formalities. I threw the pajamas across the room, and Che Yu lay gracefully on the bed with her ivory neck slightly tilted away from me. From her neck down, she covered herself with the silk sheets. As I marveled at the curved shape of her body outlined by the clinging silk, my desire for her couldn't be detained. Within seconds, I slid onto the magnificent bed and covered my bride with my burning body.

I continued to kiss her, then handled her firm breast. By now, her nipple was hard and upright, yearning to be touched and massaged. Almost too eagerly, I obliged and whispered in her ear, "Did you know that I loved you even before you were born?"

"You were only a baby, what could you know about love?" she teased, moving instinctively to the movements of my hand.

At that moment, the bed began swaying. Then suddenly, the bed frame collapsed and the mattress fell to the floor with a loud crash! I jumped up, pulling my bride up with me. Astonished, with our eyes fixed on each other, we started laughing. The servants had failed to put the wood bracing under the box spring for support.

The loud noise awoke everyone. Che Yu and I quickly donned our pajamas and robes and opened the door. Standing outside were the two chambermaids along with Che Yu's sister and half-brother. Moments later Mr. and Mrs. Chow arrived to find out what was happening and everyone shared a good laugh while the servants quickly put the stretcher board back onto the frame and secured the bed.

Actually, we had been spared a potentially more embarrassing ritual. Che Yu's two siblings had been planning to climb through our window and surprise us on our honeymoon night. This was a version of an old Chinese custom in which the door to the wedding couple's chamber was to be left open for three days and nights so that any close relatives who dared could play tricks on them and even eavesdrop. It was up to the new couple to outwit their interlopers and find the privacy to consummate their marriage.

But this time, once everyone had returned to their respective bedrooms, Che Yu and I looked into each other's eyes, where the feint hint of a smile still lingered. Within seconds, we were intertwined again and the bed held sturdy through a night of consummated desire.

Morning came with a sudden splash of light, but we rolled to the side and shut our eyes against the intruding sunlight.

It was the Chinese custom for a wealthy family to give their daughter at least one of their chambermaids to serve her when she married. Mr. Chow told Che Yu and me to select two servants who would follow and serve us wherever we went. Che Yu picked her trusted chambermaid, Ming Ming, and I chose Ahma, who was always smiling and exuded a funny, happy warmth.

Ming Ming had come to the Chow family from an orphanage at the age of 10. She and Che Yu played together in their younger years, so she understood her mistress' moods and what she liked to eat and wear. She always helped Che Yu to get dressed, but her real value was in her loyalty and unquestioning devotion.

Ahma was different. She was a free spirit, laughing all the time. She had great physical strength and could easily lift heavy boxes like the male servants. I had also detected in her a certain attraction to me, even in the days when I was courting Che Yu. She had always made sure that I received choice cuts of meat at the dinner table, and I could sense her unease whenever I came under scrutiny from Che Yu's parents.

I must admit that I enjoyed this attention. She was rather ordinary looking though and, while full-breasted, she posed no threat to Che Yu. As a young husband, the last thing I wanted was to create some sort of competition, either real or imagined, between my wife and my chambermaid. Several of the other maids did arouse my male curiosity, but I couldn't afford to be daydreaming about something I wouldn't act upon anyway. So Ahma was the perfect choice.

Ironically, one week after we had selected our personal assistants, another of the Chows' chambermaids, Lulee, slashed her wrists in an attempted suicide. Mrs. Chow found that Lulee had wanted to serve me and, when Ahma was chosen, she was inconsolable since she knew she wouldn't be able to see me once we moved out of the Chows' estate. I felt somewhat guilt-ridden since my initial reaction was to be flattered rather than horrified by the incident.

The Chows' chauffeur drove Lulee to the hospital after her misguided suicide attempt. Later, according to Che Yu's mother, the young girl began intermittently crying, laughing and uttering nonsensical words that no one could understand. She languished in the hospital for several weeks before being transferred to a mental institution. It was then that I realized Lulee's infatuation was more than a schoolgirl crush. She had some serious mental instability. I told myself to be equally cautious around Ahma since I didn't know the full extent of her feelings toward me.

Soon afterward, I took Che Yu to Beijing for our honeymoon. We visited the Imperial Palace where my late grandfather, Khan Gong Shun, the Royal Commander, and grandmother, Princess May Szee, had lived. Holding a special pass to enter the palace, we entered a domain where no one had resided since the new government overthrew the Ch'ing Dynasty more than 20 years ago. Just a handful of guards were posted at each building, the elaborate security and sense of regal pomp now just a distant memory.

The Palace grounds, also known as the Forbidden City because commoners were prohibited from entering there under pain of death, had served as home to 24 different Chinese emperors from 1420 to 1911. Gu Gong, as it was called in Chinese, is the world's largest palace domain, covering at least 74 hectares. It was surrounded by a 6-meter deep moat, with walls climbing 10 meters high on the sides.

The intricately structured towers afforded unobstructed views of the palace grounds and the city beyond, to ensure utmost security for the emperor. This wasn't an easy task, since the palace buildings contained over 9,000 rooms, which were occupied not only by the Imperial Family, but also by maids, eunuchs, administrators and even soldiers.

Che Yu and I marveled at the massive size of the grounds as well as at the ornate detail of the building interiors and exteriors. It was difficult to overlook the fact, however, that more than a million workers, including nearly 100,000 skilled craftsmen, were forced into lives of hard labor to complete the palace. During the 16 years that it required for construction, many laborers were killed in accidents related to the building of its structures.

Stone was brought in from a quarry in Fangshan, on the outskirts of Beijing. To transport it, wells were dredged intermittently along the main road from the quarry to the palace grounds. This made it possible to empty water onto the road during the winter months, and when the water turned to ice, workers would slide the huge stones into the city.

There were other instances of keen ingenuity, too. One notable example was the grand City Wall. Its base of nearly nine meters wide narrowed at the top, creating an angular shape that made it extremely difficult for invaders to scale. Che Yu and I particularly liked the imperial flower garden, Yuhua Yuan. Designed with stately shoots of bamboo, delicate flowers and soft, comforting evergreens, the garden also possessed a quiet pond for reflection and respite. This is where the Imperial Family would come to relax. My grandmother, May Szee, often cavorted here as a child.

At some point in our palace tour, Che Yu and I discovered an adjoining garden where my grandmother had met my grandfather. It meant so much to both of us to actually retrace the steps of my ancestors within the ancient walls of the royal palace.

Che Yu made a comment to me, "Ling, something is missing here. Where are all the tapestries, banners and royal garments?"

I tried to give her a plausible answer. "My dear, I am sure they were either taken by the palace officials or the Japanese. Perhaps, even the foreign countries from Great Britain that have many contacts here in the palace. These artifacts would become very valuable someday."

"Ling, did you know that my mother's grandparents owned a silk textile factory in Hong Chow, south of Shanghai? They were commissioned by the royal palace to provide all the royal garments, headdresses, banners and tapestries. The factory hired only the finest artists to create beautiful designs and embroideries. They raised silk worms and weaved garments and gowns, they used pure gold threads to embellish the design of symbols like the dragon and the phoenix. They could not sell to the public because it was exclusively manufactured for the royal families and the palace court use. During the Boxer rebellion, the gang cleaned out the priceless patterns and silk supplies. Even though their target was the foreigner, they were also against the establishments. The factory was burned to the ground and destroyed. There was nothing left from this exquisite form of creative art but the charred ashes. It was lost forever!" She sighed sadly.

After Beijing, we boarded a cruise ship to Japan and visited my mother, Dr. Namiko Khan, who worked as a gynecologist at her father's hospital. Those were happy moments, as Che Yu learned eagerly about Japanese customs and tea ceremonies. The one thing that made her uncomfortable, though, was entering the bathhouse with her mother–in–law, myself and several of my former Japanese classmates. It was utterly embarrassing for her to show her naked body in front of these people. I assured her that this practice had been part of the Japanese culture for centuries and was quite acceptable. Sensing the hopelessness of my argument, I finally gave in to my modest bride, who donned a bathing suit to enter the steaming, sulfur spring pool. I could sense that my mother liked her and admired her principles, though antiquated by Japanese standards.

While soaking in the water with Che Yu and my mother, I remembered my first trip to a Japanese bath house. Having settled into our foreign students' dormitory at Waseda University at the start of our first semester, my roommate and I were determined to visit a bathhouse. Four or five other male students offered to join us since this treat was one of the first things on all of our lists. We had heard about how the beautiful Japanese women would go to the public bathhouses and strip naked in the spring water. Since we had never seen any nude ladies in person before, we eagerly marched down to the local baths near the campus. After paying the gatekeeper, we hurried into the men's locker room and quickly disrobed, giggling and laughing so hard at the thought of what we were about to enjoy. It would be like winning a trophy, something we could brag about to other friends once we returned to China.

Side by side, we shuffled over to the hot spring and immediately spied three or four naked women, their hair pulled up in the simple Japanese manner. Though we could only see their backs at this point, and the water line was up to their waists, we grinned in anticipation.

"We'll walk around them, and then we can see their breasts," one of the boys slyly suggested.

As we walked closer, the ladies turned their bodies around in unison to see who was coming. Eying this group of skinny young lads, they began pointing to our private parts and giggling. It was then that we saw their big, full middle-aged breasts bobbing on the water like oversized tugboats. Their eyes continued to focus on us as they prattled between snickers in Japanese. I was so embarrassed by the long stares at my naked body that I awkwardly covered my privates with both hands. Though I was the first to run back to my locker, the others quickly followed. In the security of the locker room, we laughed so hard that our rib cages ached.

Now, however, after several years of frequenting the bathhouses, I calmly watched Che Yu and admitted to myself a certain amount of amusement about her shyness. My mother, on the other hand, tried to make idle conversation that would put her daughter-in-law at ease.

===================

I don't know if it was the slight air turbulence or those lingering thoughts of my mother that made my eyes open, but it was palpable. A sustained rush of blood coursed through my brain, and my hands suddenly felt a dull clamminess. Minister Tao seemed to be in that odd netherworld, his nose twitching as if in a dream.

My mother. The thought kept racing through my mind. My mother. It was then that I felt the certainty of my day's mission. I stared out of the window, nothing but darkness beyond the thick pane of glass. I allowed myself, painful as it was, to revisit that fateful episode in my life. Closing my eyes, I couldn't sleep. I could only wonder where my strange journey would end.

Chapter Four
Mama Disappears

Three years ago in Nanjing my mother, Namiko, arrived from Kyoto to visit us. She had not seen us since I took my new wife to meet her when we went to Japan for our honeymoon. Che Yu was now expecting our first baby, and mother had come to Nanjing to help her during those days leading up to the birth. The escalating conflict between China and Japan made it a very unpredictable period.

The Japanese had begun seizing some of our cities. All pretenses of good intentions had gone up in the smoke of burning buildings and the debris of life. Even Nanjing experienced waves of instability at times, with air raid horns pulsing through the city and driving the populace deeper into a gloomy malaise. Reinforcement work was underway on several of the historical landmarks, in preparation for possible bomb strikes.

During this chaotic time, most of Mr. Chow's family members preferred to stay inside his estate, under the protection of a small contingent of Chiang Kai-shek's soldiers. Though sirens screamed their warnings intermittently across the entire city, I still walked to my broadcasting company and managed to deliver the daily news reports.

One night mother told me, "Ling, with the baby due in the next few weeks, I would like to go out with you tomorrow for some medical supplies. It is not safe for Che Yu to go to the hospital, and I think it would be better for me to deliver your baby at home when the time comes."

"Mama, I am so glad that you are here with us. But I don't feel comfortable for you to go to the hospital alone. Why don't you tell me what you need, and I will get the supplies for you."

My mother was steadfast in her decision.

"Ling, I know the hospital chief of staff, Dr. Bao. He was an associate of your papa's doctor and we have been close friends and kept in touch by letters since I left for Kyoto. I would like to pay him a visit to catch up on old times. It would be easier for me to get the list of things if I go personally. Don't worry, I will be careful."

The next morning my mother walked with me; the tension in the air gave me pause, and I watched cautiously between buildings and around street corners. I was determined to accompany her to the front gate of the hospital and, when we arrived, I gave her a warm embrace. My choice would have been to continue on with her inside, but I could tell that she wanted time alone. She was back in her element and relished it.

"Mama, be careful," I pleaded. "Come home as soon as you get your list of items."

"Don't worry, son. I will see you tonight. You are the one who needs to be careful."

She gave me a warm smile as she walked inside the hospital gate and waved. I returned her smile with a forced one.

The radio station was bustling on this particular day. There was news that the Ambassador of Japan in Nanjing was being transferred to Beijing. He was also a graduate of Waseda University, and we were good friends. Troop activity around Nanjing had also gained momentum, so breaking stories were possible in every zone of the city.

When I returned home at six in the evening, I asked Che Yu, "Have you seen my mama? Has she returned from the hospital? She was just getting a few supplies for delivering the baby."

"No, I've been wondering about her all day!"

We asked around the entire estate, questioning everyone of the family members, the servants and guards. No one had seen her return. My concern was evident to all, so my father-in-law asked two of his guards to accompany me to the hospital.

Walking cautiously but briskly along the road, we arrived at the hospital and quickly ascended the steps to the second floor. Skipping the usual protocol of knocking, we entered the Chief of Staff's office and immediately demanded to see him. His assistant, Miss Fang, wandered around in Dr. Bao's office, crying and murmuring in a very weak voice.

"They charged into Dr. Bao's office with guns pointing at our heads!"

"Who are they? Please tell me. I am looking for my mother; have you seen her?" I demanded an answer.

The hysterical assistant pointed at a man lying on the floor behind the desk. Blood puddled next to his head. I bent down, turned his body over, and saw more blood on his skull.

It was Dr. Bao. I gasped as I stared at his lifeless body, sensing immediate danger.

"Where is my mother? Was she here this morning?!"

Within seconds, several more hospital staff members arrived. Ashen-faced, they observed Dr. Bao lying in his own blood. One ran quickly to his side and checked his pulse, but it was obvious that he was no longer with us.

Between sobs, Miss Fang spilled out the story.

"The Japanese soldiers – three or four of them – came in with their weapons drawn. Your mother was standing next to Dr. Bao behind his desk, looking at photographs of your late father. She had come to get some medical supplies…"

"Yes, I know. I know. Go on. What happened next?"

Miss Fang began to feel feint and gingerly eased herself into a chair where she nearly collapsed. But she continued with her story.

"The Japanese told Dr. Bao that they were ordered by their Captain to take custody of your mother and transport her to their headquarters. Dr. Bao stood between your mother and the soldiers and told them they had no right to take a civilian against her will. The soldiers told him to step aside. Then Dr. Bao reached toward his drawer for his gun."

She began sobbing, her breasts heaving with every wail.

"They shot him. Right in the head. They shot my beloved Bao. He fell right there on the floor."

By now, I was frantic, torn between comforting the poor woman or shaking her and demanding that she tell me what had happened to my mother.

"My mother, please!" I implored her.

"They grabbed your mother. She spoke to the soldiers in Japanese. Her eyes were so frightened, but her voice was very firm. She seemed to be pleading with them to let her go. They bound her hands and dragged her out. She looked back at me and said, 'Tell my son. Tell my son!'"

"And no one did anything?" I was incredulous.

"Where did they take her? How long ago?!"

"I don't know, ten, fifteen minutes," Miss Fang replied quietly. "I am very sorry. I lost Dr. Bao! I can't think."

Feeling an overwhelming sense of urgency and dread, I asked one of Mr. Chow's guards to stay with Miss Fang, but by now medics and other aides were arriving at the scene. As they rushed to Dr. Bao's body, I hurried out of the hospital.

At the entrance, medical personnel and scattered onlookers had already begun to gather. Chow Papa's other guard and I grabbed two bicycles parked there and pedaled as fast as we could to the Japanese Embassy on the next block. I kept thinking, "Where are the police? Has the whole city gone mad?"

When we arrived at the embassy, we found the gate closed and locked. I shouted angrily in Japanese to get the gatekeeper's attention.

He snapped back, "Who are you? The hours are posted on the gate. We're closed."

Two Japanese military guards also came to the gate to investigate the commotion.

"This is an emergency," I blurted. "I am a friend of Ambassador Mikara. Please inform him that Khan Ling is here to see him."

"Wait here," the gate attendant commanded in a stern voice. I immediately disliked him.

"We cannot disturb our Ambassador if he is asleep at this hour," he added.

Breathing rapidly and anxiously, I grabbed the icy cold bars of the iron gate, waiting for it to be opened.

"Please report to your supervisor what I just said. It is a life and death matter!"

Time was ticking by ever so slowly; it seemed like an eternity. Finally, one of the soldiers walked toward me with a flashlight. He shined the light in my face and said, "The Ambassador has retired for the evening. We cannot disturb him. My captain told me to tell you to come back tomorrow in the morning."

"You must wake him up! It's early. I must see him, please!"

I banged on the iron gate as the soldiers and the gatekeeper walked away from me. This got their attention, but not in the way I had hoped. One of them turned around and pointed his weapon at me through the bars of the gate. Angrily, I pushed the barrel of the rifle away, but it discharged, striking my upper left arm near the shoulder.

The soldier seemed surprised by his own gunshot, but maintained his threatening stance.

"If you don't go away, I will shoot again. This time it will be your head," he yelled at me.

Then he slowly moved the rifle's sights to my bodyguard, who appeared to be making a move toward his pocket. We were out of options, at least for the moment.

My bodyguard helped me onto the bike, and we rode quickly away without looking back. There was a stabbing pain in my heart for my mother, and another equally acute one in my shoulder. Blood was seeping through my shirt and spreading at an alarmingly quick rate. I stopped to take off my jacket, and Mr. Chow's guard helped me wrap my arm to slow the bleeding.

When we walked through the Chows' gate, the guard who accompanied me called to his colleagues for help. They carried me to my chamber where Che Yu and her parents were waiting.

"Oh, my God, you are hurt!" cried out Che Yu when she saw the blood oozing through my shirt.

"What happened? Who did this to you?!" Che Yu questioned me as she helped me to a chair. "And where is your mother?!"

Chow Papa sent for his doctor next door to tend to my wounds while I tried to explain what had transpired.

"Ling, it is too dangerous outside. I don't think it is wise for you to leave our compound again," my father-in-law warned. "I will use my informant to find out what happened and try to bring your mother back safely."

Che Yu stayed by my side and nursed my wounds after the doctor had cleaned my flesh and gently removed a few small bullet fragments from my arm. Luckily, it had missed the bone and arteries. Mr. Chow positioned two guards outside our rooms to make sure I didn't try to leave to find my mother.

Chapter Five
Chiang-Kai-Sheck

The doctor had given me an injection to make me sleep and ease the pain of my swollen arm. I don't remember how long I was out, but it seemed like days filled with blurry images and mumbled words from people whom I couldn't understand or even recognize. Che Yu was so worried that she sent for a Chinese medicine man and brewed special herbal roots for a bitter tea that she forced me to drink.

After a few days in which I faded in and out of deep sleep, my swelling had gone down, and I began to regain some of my strength. I could see Che Yu sitting next to my bed. She leaned over and wiped the sweat from my forehead with a soft towel.

"What have you found out about my mother?" I asked, the words tumbling forward in a slow, lazy cadence.

She held my hands and said, "You are still very weak. Are you up to seeing my father? I believe that he found out some news about your mother this morning. I have been kept in the dark about her, also."

"Yes, please," I begged. "I would like to speak to him as soon as possible."

Che Yu sent Ahma into the other room to fetch my father-in-law.

"Just rest. Ming Ming and I will help you to dress and we will prop you up in your bed."

While I waited for Mr. Chow, I prayed to the Goddess Quan Yin to bring my mama back safely. But I sensed that bad news was coming. Quietly, I rebuked myself for my fear and feeling of emptiness. After all, I was supposed to be a man of courage.

There was a knock on the door, and Ming Ming rose to open the door for my father–in-law who walked in slowly. Chow Papa pulled up a chair and sat beside my bed."Ling, we were so worried about you," he said, with a tenderness reserved for those about to receive bad news. "Are you feeling better now? Che Yu has been nursing you for three days now. You have given us a huge scare with your high fever. You were lucky that Dr. Lou was able to take out the bullet in your arm without any major complications."

I was growing impatient. "Chow Papa, were you able to find my mother? Please, tell me everything."

"Ah, my dear Ling, my informer spent three days searching and he even had to pay several soldiers to talk of the events that transpired. They finally told him about your mother."

"Where is she now? Is she all right?"

Chow Papa smiled warmly and patted my hand with what I hoped was reassurance. Then he told his story.

==================

This time, the air turbulence woke everyone up, even Minister Tao. Our small plane swayed left and right, up and down. One official threw up on his shiny black shoes.

I arose and went to the cockpit where I sat behind the radio operator who cautioned me about a storm coming up from the south of us into our flight path. He told me to return to my seat and strap in for a rough couple of minutes. The minutes became almost an hour, with constant turning and churning.

When the turbulence finally eased, I was exhausted but couldn't sleep. One of the bodyguards came over and handed me a cup of hot cocoa while my eyes were half closed. It was just what I needed. I leaned back in my seat and stared out at the darkness. My parents and the monks taught me to be merciful, and the image of Quan Yin, Goddess of Compassion, seemed imprinted in my memory. But I could no longer be merciful. The night of my conversation with Chow Papa, everything changed. I became a warrior.

===================

The news about my mother was relayed to me slowly, in small parcels, as one might mete out medicine. But first, Che Yu and Ming Ming were asked to leave the room so that my father-in-law and I could speak in privacy. I requested, however, that Che Yu stay. We were family.

According to Chow Papa, my mother was taken to a small interrogation house where she spent the first night. Several soldiers of high rank questioned her, but treated her humanely, though she was not offered food nor water.

The next morning my mother was driven to a local merchant's home, though the merchant and his family were nowhere on the premises. She was then brought before a Japanese captain in the home's private study. He commanded her to sit down, then began questioning her in Japanese.

"Are you Namiko from the Seito family in Kyoto?"

"Yes. Now I would like to know why you are detaining me."

The man turned around. A short, but physically fit man, he wore his khaki uniform with heavy starch and a gun and saber hanging around his waist. His glistening boots stood in sharp contrast to the dark, rustic wood floor. His face, though scarred, was not unpleasant, but its most prominent feature were the bushy eyebrows.

"Do you know me?"

Namiko strained to see any features that might have seemed familiar, but there was nothing.

"Do you know me?!" he asked with growing agitation.

"I, I'm not sure," my mother offered. She was bewildered.

"I am Shinji Ohka. I knew your family. Your ex-husband's family. Now I am Captain Ohka," he said proudly.

My mother tried to smile, but she wasn't sure if this was good news or bad. After all, her first marriage had been a turbulent one filled with many highs and lows. Mainly lows. As he furrowed his bushy brows, however, she noticed the first hint of familiarity. Vaguely, she recalled that he was a sometime friend of one of her ex-husband's brothers…a brother that had been a bad seed and an embarrassment to the family.

"Oh, yes, Shinji San."

Captain Ohka's eyes brightened with her feigned, or at least somewhat exaggerated, recognition of him. But just as quickly, the eyes narrowed. He began shouting indignities loud enough to be heard by guards standing outside the study door.

My mother decided nevertheless to play upon their past ties, minimal though they were.

"Captain, please let me go. My daughter–in-law needs me. Her baby is due in a few days. In the name of our Imperial Emperor, please let me go home."

"Namiko, you are a traitor! You have divorced an upstanding Japanese citizen and married into a foreign culture of oafs and buffoons! Now that our country is at war, you have come back to China to be with these Chinese as your family."

Captain Ohka nearly spit out the word, "Chinese," as he said it.

"Captain, that is not true. After my second husband passed away, I went back to Tokyo and finished medical school. I became a gynecologist and worked in my father's clinic along with my two physician brothers in Kyoto. My father had forgiven me and I stayed at his house with my daughter."

She paused and changed her tone of voice. "You have risen into a high position in the army and have power and authority here. You must have been a good soldier."

The captain glared at her.

"Women like you…"

Without finishing his sentence, Captain Ohka lunged at my mother and grabbed for her blouse. She pulled away as he grabbed it and part of it ripped off in his hand. The guards at the doorway turned their attention inside and began to enter, unsure of what was causing the commotion. But Captain Ohka waved them off.

"No. Everything is fine. This woman merely needs to be reminded who is in charge here."

Captain Ohka pulled my mother by the wrist and, despite her pleas and struggles, he dragged her to another room through an opposite doorway. The guards, still unsure of their responsibilities, merely watched.

Several screams were met with loud curses and, through the door, the sound of scuffling was evident. After several minutes of silence, Captain Ohka came out from the room and told the guards to return to the front of the house. They would no longer be needed for awhile.

Later that afternoon, the guards were called back, and a sullen, disheveled Namiko was handed over to them by Ohka. He asked them to guard her in a different room and to make sure she didn't try to kill herself or escape. The captain walked off, in search of dinner for himself.

They kept my mother in the house for three days. She refused to eat and pleaded with the soldiers every time they came in with the food and water.

Early on the third day, when she was taken to a small bathroom near the rear of the house to clean up and to relieve herself, she worked feverishly for several minutes to loosen the locked window. She had managed to pry it open on one end, but it was still latched from the other side. One of the guards knocked brusquely on the door to speed her up, and it so startled her that her hand slipped on the makeshift tool that she was using and she cut her palm badly. Normally, a wound of this type would have required stitching, but the guards merely wrapped it tight with a towel and threatened to kill her if she tried another escape.

Later that day, she began to run a fever and pleaded once more to be set free. Bruised and broken in spirit, she began sobbing when it became apparent that they had other plans for her. She wondered aloud whether she would ever get the chance to see her soon-to-be-arriving grandchild.

When Captain Ohka returned, he quickly tired of her pleadings and commanded his soldiers to take her out from the house and away from the compound.

As Chow Papa recounted the story, I kept waiting for the part where my mother's fortune would turn and he would smile and tell me that she had been released, a bit haggard from the experience but safe. Instead Chow Papa paused and looked at me for the longest moment.

"Your mother's soaked jacket was found two days ago by the river banks. There was a note in the inner pocket with hand writing in blood"

He forced the words from his trembling mouth. "I am so very sorry for what has happened to her and this horrific tragedy."

One soldier said that he thought perhaps she had jumped into the river to kill herself, but her will was too strong for that and her yearning to see her grandchild too great. They had hurt my mother for nothing more than being an articulate Japanese woman who had chosen to marry a man of Chinese heritage.

My head throbbed and seemed as if it would explode with agony and anger as Chow papa handed me the white handkerchief note with my mama's blood writing on it. The note said," My loving son, Ling, by the time you found this farewell note, I no longer live in this place but my spirit will be with you forever. Listen to me, this is my wish: Do not try to search for me. Love, mama." Che Yu sobbed continuously upon my shoulder as Chow Papa leaned back in his chair with a defeated sigh.

"I have sent many people to look for her along the Yangtze River and searched any of her friends, who might have been helping her in hiding, but there was no sign of her. I am very sorry to disobey her wishes, but I know that I must try before I give you this horrific sad news about your mother." Chow Papa said. "I wanted to ask you, what you would like to do next, after you have had a chance to mourn."

Ripping at my hair and tearing at my chest, I cried out,

"My God, My God, why did you let this happen to my mama? Quan Yin, goddess of mercy, where were you when my mother needed you? There is no mercy until I avenge my mother. Japan is my enemy till the day I die!"

I turned to Chow Papa and, through my tears, said, "Thank you for all you have done and for your kindness. I don't know what I am going to do yet. Che Yu, you always know what is in my heart. I would like to hear your suggestion on what to do next."

Che Yu thought for a moment and said softly, "Ling, in order to respect your mother's last word, I think we need to bring this tragedy to a closure by burying her jacket and her note. Your father bought a family plot for the Khan family by the Purple Golden Mountain. I would think your late father, Khan Bei, would like to have your mama by his side. Don't you?"

"Yes, it will be done according to your suggestion. We will prepare the funeral in a quiet ceremony for my beloved mama. Just our closest relatives at the temple. Papa was buried during the sunset hour. He and mama always watched the sunset at the Purple Golden Mountain and enjoyed the magnificent glory of the colorful sky."

Chow Papa agreed.

"It shall be done according to your wish, dear Ling. Chow Mama will arrange the funeral. Che Yu, you need to stay close to Ling and take care of him."

Chow Papa gave me a consoling pat on my shoulder and stepped out of the room.

While I mourned the loss of my mother, I stayed in our bedroom chamber most of the time. I didn't want to see anyone. It was left to Che Yu to greet the many friends who came to pay their respects. No one knew the details of this tragedy. The vivid terror of my mother's ordeal would remain seeded in my heart forever. Only Chow Papa, my wife and I would know the full extent of her suffering. The informer had been paid handsomely to remain silent.

The funeral was two days away. I was lounging in my bedroom chair, my arm still bandaged and cradled in a shoulder sling. Che Yu came in with a tray holding a vase of three peony blossoms in full bloom. Peonies were my mother's favorite flower. The tray also contained a bowl of chicken broth, steaming hot vegetable with egg noodles, two empty bowls and two sets of chopsticks and porcelain spoons.

I was glad that Che Yu had decided to join me for the light lunch. She had been trying to allow me some private time to grieve alone the past few days. Now, sitting across from me, she looked serene and beautiful in her long white gown. An inner peace filled me as I stared into her eyes and she told me that the temple had reserved the space for our private funeral.

According to my wishes, the procession would start at the temple and proceed to papa's family plot. Only the immediate family and the monks would be in attendance. I didn't want to hire any mourners or ask friends to come. Mama would have wanted to keep it small and private.

Chapter Six
Moving to the Temple

The plane had found a smooth patch between the clouds, free from the turbulence that had plagued us for so many miles. Flying in the dark of night, we were still a reasonable distance from Nanjing. I stretched my arms, then reached over Minister Tao for a bottle of brandy lying by the foot of his seat. Unfolding a white napkin, I removed a hard candy from the folds, then sank further into my seat and took a sip of the brandy. It tasted sweet, and the aroma soothed me. I knew that I should enjoy these few moments of relaxation while I could, for the road ahead was filled with uncertainties. I couldn't be sure if, after today, my world or that of my family would ever be quite the same. My mind drifted to a time when I was seven years old.

===================

It was the summer of 1917. I was living at the Buddhist temple with Master Wong, my caretaker at the time. The temple was built at the base of the famous Purple Golden Mountain, on the outskirts of Nanjing. A small mountain of only about 20 square kilometers, it nevertheless held a particular mystique for the citizens of China and provided agreeable terrain and soil for numerous plant species and wildlife. Inhabitants of Nanjing would gather on the plains leading up to the lower foothills and gaze at the mountain's beautifully changing colors during the hours of dawn and dusk.

On this day Brother Lee, a young apprentice monk, had come to the courtyard to look for me. A resident of the temple since he had been an infant, Brother Lee had been wrapped in sackcloth and dumped off at the temple door. A handwritten note tied around his tiny wrist spoke of demons possessing his spirit and of the mother who had suffered excruciating pain before dying while giving birth to him. Master Wong had taken him in and paid a local nursemaid to breast feed the child until he was weaned. From then on, Brother Lee's world was the temple. Master Wong treated him like a son, taught him literature and instructed several of the other monks to teach him martial arts. Only 10 years older than I, Brother Lee was tall and lean, but possessed a gentle spirit. Certainly no demons there. In fact, my father would use Brother Lee as an example when he spoke of avoiding superstitions and trusting my own instincts. Consequently, Brother Lee and I became true friends.

"Ling, what are you doing out here?" he asked, finding me on my haunches in the courtyard. "Master Wong wants to speak to you."

"I am trying to catch a cricket." I explained. "It keeps jumping away from me."

"You'd better come in right now and wash your hands before seeing Master Wong," Brother Lee urged.

I had been told that my father, Khan Bei, had some type of incurable disease in his lungs and liver, and he had been confined to a hospital for the last three months. Khan Namiko, my mother, was a Japanese midwife at the time. My parents had met when my father was attending Waseda University in Tokyo. They fell in love and married in 1909 and settled in Nanjing.

Before I was born, Father donated a piece of land and built a small temple for the nearby village elders to come to worship Buddha without having to hike the considerable distance up the mountain to the main temple.

Master Wong was in the lower temple hall, kneeling and praying before one of the various Buddha statues that graced the landscaped grounds. My hands now scrubbed clean, I sat quietly outside the hall. I really didn't mind waiting because even I sensed a peaceful stillness in this part of the temple that allowed one to ponder and dream without interruption from the sometimes harsh, unpredictable world outside.

Moments later, Master Wong rose up and saw me sitting there. Taking me by the hand, he led me to his chair.

"Ling, my little boy, do sit down. I have something important to tell you," he began.

"Your father's doctor said the hospital can no longer care for him. He is suffering from an incurable disease. At your father's request, your mother has made the arrangements to transport him to the main temple. Your mother is a very good nurse and, with her medical background, she is well-qualified to administer medication that will ease his pain. They have hired a servant, Archi, who is a widow and needs the work. She will be taking care of you, cooking special meals and cleaning."

Master Wong took a sip of the freshly brewed tea given to him by Brother Lee. With a sympathetic smile, he reached out to pat me on the shoulder.

"Ling, I have enjoyed your stay here with us for the last few weeks. This is a critical time for your family. Your parents have requested that you move to the main temple and stay with them as soon as possible. Superior Master Lou Ming at the main temple asked that Brother Lee accompany you while you are staying there. He will play with you and help you with your studies. He has already packed all your belongings. As soon as you finish breakfast, the two of you will start your journey up the hill to the main temple. But I will come to visit you from time to time."

"Master Wong, does that mean that my papa is dying? How much longer is he going to be with us?"

"My precious one, no one knows when that day will come. Your father is a faithful man of God. His charity has touched our temples and the communities. God is in charge of our lives. Maybe He needs your papa sooner than we expected. Promise me that you will obey your parents."

We started our short journey along the winding, gravel path that followed the creek leading to the bottom of the huge waterfall. That's where the main temple stood, at the mid-point of the mountain.

The Purple Golden Mountain was located just northwest of the city. When the sun would set, before its final descent behind the mountain, it looked to me like a giant red-orange egg yolk. I always imagined what would happen if that giant yolk would break, but it never did…merely softened in color and slid out of view. Yellow, orange and purple clouds would float against the canvas of an awesome blue sky. That's why the people named it the 'Purple Golden Mountain.'

As I looked toward the hills on this day, the sunset radiated its brilliance all around the mountain, which was usually covered with a hazy humid air, especially in the early mornings and evenings. This particular late afternoon, the golden purple haze enveloped the mountain, creating a mystical, holy presence.

I could see the temple, majestically situated in front of the grand waterfall. The Feng Shui master hired to advise the benefactor who built the temple selected this site to protect the city of Nanjing and its nearby villages more than 150 years ago.

Midway through our journey up the mountain, I found a small rabbit lying on the side of the path by a leafy bush. It appeared to have a fresh wound on one of its front legs. I gently picked up the trembling animal and held it close to my chest. Brother Lee urged me to hurry, to pick up some speed walking up the mountain.

The small rabbit shook uncontrollably in my arms, and its eyes seemed frozen in fear. Brother Lee guessed that it had been attacked by a wild animal, had managed to scamper away, then collapsed in shock. I thought the wounded leg might be broken and I used my hand to cover the quivering creature.

Slowly caressing it, I said reassuringly, "Little rabbit, don't worry. Superior Master Lou Ming is going to take care of you. Did you know that he can fix anything?'"

We finally arrived at the front of the temple, which was graced by eight tall wooden columns and an open-air portico entrance. The gigantic red lacquered columns supported a green tile roof, and hand-painted designs in vivid colors decorated each of the roof rafters. Eight large red lanterns hanging from the rafters were lighted each evening, giving the temple a crimson glow that could be seen from the foothills at night.'

In an arched hallway in the center of the main parlor, three larger-than-life ancient, carved wooden warrior Gods stood guard. They held spears, sabers, bows and arrows, and peered at guests with angry, narrow eyes that seemed to follow you as you passed by their protected domain. As a little boy, I was always frightened by these statues and tried to avoid them whenever possible. Once or twice I tried to stare back at them with an equally threatening visage, but I would soon become gripped in fear and look away as quickly as possible.

Brother Lee entered the temple first and headed straight to my papa's chamber. As I ran past the frightening warriors, through the temple arches, a young apprentice monk stopped me and said, "Welcome home, my dear Ling. Look at you; you are out of breath. You should know better. You are not allowed to run in the temple parlor! This is a holy place!" Quickly I replied, "But I have a wounded rabbit, and I need to see Superior Master Lou Ming. I need him now."

The young monk answered, "Superior Master Lou Ming is in his meditation and prayer right now. Come, let us take a look at this rabbit."

But I stubbornly kept my hold on the animal until Superior Master Lou Ming could tend to it. Waiting quietly on a green ceramic stool, I softly stroked my new pet. My eyes overflowed with tears, fearing the rabbit might die if it didn't receive immediate medical attention.

Moments later, when Superior Master Lou Ming emerged from the prayer room, I bolted across the room toward him with the rabbit in my arms. He stroked his long gray beard and studied me with his small, but unflinching eyes that made him resemble an eagle.

"There you are, Ling," he greeted me. "I am so pleased to see you. We have prepared the room for you and your parents. The servant Archi is making the bed for you. Here she comes.

"Archi, this is young master Ling."

Archi was a rotund, middle-aged woman with puffy eyes and numerous moles on her face. She smiled at me and said, "Young master Ling, I shall be taking care of your family. Just let me know what you would like to eat tonight."

I stared at her moles. Nothing seemed very appetizing.

The Superior Master interrupted her, "Young master Ling will be eating with us tonight."

Then he looked at me and said, "Ling! You have tears in your eyes. What is the matter, my little boy?"

I held the rabbit out to him.

"Oh, I see you have caught a mountain rabbit. You must set it free in the wild, as these animals are not to be kept as pets."

I looked up and spoke softly, "The rabbit is hurt. It was lying on the gravel path and could not move. I know you can help it get well. Please take care of it! I promise I will set it free when it is well again.'

Superior Master Lou Ming took the rabbit and laid it on a wooden table. Methodically, he examined the furry creature.

"This is a female bunny," he said. "Poor thing, she is only a few months old. Her leg appears to be fractured. It has been bitten by a predator, maybe a wolf or a mountain cat."

He took a deep breath and said to the nearby monk, "Brother Wu, bring me the medicine box."

Superior Master Lou Ming put an already prepared herbal mixture into a rough stone bowl, poured several drops from his wine jug, then stirred it all with a wooden spoon. Next, he used a small bowl to catch some water splashing off the rock from a waterfall just outside the temple and poured it into the grassy paste.

Looking at me, he said in his strong but soft voice, "Remember, little Ling, this water from the waterfall comes from heaven. God will heal your bunny with his rejuvenating water."

He spread the paste diligently on the rabbit's fragile leg and told me, "Hold the bunny still, Ling. I need to put a cast on her."

Then he shredded a few pieces of cotton from a clean, white cloth and, using two tiny bamboo sticks for splints, bandaged the wounded leg.

"Now, my little one, you are in charge of the patient," he proclaimed. "You can put her in that empty bamboo cage. She is not to move around until she has started to recover."

I was so excited to be the rabbit's official guardian, and I quickly announced, "I will name her Sunshine."

Chapter Seven
Life in the Temple

I brought my treasured Sunshine to a small room adjacent to papa's room and placed its cage on the floor next to my canvas cot. The maid had already put a flannel sheet on the cot and topped it off with a soft pillow and a lightweight blanket. In the room there was a chair and a small wooden chest, upon which was placed a kerosene lamp. A small, square window allowed the afternoon breezes to cool the room.

Superior Master informed me that my parents would be sleeping in the big room. I walked back to my parents' room where I had spent most of one summer by myself. I was overjoyed to know that my parents would be coming back here. Superior Master had always told me to be brave and independent. But I was only a child, and I missed them terribly.

Fresh candles dimly lit the room's open space. Through a small window I could see a part of the waterfall and feel the cool, misty air flowing into the room. The plaster and straw walls were painted in an old mustard-yellow color. I could see many cracks on the walls, with occasional strands of old straw and flecks of mud hanging from the narrow fissures. To entertain myself as I lay in bed, I often imagined the forms of cracks on the walls as different animals or other imaginary objects. They would almost seem to move, ever so slightly, amid the dancing shadows of the flickering candles.

The floor, a bit uneven in certain areas, was constructed of stone blocks common to the local area. A straw mattress, covered with a blue and white striped cotton sheet, served as the bed. I had never liked the ceramic pillow, with its hard, rectangular wedge shape. But papa told me that the pillow was cooler during the hot summer nights and its firmness offered good support for the neck and balanced our Chi while sleeping. Still, I could never understand why he liked it.

The mattress was placed on a well-built hollowed stone block base, with a large opening on one side. In the wintertime, the young monks would carry in coals and build a fire on the ash pile underneath the bed to heat the room and bed.

My favorite item in the room was a framed picture of my parents. It appeared to have been taken by a professional photographer in a studio. The photo was developed in a soft, faded sepia tone and was surrounded by a silver frame. I would gaze at the photo from different angles, at various times of the day, as it sat on a small desk. Each viewing seemed to reveal slightly different images, and I imagined in my fertile mind that my parents had prepared an entire photo album just for me.

Next to the photograph was an exquisite pearl inlaid wooden box covered with semi-precious stones. The box was filled with gold artifacts, jewelry, jade and precious stones left by my grandparents. Included among these treasures was a golden hairpin worn by his mother, Princess May Szee, the Emperor Quangxu's niece. The hairpin mesmerized me, particularly because of its tiny kingfisher feather and brilliant turquoise inlaid stone. A small pearl, set at the head of the pin, reflected the classic style of the Ch'ing period and was of the kind favored by the royal court. It was the very hairpin that my beloved Che Yu would wear on our wedding night, nearly two decades later.

In the center of the desk stood a bronze statue of Quan Yin, the ever-present Goddess of Mercy. I opened the desk drawer and took out three incense sticks, lighted them and laid them into a small, yellow porcelain bowl in front of her. Bowing before Quan Yin, I beseeched her.

"Quan Yin, Goddess of Mercy, can you make my papa well again? We have so much to do together, please don't take him away from me!"

Fearful that if I prayed for too long, Quan Yin would become bored with me and find me to be a bit annoying, I turned my attention to the mahogany bookcase where a vast collection of books that my father ordered from Japan, England and America still stood in a neat, orderly fashion. Some had illustrations and photographs, and many were Chinese history books. I enjoyed studying the pictures in these exotic books, and wondered at the strange costumes and hats worn by the foreigners. Equally fascinating were the images of the various fighter planes, battleships, automobiles and war tanks from faraway lands. Most intriguing was a Sears Roebuck catalog from America. Every page seemed to beckon with a sensational array of fashionable clothing, unusual housewares, tools and hunting gear. I would endlessly leaf through the thick book with its plethora of products, even though I didn't comprehend any of the English words or, for that matter, many of the items contained within the pages.

At this point, Brother Lee walked in.

"Ling, it is getting late. Try to get some sleep."

He led me back to the adjacent room, turned the lamp down and left me lying on my cot.

"Brother Lee, when are my parents coming?"

Stopping at the doorway, Brother Lee turned back toward me. I could see his silhouette against the crack-lined wall.

"In a few days. They have to bring the medical supplies up with them. But they are looking forward to seeing you again. Good night, my boy."

The next day seemed like an eternity. I kept asking Superior Master Lou Ming when my parents would arrive. Finally, darkness came, and the monks closed the temple gate. I knew my parents wouldn't be here this evening and, to ease my longing, Superior Master invited me to dine with him and his fellow monks again.

I reached into Sunshine's cage and petted her, letting the soft fur slide across my fingers. Then I served her a meal of water and carrots before closing the cage once again.

"Ling! It is time for supper."

This was the voice of Uncle Pigtail, the cook for the monks in the main temple. It was a Chinese custom to call the elders "uncle" or "auntie" for respect, even if not related. His long, braided hair made it obvious how he had acquired his other moniker.

I walked into the dining room, furnished with a lengthy, wooden table and several oil lamps. Two benches, long enough to seat 12 people, were placed on either side. Superior Master Lou Ming sat at the head table, and I usually sat at the opposite end. Supper this evening was simple:

vegetable soup, bean curd with black bean paste, green vegetables grown from the garden of the foothill temple and, one of my favorites, gummy rice with sweet red bean filling.

One could see the hot steam rise from the dishes, and it smelled so delicious! It was difficult to hear everyone's conversation, however, because the gushing waterfall sounded louder in the evening. Its somewhat mystical echo created a poetic mood in the otherwise nondescript dining hall.

After supper, Superior Master lit up his long, bamboo pipe and drank his favorite green tea, made from local camellia sinensis plants that Uncle Pigtail cultivated in a small, makeshift greenhouse near the rear yard of the temple. Immediately after plucking the leaves, rather than allowing them to ferment into black tea, Uncle Pigtail would steam or otherwise heat them. Following this, he would roll and dry the leaves in just the way that Superior Master liked.

Now, sitting in an elegant redwood chair with inlaid pearls, Superior Master smiled with satisfaction. I eased myself closer to him, with the hope that his good mood would prompt him to tell me stories about the temple's colorful history and about ancient China.

Superior Master asked one of the young apprentice monks to light a few lanterns in the dining room, and immediately the room was filled with warmth and a serene glow of light.

"My child, what would you like to hear tonight?"

I looked straight into his eyes and asked, "Superior Master Lou Ming, why do I have to live in this temple? Other children in school live in a normal house with their papa and mama."

I paused a moment, then continued with my questions.

"And why was I born in this temple instead of at home like my friends?"

Superior Master cleared his throat, put his pipe on the porcelain table urn and drank some rice wine. After a prolonged sigh, he stroked his flowing white beard and grabbed my hand.

"You want to know so much, my precious child!" he remarked. "Well, you do have the right to know who you are and where you came from. Let me just begin with your birth here at the temple."

Superior Master Lou Ming poured more wine into his green ceramic cup, took a good sip and lit his pipe, blowing the smoke away from my face.

He launched into his story, telling me that my mother left Japan with my father and they married in Nanjing. Next, he spoke briefly about China's turmoil and how my father had embraced Sun Yat-sen's political movement dedicated to overthrowing the Ch'ing Dynasty and reforming China into a democratic republic.

"Your father has made great contributions to Sun's movement," Superior Master said.

The story, up until now, was just history, some of which I had heard before. It was boring to me, but I dared not interrupt Superior Master because it would be considered disrespectful.

A mosquito, buzzing annoyingly at my face, disturbed Superior Master's train of thought. Brother Lee waited for the mosquito to appear again, then quickly slapped his hands together and killed the insect.

Superior Master continued, "There were riots and looting in the streets unceasingly, both day and night in the traumatic war zones of the city. Your mother worked in the hospital while your father was involved with political matters in high places. The war brought your father closer to God, and he started to depend on Quan Yin, the Goddess of Mercy, to protect him. Your father was a very powerful and wealthy man, and he was very generous to us. But he was a very poor businessman and he lost much of the family fortune by trusting the wrong people.

"When your mother discovered that she was with child, your father suggested that she stay in the temple for safety, as there was still rioting and sporadic gunfire in the city. Your father built a section of rooms here for his retreat years ago. He would visit her whenever possible. He spent very little time with her, however, as he was very politically involved with the government of the Republic, and at the same time, cultivated very friendly relations with the Japanese government."

Superior Master Lou Ming leaned back in his redwood chair and folded his hands on his lap.

"My dear boy, it is getting late," he said. "I am tired and I will tell you more about your family another day. Now, you need to go to sleep."

The Superior Master was extremely busy the next day, due to a Chinese festival. Hundreds of worshipers arrived to burn incense at the temple. Many newlyweds also visited, to receive their wedding blessings, which were accompanied by powerful fireworks. The glowing firecrackers fascinated me, as they danced around the air and made thunder and smoke in the already hazy skies.

The following night, a warm and still evening, Superior Master retired to his same redwood chair after supper and had a few sips of his rice wine, while young monks fanned him with a large, dried palm leaf.

He took a few long draws on his pipe and said, "Ling, come sit near me so you can get cooler with the fan."

I reminded him, "Superior Master Lou Ming, you promised that you would tell me about my birth."

"That's right, I did promise. Even though it is a warm night, perhaps we can stay late and catch some breezes later to cool us off. Now, I will continue the story."

Before I was born, he began, my father gave half of his possessions, including money and land, to the temple. He told the monks that the war would be a bitter one and, in case he should die, he would entrust Superior Master Lou Ming to be my guardian and the architect of my future. My father's instructions were for me to be sent to Japan to earn a degree at the same Waseda University where he had studied. The only other person in the city to trust would be my father's best friend, Mr. Tao.

Superior Master then remarked that he had been at the temple since he was 30 years old, and he had seen many unusual occurrences during that time.

"But I have never witnessed such a miracle as that of the day you were born here," he offered.

It was Spring of 1910, and a dry spell of many months had destroyed all of the crops. The village people lined up each day at the well where they would literally fight for water for their families. Remembering the late Spring afternoon when I was born, Superior Master recalled how the sky turned gray and darkness came over the city. Suddenly, thunder announced jagged lightning, as ominous black clouds covered our mountain. Within minutes, the sky opened up with pounding rain and continued steadily for several hours. The villagers had been praying for rain for four months, so this was seen as a true blessing from heaven.

Superior Master was at the main temple, with my mother, my father and a young midwife, at the time that the rainstorm began. The minute that I was born, my father wrapped me snugly in a cotton towel and gently placed me into a straw basket. He then took a wooden bowl, walked outside and held it out in the open air to catch the rainwater falling from the sky. Next, he placed the bowl of water on the table and bathed me. Proclaiming that this was God's way of saying my life would be dedicated to the people of China, he then wrapped me in another clean, cotton blanket and delicately placed me next to my mother for nursing.

"It was such an exciting evening in the temple," Superior Master remembered. "Since the rain came from heaven before you were born, your father named you Khan Ling. Ling is composed of two characters, one meaning 'rain' and the other signifying 'forest.' We all agreed that great things could be expected of you, that you would someday make the people of China exceedingly proud."

Superior Master Lou Ming patted my head. I tried to suppress a proud grin, but couldn't.

"It was after dark and the temple door was already locked for the evening, but someone was knocking on the front temple gate. One of the monks opened the temple door and looked outside. There stood a group of monks from the foothill temple…all carrying red lanterns and baskets of fruits to congratulate Mr. Khan on the arrival of his newborn baby. At that time, we did not have telephones or radio contact with the outside world from the temple. Both your father and I were astonished at how these people knew you were born!

"Master Chang, one of the elder monks in the group at the gate, told us that, right after the rain had eased, the forest was in total darkness except for a line of red lanterns moving up the trail toward the main temple. He and several of the other monks on the far end of the compound had watched the procession of lanterns as they traveled up the winding path, their glow then fading again into darkness.

"At that point Master Chang and his fellow monks began to think that it was an apparition they had seen, for how would anyone at the bottom of the hill know of your birth? So they walked back inside. But later came the knocking at the gate. It almost seemed as if these people had been swept up the mountainside by a spirit.

"My precious Ling, as you can see, you are not an ordinary child. God has a purpose for you to serve your people, and he sent the rain as a sign of mercy to our people. You are to do great things in your life. Just remember that you should be merciful even towards your enemy."

I went to bed that night and replayed the story Superior Master Lou Ming had told to me, both elated and overwhelmed by his remarks. To myself I thought, "I'm just a child, how am I supposed to serve the People of China?"

Chapter Eight
Emperor's gifts to my Grandfather

A week after I had moved back to the temple, my parents finally arrived. I ran to the front gate just in time to see two mules pulling a carriage up the path. Running toward the carriage, I called out, "Papa! Mama!"

A wheelchair was removed from the mule cart first. Mama put some blankets on the chair as two other men and two monks helped my papa into the chair. He appeared frail, but when Papa reached his arms out, I gently leaned close to his slender body and gave him a firm hug. He smiled and kissed my forehead before shaking hands with Superior Master.

All of the monks were bowing to papa to greet him. Even the nuns came out, bowed to him and wished him a pleasant stay.

Once Archi had come out and introduced herself, she told mama, "Mrs. Khan, I have the room ready." She picked up several of the suitcases and headed inside the temple. I followed Papa as my mama wheeled his chair past a breezeway to his chamber. Someone opened the wooden plank door, and mama helped papa up from the chair. She tried to stabilize him as he was standing, while Archi maneuvered the wheel chair to get it over the high wooden threshold.

"Look at the pretty white lilies, they smell so good!" mama exclaimed. "Ling, did you pick the flowers for papa? I know he likes white lilies."

"I found them by the waterfall basin this morning," I proudly announced.

"Come here, my son," papa requested. "You are so considerate. Thank you." He gave me a big hug.

Mama took out a soft pillow from her suitcase to replace the ceramic headrest on the bed. She said that it would make papa more comfortable. Soon afterward, Archi brought in a tray of food for our lunch. We sat together around a square table with wooden stools and ate a simple meal of brown rice, cabbage soup, salted pickles and green spinach with chopped garlic. Papa was relieved to be out of the hospital and excited that our family was eating together for the first time in a long while.

I was on my best behavior, sitting straight and eating all of my food. Though perhaps illogical, I feared that one false move on my part might destroy the positive energy that had brought us together once more. In the best of all possible worlds, this moment would have lasted forever.

Papa was in a talkative mood and asked me to sit by his side.

He said, "Ling, do you recognize the painting on the wall? That was painted for my parents when they got married at the Royal palace. I'm sure you remember that your grandfather was a Royal Commander during Emperor Quangxu's reign in the Imperial Ch'ing Dynasty."

"Papa, can you tell me more about my grandparents?"

My mother replied, "Papa may be tired."

"I am fine," he corrected her. "Perhaps it is time for him to know more about his heritage."

As papa began his story, I moved in even closer to him, near enough to smell the garlic on his warm breath. It made me feel at home for the first time in many months. Little did I know at the time that the insights he would tell me about my grandfather would play a role in how I viewed my own life as an adult. It would help to shape my fortitude and my decision-making, for better or for worse.

My father explained that my ancestors were farmers in a village near the southern part of Anhui Province. Of the two boys in the immediate family, my grandfather was the older, named Khan Gong Shun, he helped his father at the cotton field from a very early age, after finishing his school subjects for the day. He would also rise early in the morning at five to feed the animals, including the cows, goats, ducks and chickens. After collecting the fresh eggs in the chicken barn, he would milk the cows and goats, then pour it into ceramic jugs, which he would place in a horse-drawn cart. He loved to ride with his father to deliver the milk and eggs to the families they served.

During cotton-picking season, Gong Shun would toil in the fields until dark. Often his back would be stiff and sore, but it was the only life he knew and he savored its special moments. One of his favorite tasks was to help his mother put the cotton yarn into the vegetable dye vats and hang the yarns on the clotheslines for drying. The beautiful colors made him think of far-off kingdoms where royalty was celebrated with pomp and pageantry. Though his only schooling came from his grandparents who lived with his family, he learned literature at an early age and developed a fond appreciation for the books that he would occasionally have the good fortune to read.

In mid-story, mama handed papa a spoonful of medicine that he took with his cup of warm tea. He was very animated, waving his bony arms and hands. Barely had he taken his medicine and a sip of tea, when he resumed his tale.

"One day, while they were at a market stand," papa began, "a fortune teller saw your grandfather, who was maybe nine years old at the time. The fortune teller told his parents that he would have a bright future and would one day serve the Emperor in the Royal Palace. Your great grandpa smiled at the prognostication, but lamented that they had no extra money to send Gong Shun to the best schools for training. But the fortune teller, who was influential in the town, was so sure of the future he saw for Gong Shun that he talked among the villagers and convinced them to put up some of their own money to send him to military training."

I loved papa's stories. They were always so full of hope and grand ideas. He sipped his tea and took a deep breath. Mama gave him a hot hand towel sprinkled with imported cologne, and the room was instantly filled with a most agreeable fragrance.

"Papa, please tell me more," I begged. "What happened to grandfather? Did he do well with his schoolwork?"

"Yes, after your grandfather became 12 years of age, he was sent to a special training school to learn from the great martial arts masters and to study literature and poems with a highly respected scholar. The school was located in a remote mountain area far from his parents' home. His younger brother was the only one left to help his father on the farm.

"The only news they heard from their son was from his letters. He was not allowed to see outside people until his training was completed. It broke his family's heart to not be able to see him, and yet Khan Gong Shun was the villagers' only hope, someone who might break out of poverty and one day bring great honor to his family and his village."

Mama handed the cup of tea to papa and adjusted the awkward rubber tube sending oxygen to his nose. She watched him closely for signs of weariness, but he was lively and animated, considering his feeble condition.

He explained to me that the peasants and commoners in China were not able to rise in status unless they had relatives in high places. There were certain exceptions, however, such as scholars or warriors with leadership skills… individuals who could prove themselves by engaging in challenging tests at the Emperor's superior court in Beijing. The contestants would be eliminated, one by one, from the villages to the big cities. A final list of the hundred chosen ones was then sent to Beijing for the final tests, which lasted several months. These tests, held in the Hall of Supreme Harmony within the Forbidden City, included literature, essay, poetry, math, science, strategy, leadership ability, wisdom and common sense.

Physical abilities and fighting skills were assessed, in both the use of bare hands and a chosen weapon. The contestant was normally challenged by someone chosen from among the Royal Court captains. They would fight in the presence of the Emperor and other official judges who would grade them on style, agility, strength and physical skill.

Many young men studied and trained for years to attain this lifelong dream. It wasn't unusual, for some of those who failed, to commit suicide. Others would never return home, as they couldn't bear to face their parents who had put up their life savings for their education and training. They felt they had dishonored them and lost face among the people of their village.

I eagerly asked, "Papa, did grandpa pass the test? He went to Beijing to meet the Emperor, didn't he?"

"My dear son, be patient. I will explain to you how hard work pays off at the end. You also need to know that genes play an important role in your ability to learn, though using the full potential of one's talents is something that cannot be taught or passed down through generations. It is something deep within your own spirit. I was told by my grandparents that we are descendents of Genghis Khan who was the most powerful warrior who conquered China. Now let me return to my storytelling."

Papa went on to say that the few chosen ones who did pass the final test with high scores would be assigned to powerful positions within the Royal Court. So this Imperial Exam competition often generated more than its share of intrigue and internal conflict. Adding to the exclusive nature of these tests was the fact that Ch'ing rulers equated unusually high numbers of passing, or licensed, candidates as one of the leading causes of the preceding Ming dynasty's fall. So they were very rigid in their attempts to limit the number of successful candidates.

In addition, the State dictated certain regional quotas for geographical balance, so the available slots were highly restricted. Farming areas and small rural hamlets were at further disadvantage because of their much lesser political clout than the large cities and urban industrial regions. As such, the odds were stacked considerably against Khan Gong Shun.

Consequently, it was no surprise that a competitor from a village in the same region as Gong Shun tried to spread false rumors about him. The young man told of how, as a child, Gong Shun would slip into the surrounding villages at night and steal some of the prized laying hens. It was said that Gong Shun's family made a tidy profit off of egg sales in their village, due to the large number of quality chickens in their barns. This competitor claimed that, at one time, he had stationed his rather large dog in the henhouse to guard the chickens against theft. When Gong Shun crept into the chicken coop late one night, the dog surprised him and a brutal fight resulted. Gong Shun finally strangled the hound, but not before he received several large gashes across the inside of his left hand, below the thumb. The real truth about the narrow scars on Gong Shun's hand, however, was much less dramatic. He had received them while stringing fence wire around his parents' small vegetable plot.

Fortunately, Khan Gong Shun's reputation for honesty preceded him, and his accuser revealed a number of inconsistencies in his story. And because strength bestowed legitimacy in those days, it didn't help the accuser's cause when he was bloodied and rendered unconscious while fighting a test with one of the Royal Army Captains.

Gong Shun, on the other hand, received the highest honors. He not only passed the literacy test with a top score, he also demonstrated his fighting skills by winning his contest with one of the captains. After his impressive display, the Emperor Quangxu even asked him to remove his armor to show his physical attributes. The judges all agreed that Khan Gong Shun was to be chosen to enter the Royal Court in Beijing and serve in the Emperor's palace. He later went on to become a palace favorite, even with the devious and opportunistic empress Cixi. A self-proclaimed artist who loved to cultivate black peonies in her nursery greenhouse and paint in her art studio, she sometimes invited Gong Shun to collaborate with her on poetry and calligraphy.

"Papa, that is a great story!" I cried out. "I wish I could have known my grandpa, the Royal Commander!"

I stood up, went to my room and brought back my wooden toy sword. In front of my audience, I made several fighting moves that I had learned from Brother Lee during his martial arts instruction. My mother and father laughed, and I was glad that I made them happy.

"Ling, your papa needs rest," mama said. "Why don't you go and play outside for the afternoon."

Chapter Nine
Papa's last days

Minister Tao touched my arm and startled me from my deep thoughts, "Major, would you like to share?"

The minister proffered a tiny canister, which contained sardines in tomato sauce. In his other hand, he held a small bag of crackers.

"We will be landing soon. But it is late, and you may not have the chance to eat again until morning."

I smiled my thanks, took one of the sardines from the canister and laid it on one of the stale crackers. It was surprisingly good, but then I hadn't eaten in quite some time.

Looking out through the window at the all-encompassing darkness, I thought of the significant decisions that lay ahead. Minister Tao and I would work on our meeting report drafts in the morning and compare our notes. We would need to present our findings to the department chief as soon as he arrived at headquarters. We knew that he often stopped in the morning to enjoy the pleasures of a young shop girl who lived several blocks from our office building, so he probably wouldn't be at his desk until mid-morning. But there would be no sleep for me this night. The meeting with Admiral Saka had, for the most part, been an unmitigated disaster. The alarming speed at which the Japanese had been occupying our villages lately was reason for concern. It would have been nice to report that our "allies" to the east were considering a less ambitious plan, but I would have to utilize some highly creative phraseology to provide even the slightest hint of optimism. Suddenly, the sardine didn't taste so good.

But there would be plenty of time for consternation and head-scratching when the plane set down, so I determined to put the meeting with Admiral Saka out of my mind until then. Besides, I found myself drawn back to those thoughts of my early formative years...the times that helped to define the decisions I would make today and in the days ahead.

I thought again of papa.

=====================

Dr. Chang came one day to the temple in a horse-drawn carriage. I went to greet him.

"Dr. Chang, what is your horse's name? He is so beautiful, and his hair is so shiny and smooth."

"Ling, I call him Old Faithful. He has been with me for six years now. I cannot get up here without him. Animals are so loyal to you."

He smiled, and I took that as a sign that I could pat Old Faithful's forehead.

"Is your father doing well?"

I wasn't sure how to answer, so I helped him to pick up a medicine package and we both walked to papa's room. When Dr. Chang went in, I stepped back into my room and took my rabbit, Sunshine, out of her cage, then returned and waited just outside my father's door. Sunshine had already become quite attached to me and had become my shadow whenever I let her run free, which was increasingly often as her leg healed.

The door opened slightly, and I heard Dr. Chang tell my mother, "Mrs. Khan, you have been doing an excellent job taking care of your patient. I would expect no less, considering your medical training and background. And he is right; he seems more comfortable staying at the temple than in the hospital. I have left you enough morphine for the rest of the month. There is a fresh tank of oxygen when you need it.

"Doctor Chang, thanks for coming," papa said. "I seem to have an increased appetite. The vegetarian dish is too bland. Could I have a juicy steak and a roast chicken for my next meal?"

"Mr. Khan, this is great! It is a good sign that you are getting your strength back. By all means, eat whatever you want and enjoy it. Just don't overdo it."

My mother flinched. "We don't have any meat here. Could I send Archi to ride with you to the market and buy the food that Bei likes. She could hire a rickshaw back."

"Not a problem. Make sure Bei drinks lots of water. And don't cook the food too salty."

Dr. Chang opened the door wider and turned to go. Mama followed him out and gave Archi a list of things to buy.

"Archi, will you also get Ling some strawberry lollipops and some butter cookies?" mama asked. "He has been a good boy and deserves a treat." As she handed the money to Archi, I smiled discreetly. I had learned a good lesson…there are often rewards for merely staying quiet and showing patience.

After Archi and Dr. Chang left, we took papa in his wheelchair to the temple garden. A few stray geese flew overhead. Papa shot me a look that was filled with mirth.

"Remember the first time that you and I went hunting? You shot many trees instead of the birds. Master Wong says that you have become a good marksman now. Perhaps you could bring a pheasant home for dinner some day. Or would it still be a large oak branch?"

It felt good to hear papa laugh.

"Isn't this place beautiful?" he said. "I will die in peace here. Namiko, I have purchased our burial plots a few hundred yards from here. You should go with Ling and see what I have chosen for us. I would feel very comfortable resting there, knowing that my next heirs would receive blessings for generations to come.

"Look at the beautiful sunset. It is ever changing, just like our lives. Namiko, I want to be buried at the sunset hour. Promise me, will you?"

"Khan Bei, my husband, I will honor your wishes. But let's not think too far ahead. It is getting windy, so maybe we should go in. Besides, I need to go to the kitchen to prepare dinner. Archi should be back soon."

That night, we had a memorable dinner in our room. Mama cooked the steak with Worcestershire source and sautéed onions, just as papa liked it. Brown rice and green beans provided the perfect accent. It was delicious, but midway through our meal, papa began feeling some pain. Mama administered a dose of morphine to ease his discomfort. As a result, he slept for hours.

"Mama, will you stay with me awhile and tell me stories?" I asked.

My mother prepared a tray of cold lemonade and some snacks, which she brought to my room. She looked over at Sunshine.

"How is the rabbit doing? She's so adorable."

I didn't stop to answer. I was too eager for a story.

"Mama, can you tell me about how my grandfather, the Royal Commander, met the Princess?"

Mama smiled and nodded, then took a sip of her lemonade. She picked up a butter cookie and handed it to me, while a slight breeze carried the cool waterfall mist into the room.

"Ling, child, did I ever tell you how handsome you are? You are growing up to be a gentleman. You have been engaged to marry the Chows' daughter, Che Yu. I don't want you to mingle with other girls in school. Do you hear?"

"Yes, mama" I said, but I had no idea what she was talking about. Who's interested in girls, anyway, I thought.

"Your grandfather, Khan Gong Shun, even though he mastered the skill of armory, was such a charming poet," she began, "entertaining the Emperor, the Empress and their guests with his poetry at festive gatherings. The Emperor trusted him, and the Empress Dowager Cixi, as you know, was also very fond of him.

"In China, young women were not allowed to reveal themselves in front of men unless it was a celebratory occasion and they were accompanied by elders of their own sex. On this particular occasion, it was an unusually cool summer evening. Your grandfather, Khan Gong Shun, had just finished a meeting with the Emperor and was walking out of the Royal Court along the pathway to his office.

"That same evening, the princesses and their maidens were playing in the west court garden, surrounded by tall cypress hedges that separated it from the men's world in the palace. The garden's pond boasted blooming lilies and summer flowers showing off their colorful blossoms and emitting their full, rich fragrances. Some of the princesses were standing at the small red and green bridge that crossed over the lily pond and watching a school of goldfish fighting for food that the girls had dropped from above.

"The princesses, who were granddaughters of the Emperor Xianfeng, laughed giddily, their small cherry-colored lips glistening against their shining white teeth. The cool breezes occasionally brushed against their ivory necks and glossy black hair, making music of their dangling gold earrings that swayed back and forth in the soft wind.

"The eldest princess, May Szee, was only 16 years old. She and her sisters were wearing their casual garments that evening. May Szee's peach silk gown featured long flowing sleeves and a light apple green vest delicately embroidered with pink and red flowers. Her shiny black hair was bundled up with a few long combs made of amber and accented with a dazzling mother-of-pearl inlay.

"A colorful butterfly flew over the bridge, and Princess May Szee, followed by her sisters and maidens, gave chase. It flew past the garden hedges, and May Szee ran after it through a narrow opening where she tripped and fell directly in front of Khan Gong Shun. He quickly reached out to catch her in his arms, dropping the documents he was holding onto the ground.

"As he apologized profusely for walking into her path, May Szee looked up from his arms and saw a magnificently regal man with olive skin and a captivating smile.

"'Oh! It is entirely my fault,' she blurted out. 'We were chasing that silly butterfly and I lost my balance.'

I always giggled when I heard that part. Mama had actually told me this story before, but she had a way of always making it seem new and different. Several passages never changed, however, because she knew how much I enjoyed them. And now that papa had told me more about Khan Gong Shun's earlier life, it intrigued me even more.

"Her two other sisters and the maidens hid behind the bushes and peeked through an open spot among the branches to witness this most extraordinary encounter.

"Immediately, May Szee covered part of her face with her peach-colored silk handkerchief and looked down toward the ground shyly. Slipping gently out of Khan's grasp, she ran back into the garden with a motion so graceful and swift as if she were a feather carried away on a whispery wind.

"Khan was speechless; he had never seen such a beautiful young creature. His heart pounded like a war drum and his face felt warm and flushed, while a sweet fragrance lingered on his sleeves and in the surrounding air. He assumed that she was one of the maidens in the palace, for he had not seen any of the Emperor's brother's daughters since they were younger children, running around the palace during special holiday celebrations.

"After collecting up the documents scattered on the ground, Khan composed himself and started walking. He sensed what seemed like a thousand pairs of eyes peering out at him through the bushes, and he heard the faint giggling and laughter of the ladies as he walked away toward his office."

Papa inadvertently interrupted the story with a groaning sound. Both of us went to check on him and saw that his oxygen tank was almost empty. I helped mama to re-attach the new tank to the rubber hose. Papa never opened his eyes as mama also adjusted the glass bottle dripping fluid into his vein. She took my hand tenderly and we walked back to my room where she resumed her fascinating story about my grandfather. For a seven-year-old child such as I, this was truly a grand adventure.

"Everyone was talking about this event amongst the ladies' court," mama said. "Several days passed by. Then one evening, Princess May Szee was alone with her auntie, Empress Long Yu, a delightful and gracious lady who had been one of the concubines in the palace some years ago.

"May Szee was curious about the story she had heard about Long Yu, and she asked her how she met May's uncle, the Emperor Quangxu.

"Long Yu sat on a marble bench under a fragrant climbing rose trellis and looked admiringly at the lovely courtyard before beginning her story. She told of how it had been right there, in that very spot, where it all began. Until then she had been locked up in the concubine quarters for two years without every glancing on the Emperor. She had felt sad and hopeless.

"One night, she went to the garden where the concubines were allowed to visit and she wrote a poem about her sorrow and the pity that she felt for her misfortune. When she heard something in the nearby cypress hedges, she got up to investigate. There she saw a handsome young scholar who appeared to be admiring the summer greenery.

"'Oh, excuse me,' she said. 'You startled me. We don't often see gentlemen in this area of the courtyard.'

"'Yes, that is why the hedges are there,' the scholar replied. 'Ladies do not often look between the hedges, either.'

"This made Long Yu blush with embarrassment. Sensing her unease, the young man quickly changed the subject and asked her about the paper in her hand.

"She told him it was a poem about her longing to meet the Emperor. The verses, she said, contained much sadness. But when he asked to read it, she shyly declined.

"For the next few weeks, she would sit out at that very spot and write her poetry. Almost without fail, the scholar would show up and, from the other side of the hedges, call to her and ask to read her poems. Finally, one day Long Yu parted the hedges and allowed him to read her verses, and he was quite impressed. Handing the paper back to her, he looked warmly into her eyes.

"'And how shall I address you, my beautiful lady?', he said.

"She replied, 'My name is Long Yu, I came from Suezhou.'

"He told her how many beautiful ladies and famous poets had come from Suezhou, then asked why she had written such a sad poem.

"She said that her father had died when she was only 10 years old. Her mother had been an opera singer and actress. Two years ago, soldiers had come to their house in search of young girls to become concubines for the Emperor. So Long Yu was taken away from her mother when she was only 16 years old. Ever since, she had been living on the west court of the palace where she studied poetry, writing, singing and dancing…the very talents that her mother had possessed. Long Yu had been one of the best students among the girls but, because one time she had accidentally angered one of the head eunuchs, she had never been given an audience with the Emperor."

"Did Long Yu want this man to introduce her to the Emperor?" I asked.

"Yes, but the more she sat with the young scholar, the greater her attraction grew for him. She felt as if her heart was about to jump out of her body. He was such an intellectual gentleman, with the kindest eyes. But after that encounter, he did not return.

"As Long Yu told her tale to young May Szee, her eyes welled with a certain wistfulness, but the lovestruck girl encouraged her to tell her all about this magical encounter. She was clearly intrigued by the scholar and hoping for a happy ending."

I looked wide-eyed at my mother. Her story had almost made me forget about my father suffering in the next room.

"Tell me what happens next, mama."

"Well, after two weeks, one of the eunuchs came to Long Yu's chamber with several maidens. He told her that she must take her milk bath and choose a gown to wear. He told her, 'Tonight you are going to meet the Emperor!'

"Long Yu could not believe what she had just heard. In her heart, she wondered if the gentleman scholar had been the one to arrange the meeting. This made her both happy and sad, because she did not want to believe that the scholar would give her up so easily.

"But the excitement of the moment overtook her, and she gave herself freely to the preparation process. First, a eunuch brought her to a private chamber where she was ordered to disrobe."

I was transfixed. For most it would seem like a fairy tale, but this was the story of my ancestors, so it held me particularly spellbound.

"Her underclothing, too?" I asked.

"Yes, the eunuch and a maiden examined her entire body, even running fingers through her hair to make sure she wasn't hiding any sharp objects or poison that could harm the emperor. The maiden then took out a silk padded blanket and covered Long Yu's body, at which point the eunuch walked her to another chamber where more maidens were waiting for her.

With these young girls helping her, it took Long Yu almost two hours to prepare her hair and attach the large headdress. She selected a beautiful light mint green gown, trimmed with soft pink silk banding. The eunuch presented a tray of jewelry and hairpins. They decided which one she should wear in her hair, and they adorned her with pearl and jade earrings and bracelets.

"After Long Yu met the eunuch's approval, they led her through a courtyard, past a row of marble steps, to the Great Room. There she waited in an elegant greeting hall embellished with high ceilings and sculptured columns. A group of people had already gathered to witness the encounter, one of many that the Emperor held regularly with his potential concubines.

"Suddenly, the guests bowed and called out, 'The Emperor approaches!'

"Moments later, the palace captain called for all of the guests lying prone on the cold marble floor to rise.

"Next, the eunuch and his assistants brought Long Yu into the hall where they approached the emperor. Her face was still lowered at this point. But when they asked her to lift her head, she was awed by what she saw. It was the handsome scholar that she had met by the hedges. He was, in fact, the Emperor!"

I laughed loudly and clapped my hands. What wondrous stories my mother told! She continued.

"Long Yu felt weak from the shock and almost collapsed right where she was standing. It seems that the Emperor enjoyed dressing in certain disguises so that he could walk through the palace grounds without being approached by strangers such as the numerous staff members, would-be concubines and others.

"Within days, Long Yu moved into Emperor Quangxu's palace chambers with him. He loved her even though she never was able to bear him any heirs. She was petite and slender with an oval-shaped face, perfectly balanced eyes, a small nose and full, luscious lips. Her smiling countenance accentuated her kind and gentle nature. But, of course, it was essential for emperors to bear sons that could carry on their lineage, so at some point Quangxu took on other lovers."

"Mama, what happened to the ladies that the emperor turned away?"

"Oh, they were led back to the examination chamber, made to disrobe again, then checked to make sure they had not secretly stolen anything while in the emperor's presence. They would then be sent back to their palace quarters. Other than performing for various court events, they would never see the emperor again."

A sad sigh escaped from me. Sensing my disappointment, my mother continued.

"On another day as they strolled in the garden and fanned themselves for relief from the humid air, Long Yu asked May Szee about the incident in the garden and inquired as to whether she caught the butterfly after all. May Szee understood the real meaning of her question and blushed a bright shade of red before admitting that the butterfly flew into her stomach instead."

This time, I let out a full horse laugh. Mama smiled at my amusement with the story.

"May Szee said that she had been feeling very strange and light-headed lately and wanted to know what was wrong with her.

"Auntie Long Yu was sure of the reason…her niece was in love with the nobleman!

'Who is this man?' Princess May Szee asked. 'He is so striking and strong. I remembered that I had seen him at the emperor's court a few times. My sisters and I were looking through the carved wooden screen behind our grant auntie, Dowager Cixi, who was seated behind uncle's throne in the court. I heard him discussing court business with our uncle. But that was a long time ago.'

"It was then that Long Yu said that your grandfather's name was Khan Gong Shun, the Emperor's trusted confidant…a brilliant man who shared the Emperor's same philosophies about reforming China. She went on to say that neither the Emperor nor your grandfather had the blessings of May Szee's grand auntie Cixi, the Dowager, when it came to politics. In fact, she violently opposed any mention of reform and had her eunuchs watching every move that the court made."

The temple was asleep; only the chirping sounds of nearby crickets broke the quiet. My mother paused and stood up to stretch, then walked back to check on papa. Though it was late, I had plenty of energy and a visible eagerness to hear the story in its entirety. So after sipping some of her lemonade, my mother continued.

"The time had come for the Emperor to give a festive party celebrating your grandfather's promotion to Royal Commander of the Blue Feather. His parents, who lived in a village in Anhui province, received a summons from the Emperor to travel north to the palace for this honorable occasion. Everyone in Anhui province was proud that Khan Gong Shun had risen from his humble, peasant background to become a Royal Commander.

"During the celebration of Khang Gong Shun's prestigious promotion and recognition with the formal edict, the Emperor announced that he would give his niece, Princess May Szee to Khan Gong Shun in marriage.

"In addition to the title, Emperor Quangxu awarded your grandfather many fine treasures from the palace. Among the gifts were two royal scrolls featuring the Emperor's seal and inscriptions in both Chinese and Manchurian. He was also given an art scroll and a painting of black peonies hand-painted by the Dowager herself, who had been taught the art of water coloring by a series of famous painters. This painting of the black peony was considered a national treasure and surely meant that Dowager Cixi expected great things of your grandfather."

I sat there open-mouthed.

"Wow, mama, does that mean I have royal blood in me? Perhaps one day I will be a warrior too."

"Little one, it is time for you to go to bed. I need to check on your homework exercises before I retire. Sweet dreams, my love."

She gave me a big hug and kissed me on my forehead. I was very tired, but I pondered the wonderful story that mama had told to me. Imagining what life was like at the palace allowed my imagination to soar in the rarest of places. I thought wistfully about the elaborate ceremonies, the unusual superstitions and palace protocols, as well as mama's descriptions of the palace's sleek stone floors, brightly painted wood, the brilliant colorful rugs and pungent incense burners sweetening the air. In my mind, I could actually hear the drum rolls and the regal music, not to mention the swishing silks of the courtiers, concubines and eunuchs as they walked quickly on their way to intriguing appointments within the walls of the Forbidden City. And even though I didn't know what a concubine was, I thought it would be grand to have a playmate such as that who would share a bedroom with me each night!

Chapter Ten
The funeral

My father was taking a turn for the worse. He was in constant pain when awake, so he took generous amounts of morphine and slept most of the time. I would watch my mother cry quietly in my room, away from my father so that neither he nor his spirit could see her weeping.

One afternoon, while papa was resting, I asked my mother if she wanted to go with me to the cave, to my "secret" place.

"Ling, I have heard so much about the cave," she said.

"I would very much like to see it."

"Mama, you need to put on rubber-soled shoes. The rocks are slippery. And bring a sweater too. It is cold in there."

I led my mother down the gravel path instead of along my normal route, which was more difficult to navigate though inherently more interesting for a young boy. When we reached the basin of the waterfall, I said, "Mama, hold on to my hand and I will guide you to the cave. It is going to be wet before we enter."

Mama was a good sport, as we passed under the rushing waterfall to enter the cave.

"Ling, you are right, it is cold and damp in here. Look at these interesting wall paintings. Did you paint them?"

"Yes, I wandered down here alone in the summertime when I was bored with the temple activities. Here is the rock that Papa and I used to sit on when we talked. He showed me how to paint the wild animals with the special paint he gave to me."

I studied my mother and wondered whether to tell her the delicious secret of this place. But then I thought, well of course she knows. Even so, I felt as if I were ushering her into a private world with my next question.

"Mama, did you know that my grandfather Khan Gong Shun, the royal commander, is buried here? His parents brought his body here because of the treachery that happened in his home village. You see the large block of stone at the end of this cave? He was buried inside a tomb there, secretly, so the villagers would not disturb his body. It is sealed and I have never been in there. Papa and I burn incense at the entrance to pay respect every time we are here."

Mama just smiled and rubbed my head, but didn't say a word. She didn't want to spoil my moment of self-importance, even though she obviously knew about the palace conspiracy that led to my grandfather's poisoning, and the willing villagers who had helped kill their generous native son because of their insatiable greed.

It seems that Empress Dowager Cixi's vehement opposition to the sweeping political, legal and social reforms that Emperor Quangxu wished to impose festered for some time. His establishment of a modern university in Beijing, the construction of the Lu-Han Railway and his proposed system of western-style budgetary management began to create a thorny, uneasy partnership. It ultimately soured the previously solid understanding that Cixi had formed with Quangxu. This problem, in turn, carried over to Khan Gong Shun, as well, because of his closeness to Quangxu who treated him almost like a brother.

To nullify Quangxu, Cixi orchestrated a successful coup d'etat, with the help of a General Ronglu. She had Quangxu exiled to a palace on a small island linked to the Forbidden City by a controlled causeway. Not long afterward, Khan Gong Shun and Princess May Szee visited his hometown where the local officials honored him with a banquet. The next day, he became gravely ill en route to pay his respects at the Purple Golden Mountain. He died just before he and his family reached the mountain foothills.

I remembered that my father had also told me how Cixi had not only bribed several of the local villagers to assist with the poisoning at the banquet, but she had also hired a small group of Manchu clan elders to slaughter several roasters and sprinkle the chickens' blood around the outside of Gong Shun's family house. This curse served as a prelude to Gong Shun's death the next day.

"Papa said that when they rode in the horse-drawn carriages to Purple Golden Mountain that day when grandpa took ill, the banners of the Royal Ch'ing flag were flying proudly ahead of them, held by riders on beautiful horses. They didn't know then that grandpa had been poisoned."

I picked up three sticks of incense from a nearby box and lighted them. After bowing three times, I gave the sticks to mama.

She bowed and said, "To honor you, Khan Gong Shun, we are here to beg of your spirit and your ancestors' spirits to protect your son, Khan Bei. Please don't take him away from us. He is too young to leave this world. My son and I beg of you to let him stay with us a little longer."

I took out my paintbrushes and wet the paint with the water dripping down along the cave wall. Using my rudimentary skills, I painted a warrior in full armor, with swords rising from his hands, on the stone block that was the entrance to my grandfather's tomb. That was the image I had always visualized of him.

"Ling, that is a very nice drawing," mother complimented me. "You have quite a collection of paintings here. One day we should bring a photographer down here to take pictures of your artwork. But it is getting late, I think we should go back up and check on your papa."

It was so quiet in papa's room except for the wheezing sound of his weak breathing. When my mother touched him, he opened his eyes and tried to say something to me. Mama held me up to his bed and let me snuggle with him. He was so frail as he held onto my hand that it almost frightened me. I felt guilty that the touch of my father's bony hand made me uneasy. But I loved the warmth of his breath.

The next morning, I woke up next to papa, who lay cold and motionless on the bed. Mama was silently crying next to his body, which was covered with a silk blanket. I got up quietly and moved toward the foot of the bed.

"Ling, papa left us last night," said mama, "but he was happy to have us close to him. Superior Master is coming in to bless your papa's body soon. We are in mourning; you need to put on this white garment."

Mama handed the garment to me. Surprisingly, I didn't cry. I was sad, but I still couldn't imagine that my papa was gone. People began coming into the room to prepare his body, and I was told to go to the temple hall to pray.

=====================

Through the early morning gray, the lights of Nanjing were muted at best. City officials, taking the most prudent route, had recommended that only essential lights remain on throughout the night in fear of possible bombing raids by the Japanese. Even so, above the city I could make out the silhouettes of some of the more familiar buildings as we roared toward our landing spot on a private airfield just north of the city. Soon the whirring sound of the landing gear would pierce my ears, but for the moment there was a certain sense of calm before I would have to face the unpleasant reality that awaited me back at my office. I closed my eyes and let my mind wander for a few more precious moments.

=====================

Papa's funeral was deeply ingrained not only into my brain, but also into my soul on that solemn day.

Several years earlier, he had contacted the best Feng Shui master in the district to help him select the burial site for the Khan family. Though only about five years old at the time, I remember walking around the base of the Purple Golden Mountain. The Feng Shui Master held a compass and an eight-sided chart wheel in his hands. He pointed his compass in different directions and studied the various sites. After what seemed like hours of intense study of the compass and the wheel, he finally spoke.

"Mr. Khan, this is it. Right here at this site. You shall have the tall mountain for your backdrop to protect you from the north wind; in front of your family plot is the winding, running creek. Water is a living element from God and it will bring peace, harmony and prosperity to your future generations. You will see the sun rise from the east each morning and set to the west in the evening. The tall trees from both east and west will offer natural protection for your site. These trees have been here for centuries, unfolding their ancient wisdom and sense of endurance that will bring longevity to your family. You and your descendents will enjoy a life cycle of many blessed days to come."

My father was quite happy with the final determined site. He had wanted it to be close to his own father's burial plot, yet with its own unique sense of balance and continuity.

"Good," my father had exclaimed. "I will make arrangements with the Nanjing government to purchase this lot. I would like to have at least three hectares so that this would be the Khan's sanctuary near the temple and surrounded by the tall pine trees of my favorite Purple Golden Mountain."

"Mr. Khan," announced the Feng Shui Master, "I am going to mark the family plot with these sticks. You should be buried with your head facing north. Regarding your loved ones, we will have to calculate each individual's birthday, as well as their exact birth time and place to determine each coffin's final resting location."

"This is good enough for me," my father said. "I will purchase this land so that it can be a blessing to my generations to come. Whether they want to use this plot or not, I will leave the rest of my family to decide their own destiny when their time comes."

Many people came to the main temple on the day of papa's funeral. They gathered together at the temple hall to start the procession, their heads bowed in tribute as the pall bearers carried my papa from his chamber in a plain wooden coffin. The coffin was adorned, however, with a yellow silk banner, embroidered in purple with the Ch'ing Dynasty royal family emblem.

The temple gong rang nine times and the procession proceeded past the waterfall, downhill toward the west side of the temple. It followed the narrow gravel path, which had become so familiar to me during my daily walks up and down the hill each summer while staying with Superior Master Lou Ming. Hired mourners walked in front of the procession, wearing white robes and hoods. They made very sorrowful sounds and cried out my papa's name. Some actually sobbed, the tears running down their cheeks like water down a rain gutter. I couldn't understand why we had to hire strangers to cry for papa's death. He had many close friends who dearly loved him and missed his presence at this sad hour. The paid mourners seemed to cheapen the event in some uncomfortable way.

The Buddhist temple monks, led by Superior Master Lou Ming,

walked at the front of the coffin, which was held aloft by four men wearing white tops, white trousers and light straw hats. They carried the coffin on two thick wooden poles threaded with heavy ropes that wrapped around the casket. The monks chanted in unison and rang their heavy brass bells occasionally, while incense smoke filled the air. I could smell the pungent aroma of cinnamon and sandalwood in my nostrils.

Our servant, Archi, was among a group in black and white clothing behind the monks. She brought with her two men who claimed to be my papa's relatives from Anhui province, though I had never met or heard of them before. Archi's moles stood out in stark relief against her round face, giving her the look of an Asian caricature.

As we approached the burial site the sky turned dark and ominous. Soft raindrops soon began landing on our heads when we approached the open hole at the gravesite. The crowd of people stood in silence around my father's coffin, which rested against a rather large mound of dirt.

I held my mama's hand tightly as the monks performed the Buddhist burial rituals. Dressed in a pale garment and a white veil, she tried to choke back her tears, but her eyes were red and swollen from grieving the night before. While the monks swung their incense urns back and forth, chanted and sprinkled ashes on the wooden box, I tightened my grip on my mother's hand. I remember thinking about my father's engrossing stories and our walks out to the woods where he taught me how to hunt foxes and wild birds. I had told myself that I wouldn't cry; I was a big boy. So whenever I felt the hint of moisture seeping from my eyes, I would think about another adventure, some real and some just imagined, with my father.

Finally, mama let go of my hand and knelt before papa's coffin. She removed the Royal Court banner from the coffin lid, folded it neatly, then watched as the men lowered papa into the deep hole.

Almost instantly, people began shoveling dirt on top of papa's casket. Mama wept quietly and the sky grew darker. I thought, for a moment, that the clouds would open and the rain would race down in torrents, interrupted only by deafening cracks of thunder and bristling, jagged bursts of hot lightning. But instead, a light drizzle descended on us, the gray clouds remained almost shapeless and the wind was as still as a field mouse. Hardly the kind of ending I would have expected for my father, the effervescent Khan Bei.

The people all left, one by one, including Archi and her friends who seemed to fade into the misting rain. Only the monks remained, chanting and lifting their hands to the sky as they knelt on the wet, muddy grass.

After the men shoveling dirt into the hole finished their task, I wrapped my arms around my mother's soaked body from behind and clung to her tightly. My heart hurt to think of my mother so alone, but also to wonder what would become of me. Where would I go now?

Superior Master Lou Ming helped mama to her feet and asked her to follow them back to the temple. Once inside the temple, mama took me to our quarters and removed my wet clothes. She dried me with a warm towel and rubbed my body vigorously to keep me from shivering, then helped me to put on a new set of white clothing, the official garments of mourning.

Mama's long black, wet hair draped around her shoulders. I could see the rainwater still dripping off the moist strands as she knelt at papa's former bedside, her head now buried into the silk comforter. There was silence all around, and I dared not speak a word nor make a sound. Kneeling down next to her, I leaned my head onto mama's cold and trembling body.

Chapter Eleven
Time with my parents

When I awoke the next morning, I found myself sleeping in the same bed where my papa's lifeless body had lain just yesterday. Mama sat next to me and stroked her hands on my hair with a warm, loving touch.

"Good morning, Ling. You slept like a baby all night."

"Morning, mama." With an anxious frown, I asked, "What are we going to do without papa? Where are we going to live?"

"We are not going to worry about this right now. I need time to sort things out and we will stay here a little longer."

Just then, there was a knock at our door. Brother Lee, the young apprentice monk, spoke softly behind the door.

"Mrs. Khan, is everything all right? Superior Master Lou Ming would like to speak with you some time today whenever you are ready." Mama walked toward the door, which was slightly ajar.

"Please tell Superior Master Lou Ming that I will meet with him as soon as I change my clothes."

After Mama changed to another white garment, she bent down to kiss me on the forehead.

"Ling, dear, I will see you after I speak with Superior Master Lou Ming. There is a fresh white garment for you at the foot of the bed. We are in mourning for three months, so you are to put away all of your colorful clothing for awhile."

After dressing and, with Brother Lee's help, reluctantly putting my colorful clothes into a woven basket and covering it with a black cloth, I walked toward the kitchen. Brother Lee had given me good news…Uncle Pigtail was making fresh hot buns, my personal favorite.

I walked quietly into the kitchen where Uncle Pigtail was lifting a bamboo steamer from the hot water pot. The rising steam sent its tantalizing aroma into my nostrils.

"My dear Ling, are you all right?" Uncle Pigtail asked. "I hope you didn't catch cold yesterday."

"I think I am all right, Uncle Pigtail. Can I have some hot buns now?"

"I made a fresh batch just for you. Here are some pickles, if you like. I milked the goat this morning, so you may also have some milk."

Uncle Pigtail watched me eat and wiped his eyes with his freckled, olive-colored hand. He took out his handkerchief to blow his nose, making a sound so loud that it scared the little sparrows loitering by the open kitchen window. We both laughed as they flapped their wings frantically and flew away. It felt good to return, even briefly, a smile to my face.

"Your father was a good man," Pigtail said. "We are going to miss him! He had great plans for you and your future."

"What plan, what future? Uncle Pigtail?"

"You must wait, child, until Superior Master Lou Ming finishes talking with your mother and she will tell you all about it."

Suddenly, Pigtail remembered something. "Ling, have you seen your servant, Archi, since the funeral? She never showed up in the kitchen last night or this morning."

"I don't know where she is," I replied.

Returning to papa's room after breakfast, I decided to look for Archi while waiting for mama's return. My first stop was the storage door in the bedchamber where papa kept his belongings. I was shocked by what I found or, more correctly, what I didn't find.

All of papa's clothing and mama's fur coats and fine dresses were gone. The storage room was totally emptied out. Even my father's important documents and precious jewelry boxes were missing, as well as his shot guns and hunting rifles.

I ran out and intercepted Brother Lee in the hall.

"Come, Brother Lee," I grabbed his hand and led him to papa's room.

"Where are all my papa's and mama's belongings in the storage room? They have disappeared!"

"Dear Ling, let me take a look." Lee opened the storage door to check, and his eyes opened wide.

"Oh, no! Everything is gone! Let me find out from the other monks who stayed at the temple while we went to the funeral procession yesterday."

I waited for mama to come back so I could show her the storage room. Brother Lee never returned with any news, so I just sat on papa's bed for what seemed like an eternity. Tears threatened to flood my eyes; I felt so alone and helpless. I wanted to go to my cave where papa used to sit with me and tell me stories.

Unable to sit still any longer, I ran out of the temple and climbed down the rough rocks, following the narrow stone ledge next to the waterfall, which led to my secret summer cave hideout. The waterfall continued to roar at the entrance to my cave.

This was the place where papa and I used to bring our kills, and I would draw the bird or the small game animal on the rock walls with a special paint. Papa told me that the paint was very expensive, made of vegetable dyes and precious stone powder that would make it last forever. Anyone who discovered this cave after hundreds of years, he said, could still see my paintings on the cave wall and would wonder who painted them. They could see the story I painted of my happiest days and saddest moments.

"Today," I told myself, "I will paint my papa next to the circus ring and a flock of flying geese."

I took out the paint brushes and mixed the powder with a few drops of the water splashing off the rocks. After I had finished, I washed the brushes clean by putting them under the waterfall. Carefully I put away the art supplies in the small box that papa had given to me and hid it in a subtle gap between the rocks.

Sitting on my favorite boulder, I gazed at the cave wall and studied the just completed painting. Papa lay in a wooden box with the trees behind him and dead animals lying all around. The geese were no longer flying, but lying motionless beside papa's box. It was a painting that spoke only of grief and so, for the first time since papa's death, I began to cry.

Around me, all was silent except for the rushing sound of the waterfall. My mind drifted back to the good times when papa was alive. I remembered as far back as when I was four years old, staying with mama and papa in a luxury hotel suite in the center of Nanjing. It was possible to order anything I wanted from the front desk simply by pulling a long rope that stretched between the floor and the ceiling. The Westerners called it "the butler's belt." The bellman would come up to our third floor suite and ring our doorbell.

"Master Ling, what can I do for you today"? he would ask with the most proper diction.

"Can we go to the playground?"

"Let me check with your father, who is in the smoking room with some of his friends. If he says yes, then I will take you."

We would walk to the park playground where I loved to sit on the swing as the bellman pushed me gently from behind.

"Higher! higher!" I would shout. I wanted to be as close to the clouds and blue sky as possible.

My father had given me a bright orange ball, about the size of a small balloon, that I used to kick and chase in the park. The bellman, who was a good sport but not much of an athlete, would sometimes be cajoled into knocking the ball around with me and I always delighted in pushing the ball past him with a clever leg movement or head fake.

One time I slipped past him while toeing the ball like a soccer player, then turned back to smile and gloat. Instantly, I tripped on a loose tree root and fell, then began crying, probably more from embarrassment than from actual pain.

The bellman, whom I secretly named Swim Cap because of his short-cropped black hair, came to my aid and picked me off the cold ground.

"My dear Master Ling, you have a cut on your knee. Can you walk back to the hotel?" He wiped my tears, wrapped his white handkerchief around my knee and secured it with a knot. I stopped crying, for it was really only a small scrape, and let him hold my hand as we walked back to the hotel.

The bellman stopped at the front desk and pulled a first aid kit out from one of the cabinets. He dabbed a cool yellow liquid on my scrape, then covered it with a sterilized pad and bandaged my knee. I looked like a wounded soldier, and it actually hurt worse now that the bellman had applied the liquid and stretched bandages over the tender area. Even though I was hurting a bit, I tried not to hop with one leg so that I wouldn't get Swim Cap into trouble. If papa saw that I'd been hurt under Swim Cap's care, he would surely scold the well-meaning bellman. So I went to one of the dresser drawers in my room and changed to a long pair of trousers.

Mama worked in the nearby hospital where she handled the delivery of newborn babies. Sometimes she would have to leave in the middle of the night, but we were happy together. Or so it seemed.

I don't remember when things began changing between papa and mama. Many nights, my father wouldn't come home. My mother would suffer silently, but even as a child I could sense the apprehension and the loneliness.

One day when papa returned to the hotel suite after three days of absence, I heard mama tell him behind the half- closed door, "Bei, you know how much I love you. And I never ask about other women. I don't want to know. But it is not good for you to hang out with your opium-addicted friends. You have been complaining about the pain in your head and stomach now for some time. I would like for Dr. Chang to come and check it…to make sure everything is all right with you."

Papa coughed hard and cleared his throat. "I am not feeling well these days. Perhaps Dr. Chang could come over and give me some pain medicine."

One day, I came home from kindergarten and found my mama in the room packing our clothes.

"Mama, are we going for a trip?"

"Ling, mama has a new place to live and you are coming with me. It is next to a park and close to my hospital. The school is only a block away and there are many great shops along the street. We can eat out and go to the playground after I come back from work. There is a lady next door, Mrs. Kwan, who will take care of you while I am at work."

"But what about papa? Is he coming with us?"

"My dear, this is a grown-up people matter. You don't need to know now, but papa and I love you very much. Your papa wants to stay at the hotel alone for a little while. You could visit him anytime you want."

The flat we moved into was not as elegant as the hotel suite. It was a small room furnished with two twin beds separated by a drab nightstand. At least the toilet flushed in the bathroom, and the tub held water. Mama always put an imported vanilla fragrance bubble bath into the tub and let me splash the bubbles onto the walls. Sometimes the bubbles warped into shapes similar to the animal paintings in the cave. I had already grown fond of drawing, and mama hung many of my school paintings on the wall above her bed.

True to her word, we went to many new restaurants where we always tried different exotic dishes. Being Japanese, she loved to eat the raw fish favored by her fellow countrymen. I was especially proud that I had learned to acquire that particular taste as well. There were only a few foreign restaurants in the city, but we sampled many different types of food, including French, Italian, Russian and German. Besides Chinese and Japanese food, I liked the Italian dishes best because of their rich red sauces and creamy cheeses.

Papa would send a car to pick me up and drive me to his hotel on holidays and some weekends. He always indulged me and even took me to see puppet shows and the circus whenever it came to town. I loved being pampered by both of my parents separately, but it wasn't the same joy that I had experienced in the past when the three of us did things together. A part of me resented that that had been taken from me.

In the summertime, papa wanted me to stay in the lower temple for three weeks of summer school at the nearby missionary school. Then I was to go to the main temple to spend time with Superior Master Lou Ming to learn literature and history as well as to play around the surrounding woods.

Sometimes papa would come to the temple and take me hunting. He gave me a shotgun as a birthday gift when I turned six, and when I killed my first bird, a solitary starling perched on a weathered tree stump, he applauded me. Deep down, I felt remorse because the bird seemed so content as it warmed its feathers in the midday sun, but papa's boisterous approval overwhelmed those feelings and made me feel giddy with a sense of accomplishment. But even as I sat in the cave, thinking back, I wondered if the bird had had a family waiting for him. I preferred to think of him as a loner, possibly even up to no good.

Even this made me sad and I realized, at that instant, that Archi had packed mama's and papa's clothes and left with the two strangers. I thought of her wearing mama's fur coat, and I bit my lower lip to keep from crying again.

Chapter Twelve
How my parents met

By the time Minister Tao, myself and several other officials had disembarked from the plane, dawn had slowly pulled away the curtain of darkness. Standing straight up for the first time in several hours, I realized how stiff and rigid I felt. I welcomed the brisk walk to one of the military jeeps waiting for us. Minister Tao yawned and followed me to the vehicle, but I asked if he would mind catching a ride with one of the other officials. I had this yearning to return home for an early breakfast with my family before heading into the office for what would surely be a trying day.

The jeep took me straight to the Chow estate. Che Yu was already having breakfast with her family. They were happy to see me and set another plate at the table. Without waiting for much small talk, I began devouring the meal set before me.

"Ling, those people on the plane did not feed you? You look like you have lost some weight."

Everyone laughed, for I had been gone for less than two days, though Chow Mama spoke to me with a concerned look because she thought food was one of the most important things in life...especially for a growing boy as she still regarded me.

After breakfast, I excused myself and went back to our room with my wife. Ming Ming brought our daughter, First Treasure with the given name of Kay, into our room. She was very tiny but had large, beautiful eyes. I held her in my arms, rocked her and kissed her tummy. Something didn't smell quite right, though, and I quickly handed her back to my wife.

"Men, you are all alike," she laughed. "You only want to play with them when they are fresh and clean. We women have to do everything."

Knowing that I wanted to spend time with her, Che Yu rang the bell for Ming Ming, who took the baby away to change its diaper and leave us alone. Next, she called in Ahma and asked her to prepare a hot bath for me.

The bathroom filled with hot steam as Che Yu gently undressed me and helped me into the tub. Sitting outside the tub, she used the sandalwood soap to lather my body. A sweet fragrance filled the room, and my young bride's face appeared flushed from the moist heat in the room.

"I missed you, Ling," Che Yu said shyly.

"It was just a short trip, but I know what you mean," I replied. "There is so much confusion and uncertainty going on right now."

I pulled Che Yu closer.

"Listen, I don't want to alarm you, but there are troubling times ahead for the city. We must all begin to make some contingency plans, in the event that the Japanese attempt an occupation of Nanjing."

The horror on Che Yu's face was unmistakable.

"But you said that the meeting would go well, that you and Admiral Saka were old friends."

I took her hand in mine.

"Friendships cannot always stave off the destiny of wars. We are in a very precarious position, and I must deliver my report to Department Chief Lin later today."

I thought about Che Yu's half-brother, Che Ming, who had had disagreements with the Japanese on various real estate dealings. At the very least, they would confiscate his properties if a full-scale invasion took place.

"And Che Ming,?" I asked. "Is he concerned at all for his safety?" Che Yu didn't answer, but moved closer toward me and stroked my hair. She was clearly worried. I tried to downplay my fears.

"Come on, now. It is not going to happen today, tomorrow or even next week. I am just saying that we need to remain cautious and make a few preparations."

I pulled her closer to me, and we kissed. The soap slipped from her hand and fell into my tub water. When she tried to fish it out, her breasts touched my body and I could see the outline of her nipple against the wet fabric of her blouse. Slowly, I unbuttoned the blouse and removed it, all the while marveling at her smooth, ivory skin.

Touching one of her breasts, I asked her, "Che Yu, are you still nursing our baby? Your breast is so full and round."

"You have turned into an expert in making babies," she answered. "Our doctor checked on me yesterday since I had been three weeks late on my monthly cycle. He suspects that I am pregnant again."

All of that day, as I crafted the words in my report, my mind kept turning back to Che Yu, and the possible birth of our newest child. Perhaps it would be a boy this time. I rushed about my office, taking care of business as quickly as possible. I had determined to arrive home early tonight. Not only was I tired from the long journey, but I had this continual desire to spend my moments with Che Yu.

The evening's dinner was roasted quail with rice, in a sweet orange sauce. Despite worries about what the Japanese might do next, it was still relatively easy to find good meats at the market, especially for those with considerable means.

After savoring the meal with Che Yu and her parents, I poured myself a glass of brandy and retired to a small sitting room with my wife. She put a hand gently on my shoulder.

"Ling, will you tell me a story about your family?"

My mind drifted back to where it had been earlier in the day…to that time at the temple, just after papa had died.

"After my father passed away, mama and I stayed at the temple for a few more weeks," I began. "It was then that she brought up the subject of my future and my father's educational plans for me. It seems that papa had laid out specific instructions that had been witnessed by Superior Master Lou Ming.

"One night not long after papa's death, Superior Master invited mama and me to sit with him in the dining room. After Brother Lee served tea and almond cookies to everyone, Superior Master sighed deeply. Mama put me on her lap and wrapped her arms around me in anticipation of what he was about to say."

"Was it good news?"

"Well, he mentioned my father's long-time trusted friend Uncle Tao whose son, Tao Yee, was a schoolmate of mine. We had played together at the temple the year before and become very good friends.

"Uncle Tao had been my father's roommate at Waseda University many years before and they had become like brothers together. Superior Master told me that Uncle Tao had agreed to be my caretaker and to see that, when the time came, I received the best possible education at Waseda University. I was to begin living with his family that very fall."

"But you were only seven or eight years old."

"Of course, I was shocked and could not contain my anxiety. I asked Superior Master why I couldn't stay with mama, who then lifted me up and put me in a chair in front of her. She told me that she had asked the same question and had told my father, 'Dearest Bei, why can't I take care of my own son? I could take care of him in Nanjing or I could take him back to Japan, stay with my parents and give him the best education he deserved.'

"But papa had told her that, because she was Japanese, we would not be safe here in China together. Then he reminded her that I was Chinese and that I needed to learn the Chinese customs here in my homeland. He thanked her for sacrificing her own dream goal of being a doctor and instead becoming a nurse and a mother. And he told her that it was time she went back to Japan and finished her medical degree in gynecology, her field of study. Then he made her promise that she would return to Japan, or he would not die with his eyes closed. It broke my mother's heart, but she felt it was her duty to honor my father's wishes."

Che Yu smiled a sad smile and put her head on my shoulder. I ran my hand across her soft hair and continued with the story.

"Superior Master Lou Ming went on to tell mama that, years before, Uncle Tao needed to borrow money for the purchase of a newly chartered bank headed by your father. It was my own father who loaned Uncle Tao the amount needed to purchase fifty thousand shares of the stock. My father and yours owned the other portions of the shares, and Uncle Tao was to pay papa back with interest in 10 years. He was out of town when my father passed away and was unable to attend the funeral, but informed Superior Master by messenger that he welcomed me into his family's home until the day I would leave for college. All of my living and educational expenses were taken care of by my father's investment in the bank. Uncle Tao also said that he would take me to meet the Chows and my fiancée… that was you, of course. He mentioned to Superior Master that he had heard she was a very pretty little girl."

I looked down at Che Yu, but she had fallen asleep after a long, tiring day. Not wishing to wake her from her peaceful slumber just yet, I continued to think back on that important time in my life.

That night when I first heard that I would be living with the Taos, mama slept with me and held me tight. I longed for her warmth and the scent of her soft breath. I felt secure and safe when she was near me. It was the one thing…the most precious thing…that gave me any sense of stability. Unlike papa, whom I also loved dearly, mama was someone I could always trust to be there. Or so I had hoped.

The next morning she packed her remaining belongings and bid me good-bye. She was to board a ship to Japan where she would prepare for her medical school in the Fall. I remembered that my father's mother, Princess May Szee, had left him, too, but only after raising him undercover in Nanjing because she feared returning to Beijing after Khan Gong Shun's poisoning. When my father was ready for college, May Szee sent him off to Waseda University and she went to live in a convent where she died only a few years later. I envied my father's years with his mother and even imagined myself in his position, with my own mother depending on me to keep her identity hidden from the wrath of Empress Dowager Cixi. I thought about how exciting it must have been for him to share such a delicious secret with his mother, though in truth their real existence together in Nanjing included the many routines of day-to-day living. Even so, it fascinated me to think of how deep and meaningful their private conversations must have been.

My mother and I both cried and held each other close. The horse-drawn carriage had been waiting for a considerable amount of time at the front temple gate. So Superior Master hurried us along. They bid each other a cordial, heartfelt farewell, both bowing to one another before she stepped up onto the carriage.

"I love you, Ling, I will write to you," mama called to me. "Please ask Uncle Tao to send me pictures of you."

I ran after her carriage until it turned the corner of the winding road and disappeared behind the thousand-year-old trees, tall reeds and bushes of the lush green bamboo forest.

I walked slowly back to my room and sat on my bed. Determining not to cry anymore, I began remembering the story of how mama met papa in Japan.

While he was studying there, he first saw my mother, Namiko, in the university library. He was standing near a well-stocked bookcase and searching for a particular reference manual. As he lifted up his eyes to glance around the room, he saw a beguilingly beautiful young student sitting at a table midway across the room where she was writing notes from a stack of books in front of her. Khan Bei was immediately taken by her fair skin, slender eyes and perfectly oval face with well-balanced features. Her hair was long, shiny and black, accentuated by a colorful hair band on top.

Gathering his books, Khan Bei summoned his courage and walked toward the young woman's study area. His heart pounding heavily, he seated himself across from her reading table and pretended to flip through his books. Occasionally, he would lift his head to peek at the beautiful Japanese girl.

Khan Bei had met many young ladies at parties and functions, but had never felt quite so awkward and uneasy before. This time when he turned his eyes toward her, she looked back and their eyes met. Electricity ran through both of their bodies in a deliciously unnerving way. Both lowered their heads and pretended to study their books.

Though they were clearly drawn to each other, their cultures prevented them from saying anything. So they met at the library like this for almost three months without speaking a word to each other.

Khan Bei's roommate and lifelong friend, Tao Yee, told him one day, "Khan Bei, how can you stand this? You think about that girl constantly and your grades are dropping. You need to do something about it. Draw some courage and ask her out; the worst she can say is no. At least you will get an answer."

Two weeks later, Khan Bei saw her again at the library. After wrestling with himself in his mind for nearly a half-hour, he still couldn't force himself to speak to her. Suddenly, she picked up her schoolbooks, placed them into a cotton bag and left the table. Instinctively, Khan Bei jumped up and began to follow her. When he reached the glass door exit, he realized that it was raining hard outside.

Bei saw the young girl standing under the canopy, the rain and wind blowing on her skirt and white lab coat. Taking a deep breath, he opened the door and went outside to stand next to her.

"Hello," he managed in his best, but still noticeably accented Japanese. "The rain is getting worse and I don't think it will stop for a while. Would you like to go inside to wait instead of out here, Miss?"

The young woman nodded her head and they both turned around and slipped back inside to the library vestibule.

"Hello, my name is Khan Bei, I came from China to study law. I noticed that you come to the library quite often. Could you tell me your name?"

"My name is Namiko Seito. I am in the first year of medical school and plan to be a physician."

The words ran together quickly, almost as if the two had been practicing them for months, only to let them tumble forth all at once when the opportunity finally arose.

After the rain had subsided a bit, Bei offered to walk her to her dormitory. Taking off his coat, he covered both of their heads from the light drizzle on their way back to her living quarters. Whenever they accidentally touched during the walk, they both felt the bristling sparks of attraction.

The next time Khan Bei saw Namiko at the library, he boldly walked up to her table and, addressing her again in Japanese, asked what she was studying. She replied that she was preparing a resume to work in a nearby hospital for the summer, as a training ground for her medical ambitions.

"I do admire your determination!"

Khan Bei spoke more loudly than he had intended, causing other students to look at him in a disapproving manner. So he leaned over and whispered into Namiko's ear, "It is so nice to see you again. If you have time, could I interest you in joining me for tea afterwards?"

Namiko blushed and responded only with a smile, then went back to writing her resume.

Later, pushing the glass door forward and walking outside, she saw Khan Bei waiting there on the library steps. Her heart dropped, and the temptation and desire to know this handsome, young Chinese student was overwhelming.

"You are still here, who are you waiting for?"

Bei gave her a warm smile. "I am waiting for you, Miss Seito. I will not leave until you accept my invitation for tea."

Even though Namiko politely demurred and spoke of a conflicting appointment, Khan Bei summoned his courage and invited Namiko to a school dance scheduled for the following weekend. Hesitant at first, she finally agreed several days later after encouragement from her roommate.

Their date became the first of many. Khan Bei was funny and charming, full of energy and imagination. Namiko grew to adore so many things about him. They talked of his ambition to return to China and to help Sun Yat-sen overthrow the corrupt Ch'ing Dynasty. She laughed at his clever impersonations of famous people, both in the entertainment world and politics, and he reveled in the white heat of her smile and her knowledge of medicine and, more importantly, people. In a very short time, they had become the best of friends.

One cool Spring afternoon, they met at a public park for a casual picnic. From the very outset, Namiko appeared troubled and downcast. Khan Bei could sense it and he tried to probe what was bothering her.

Namiko's eyes teared up. "Khan Bei San, I have a confession," she said in the formal tone common to the Japanese, especially the women. "It is something that I must not keep from you any longer. I am a married woman, with a one-year-old baby girl. She is staying with my parents while I am attending medical school. My parents forced me to marry Mr. Yahata six years ago. He is a very controlling man, without much interest in my medical ambitions. Though he promised my father that he would allow me to go to medical school after we got married, he changed his mind and wanted me to work to support him in his dentistry studies. I reminded him of his promise and, just so that he would not lose face with my father, he finally gave in and allowed me to sign up for medical school. He does not even live with me anymore. Most of his time is spent with a favorite geisha, but that is all right because he was never home much anyway."

She looked at Khan Bei for some sort of reaction. When he didn't speak immediately, she continued, her nervousness clearly apparent.

"I am studying very hard and hope one day I will be independent and able to divorce Mr. Yahata. There was never any love between us. He is a very difficult man to live with because he does not give of himself. Living with him was like living alone."

"What are your plans then, Namiko?"

"I want to divorce my husband and go back to Kyoto to work in my father's clinic. My husband is doing his dentist residency here in Tokyo and will probably stay here, but I never see him. My parents knew about my marriage troubles, but pride has kept them from allowing me to file for divorce."

Namiko lowered her face and began weeping.

"Don't cry," Bei said gently. "I am so sorry for what you have been through. I admire your determination to continue your medical school despite your difficult situation."

Bei lifted her face and kissed the droplets of water from her cheeks.

"Namiko, how do you feel about our relationship? You should know by now that I care about you very much."

"Khan San, I am so happy when I am with you. You bring hope and laughter to my withering life."

Khan Bei grabbed her hands in his.

"I was in love with you the first time I saw you," he admitted. "We have so much in common and I want to spend the rest of my life with you."

Namiko shyly pulled her hands away from Bei to avoid any embarrassing glances from the bystanders in the park.

"Khan San, I am so confused. I am a very librated woman who loves your ideas and ambitions, but our cultures are so different. I obeyed my parents' will to marry someone I did not love. But am I supposed to bear this for the rest of my life because of obedience to my elders?"

Bei looked at her with compassionate eyes. He leaned close to Namiko and whispered to her, "I know what I am about to ask you will shock you. But I must say it now. Will you have the courage to leave your husband now and become my wife? We could take your daughter to China. And I too have a confession.

"I was married once before and also have a daughter. My wife died of smallpox five years ago, and my relatives are taking care of my little girl while I am in Japan. I have never met anyone who could make me so happy and complete. It would give me the greatest honor if you would agree!"

Namiko looked at Khan Bei and responded only with her tear-filled eyes, but he could sense her appreciation and fondness for him. Throwing caution to the wind for the briefest moment, they embraced tightly.

Finally, Namiko's sense of propriety overcame her and she pulled away. They both got up and began walking back to the dormitory together. Namiko was the first one to break the silence.

"I know that it would pain my parents' hearts. Divorce is considered a very shameful deed. They might disown me because I would bring dishonor to the family. But my love for you is greater than those worries."

Khan Bei's face brightened. "Does that mean..."

Namiko continued, "I will follow you wherever you go. I am willing to take the chance and break the news to my parents during summer break."

Inwardly, she abhorred the thought of breaking her parents' hearts, not to mention asking their permission to file for divorce from her husband. This was considered to be one of the most dishonorable acts that a wife could do, especially if she initiated it herself.

Khan Bei had only one more year left before receiving his doctorate in law, and Namiko was concerned about being separated from Bei when he returned to China while she remained in medical school in Japan. After much discussion with Bei, she decided to switch to nursing school and graduate at the same time as him. This could be another potential point of contention with her parents, though when she moved to China she could become a nurse with her extensive medical knowledge and find a respectable job in a hospital there. It was a great sacrifice on her part, but she couldn't bear the thought of separation from the man she loved. There would just be too many variables for things to go wrong if she stayed in Japan.

Namiko went home for a month to be with her daughter and her parents. When she finally broke the news to them, their response was predictable.

"How dare you think of filing for divorce!" her father screamed. "Do you know that our family would be the laughingstock of Kyoto? We did not raise a daughter to shame us!"

"I know I have dishonored you and disappointed you," Namiko began. "But you know that I have been through so much with this arranged marriage. My husband does not love me, he is verbally abusive and frightens me on a physical level as well. I just cannot bear to have my life ruined because of a marriage that was a horrible mistake. Please forgive me!"

"Disgrace! You are not my daughter!" her father angrily shouted back. "I want you out of my house!"

With that, Namiko's father angrily threw her belongings out onto the street while her mother watched the tragic scene with tears in her eyes.

Namiko moved in with a girlfriend and met with her brothers periodically to check on her father's mood. Both of her older brothers were physicians and part of the medical team in their father's clinic. They seemed to sympathize with her situation, although the unconventional approach for a woman to divorce her husband and marry a man of a different race wasn't socially permissible in the Japanese culture.

Finally, through family meetings and discussions of all the benefits and drawbacks, Namiko's father reluctantly gave her permission to leave her husband, but she could never return home again. They would keep and raise her daughter, Khanako. The divorce was devastating for her husband's ego, especially since he was to become a dentist within the next year. When she was finally set free from the marriage, Namiko finished her nurse's training and took work in a local hospital while waiting for Khan Bei's graduation.

Later, my parents married in Shanghai and settled in Nanjing. There, my father followed Sun Yat-sen's political concepts of working to overthrow the Ch'ing Dynasty and reform China into a democratic republic. China was in turmoil; civil war had broken out everywhere, with powerful warlords choosing sides and controlling large numbers of troops. The Boxer Rebellion, with support from Empress Dowager Cixi, was in full swing, with foreigners attacked for "crimes" as trivial as violating Feng Shui.

The Boxers, also known as "The Righteous and Harmonious Fists," were in fact a religious society with animistic leanings. They practiced numerous rituals and used magic spells that allegedly protected them from pain. Their goal was to drive out all "foreign devils" and to usher in a new Golden Age for Chinese society. Though Cixi attempted to exploit the Boxers and other secret societies as a way of fomenting chaos that could be blamed on others, the regional governors made strong efforts to maintain order and limit the Boxers' influence.

No fewer than eight foreign countries found themselves in some semblance of war with China and the Boxers, and they took swift action. When the rebellion ended in 1901, these foreign entities exacted punitive terms that led to millions of dollars in compensation from the Chinese imperial government. Through it all, Japan was hard at work remaking itself as our "allies."

Chapter Thirteen
The White Lantern

A preponderance of work awaited me at the office, particularly since I had been away for several days and yesterday had been spent preparing my report about the disastrous meeting with Admiral Saka. Still, I had this overwhelming urge to drive up to the Purple Golden Mountain, pay my respects at the temple and visit my mother's grave. My remembrances of her the night before weighed heavily on my heart, leaving me with a profound sense of loneliness.

I determined that if I left at daybreak for the temple, I could still return to my office and finish a considerable amount of paperwork. No doubt Chief Lin would want to discuss my report at length, but his sporadic appearances at the office had grown tiresome for me. I reasoned that his mind would probably be on his mistress anyway, rather than wondering about my whereabouts.

Having firmed up my decision, I set out by automobile for the temple after a breakfast of tea and a hot bun. Only Chow Mama was stirring at that hour, and she seemed pensive and somewhat removed from my bustling about in the kitchen. Sensing that perhaps her indigestion was kicking up again, I said no more than "hello" and was soon on the road to the temple.

Though my drive to the temple was uneventful, I couldn't help but feel a sense of uneasiness. Perhaps it was my imagination, but I had begun to see more and more Japanese faces here in the city lately. Japanese dignitaries, bureaucrats, military officers and others increasingly used the term "official business" to explain their growing presence. I had seen what had happened in Manchuria in 1931, when the Japanese had begun their occupation and set up their own puppet state there. Not even complaints from the United States government, nor teeth-gnashing at the League of Nations could keep the invaders from removing the last remaining Chinese administrative authority in the region. Within months the Japanese had established de facto control and were already looking longingly southward.

Now, after my discussion with Admiral Saka, I realized more than ever how all of the pieces seemed to be falling into place for similar escapades in China's major cities such as Beijing, Shanghai and even Nanjing, the capital. After all, we had been living on edge here for three years now. My murdered mother was proof of that.

Internal fighting between various factions of the Chinese government further weakened its ability to curb Japan's expansionist vision. It was easier to appease and compromise than to engage in an all-out war with a stronger, more technically advanced enemy. As a result, intermittent skirmishes among the Chinese government, independent warlords and Japanese troops were commonplace. In truth, the political power of the nationalist government only extended around the area of the Yangtze River Delta. The other parts of the country were under the rule of regional powers. This gave the Japanese a pretext for helping China establish "stability." They would often either buy or develop, through their artifices, special relationships with these regional entities to undermine the nationalist government. It was easy to find men willing to collaborate for a reasonable fee. And as I drove along on this warm Spring day, I wondered who among the many faces that I saw might, in fact, be amenable to such a deal. The thought of it filled me with rage, especially considering my gravesite destination.

Once I arrived at the temple, I first paid my respects to Master Lou Ming who had suffered a mild stroke several months before. In the course of his recovery, he had contacted pneumonia and nearly died, further complicating his return to normalcy. On this particular day, he was in good spirits, though his slurred words provided a grim reminder that time waits for no one…not even the most eloquent of storytellers.

We spoke of old times and shared a few heartfelt laughs together. His mind was, for the most part, exceptionally keen except when he asked about Sunshine's health. In the politest of terms, I reminded him that I had set my dutiful rabbit free in the woods on the day that I left the temple as a boy. He smiled with a knowing nod, no sign of embarrassment in his face, only a philosopher's recognition that the mind is made of simple tissues that inevitably break down with age.

Once outside again, by myself, I eagerly breathed in the mountain air. I could see the new observatory, built three years earlier and set cozily amid dense foliage just below the summit. It was said that the views of Nanjing were spectacular from that vantage point, but I had never ventured to the observatory entrance. I thought it to be an intruder of sorts, an unwelcome guest that brought with it scores of sightseers who would never know nor appreciate the secrets of the mountain as I did. In truth, it was a beautiful structure with a softly rounded dome and an impressive array of research equipment and instruments. And on this day the mountainside trail leading up to the observatory was devoid of foot traffic.

Walking slowly toward my mother's gravesite, I scanned the vegetation in hopes of spying a late-arriving tiger butterfly. Found only in Nanjing, they displayed exquisite black and yellow patterns on their wings that looked remarkably similar to tiger stripes. Since they traditionally make their appearance during the month of March, I knew the chance of seeing one at this late stage of Spring was remote. So I sat for a moment, merely pondering my familiar surroundings.

Later, kneeling at my mother's grave, the anger that I felt on my drive out to the temple had dissipated. I remembered, almost dispassionately, the day of my mother's funeral. It had been a very quiet ceremony, held at the temple during the sunset hours when the sky filled with a palette of amber and purple colors.

Chow Papa, Chow Mama and several of our close relatives all stood before mama's mahogany coffin. Che Yu had arranged for the top of the coffin to be draped with white and pink peonies. Master Lou Ming, his monks and nuns walked in a circle around the coffin and prayed, all the while sprinkling holy water and swinging incense, which filled the gravesite with a familiar sandalwood aroma. We each held a red rose that we placed on top of mama's coffin before it was lowered down into the dull brown hole next to papa's grave. That was when I had knelt before my late parents' caskets and vowed revenge for my mother's cruel, untimely departure.

Leaving before the arrival of darkness, Chow Papa and Chow Mama asked if Che Yu and I wanted to stay a bit longer because they could sense my strong urge to linger at the gravesite. When I finally got up to leave, Che Yu and I thanked Master Lou Ming and took a horse drawn carriage down the familiar path to the base of the temple where Chow Papa's chauffeur was waiting for us.

We drove along a newly paved road along the riverbank, in total silence. Finally, up ahead I saw a huge willow tree that brought back something significant from my childhood memories, and I asked the chauffeur to stop.

"What is the matter, Ling? Is everything all right?" Che Yu broke her silence.

"Che Yu, when I was a child of six, something very dramatic happened around that willow tree," I said, pointing toward the riverbank below. "Give me your hand, I will take you down the little path."

Just in front of the willow tree, I found a flat rock and brushed it with my handkerchief, then motioned for Che Yu to sit down.

"Ling, what is on your mind? Can you tell me?"

It was then that I told her my story about a time, during the year 1916, when the civil war in China had caused major cities to deteriorate into gun battles and looting. It was still safe outside the city, however, especially the area around the temple. As a six-year-old boy, I walked two miles to school each day along that riverside.

On this particular cold and windy January day, the school was holding a late afternoon function in which the students were performing for some missionary guests. After the show, I packed up my school books in a large handkerchief, which I tied into a sturdy knot and carried on my shoulder. The teacher lit a white lantern for me to carry on my journey back to the temple, then closed the school gate behind me.

As usual, I walked and hopped along the river path. The air was frosty, and misty raindrops dampened my little straw hat. I was careful not to let the drops smother the flame in the white lantern because there were no street lights to guide my way, and only a few locals lived alongside the river. Humming the song that we had sung at the school performance, I could see the smoke rising from the chimneys of the shabby structures across the river.

As I passed the large willow tree by the riverbank, I felt the frigid air cutting through my cotton-quilted jacket. When the rain began to strengthen, I ran under the willow and looked up at the half-moon, which cast a subdued light on the tree.

Suddenly, I tripped over the gnarled tree roots, and my schoolbooks dropped into the dark, wet mud. Somehow, though, I was able to maintain my grip on the twisted bamboo stick that held the lantern. At that instant, I could smell an unusually sweet fragrance in the air. Puzzled, I held out the lantern to examine my surroundings more clearly. The mysterious fragrance smelled like a lily, but it would be extremely unusual for any flower to be blooming at this time of the year.

My curiosity took hold and I continued to search for the source of the aroma, but all I could see were dry bushes and small mounds of dirt piled around the willow tree.

All at once, a piercingly cold air brushed across my neck from behind. I felt so afraid that I immediately darted from under the tree, picked up speed and rushed toward the faintly lighted temple still far in the distance. Finally approaching the temple gate, and completely out of breath and shivering from the cold, I reached as high as I could to grab the huge, bronze doorknocker and called out, "Brother Lee, I am home! Hurry, please open the door!"

It was reassuringly comfortable and warm inside the temple living quarters. Brother Lee, the apprentice monk, helped me remove my wet jacket and placed it over a large, mustard yellow ceramic urn containing hot coals that warmed the room. I put my numb little hands on the rounded edge of the urn to heat them up.

Food was already on the table. Even though it was lukewarm, I was so hungry that I ate seven vegetable dumplings, a bowl of turnip soup and, for dessert, a scoop of my favorite sweet gummy rice filled with red beans.

Feeling the contentment of a full stomach, I drew closer to the fire where Master Wong sat and slowly drank his green tea.

"Ling, my child, how was school today?" he asked.

I excitedly told Master Wong everything that had happened in school, even singing a refrain from our song performance. Then I inquired, "Master, does the lily flower grow in the wintertime?"

Master Wong smiled gently and stroked my head with his lean, bony fingers. "Of course not, my child, why do you ask?"

I related to both Master Wong and Brother Lee the events that transpired during my walk back to the temple.

Master Wong took another sip of the green tea and covered the teacup to keep it warm.

"Some 30 years ago," he began, "there was a well-established merchant family named Zhou that lived in a nearby village. They had a beautiful 17-year-old-daughter, May Ling, whom the father had arranged to be married to a wealthy banker who lived across the river. But May Ling and her young home school tutor had secretly been in love for several years.

"After the marriage arrangement was announced, the family busily went about getting May Ling's dowry together. The household maids sewed new dresses and gowns from Mrs. Zhou's collection of colorful silk fabrics. They added pearl embroidery and embellishments of gold and silver threads throughout the silk garments. Gold and jade jewelry from the family heirlooms were chosen as complementary accessories. A servant was even appointed to serve as May Ling's chambermaid once she was married.

"The young bride was utterly heartbroken that she would not be able to unite with her true love, but it was the Chinese custom that the children must obey their parents' decisions regardless of whom they personally wished to marry. Well, May Ling refused to eat for days. Finally, the servants were ordered to force feed her so she wouldn't be too thin on her wedding day. That certainly would have been an embarrassment for Mr. Zhou, causing him to lose face with the groom's family and the village at large.

"As the wedding date drew near, May Ling told her parents that, although she was grateful for her wonderful education and her loving upbringing, she had misgivings about the man she was about to marry. Since she had never met him, she could not be sure if he would love her and treat her well.

"After a fair amount of begging and tears, May Ling buried her head against her mother's bosom. Tears swelled in the mother's eyes as well, and Mr. Zhou extended a hand to lightly touch May Ling's head. In his gentlest tone possible, he reminded her of the long, exhaustive search he had undertaken to find the best candidate, with just the right bloodline. The Han family, with its successful banking business stretching over two generations, fit the requirements perfectly.

"He assured May Ling that, having met the groom and his family, he knew that she would be pleased with the choice. Then he reminded her of the disgrace it would cause their family if May Ling were to back out now. Before he went into another room to smoke one of his hand-rolled cigarettes, he encouraged his daughter to start eating again. It was imperative that she gain some weight before the big occasion.

"May Ling yearned hopelessly for the touch of her star-crossed lover, the tutor whom she missed desperately. She remained in her bed and sobbed throughout the night, unable to bear the thought that she would never see him again.

"Her tutor, Mr. Chong, wrote a letter to May Ling in which he outlined how she might escape from her home and elope with him. They planned to travel on foot and hide in his cousin's home for several days. Later, they would take a train to Shanghai where they would make a new life for themselves.

"Unfortunately, Mr. Zhou found out about the plan and had Mr. Chong intercepted and sent on a freight car to Mr. Chong's family home in the Guangxi Province, several days journey by rail from Nanjing.

"On the day of the wedding, the Zhou family prepared their daughter for her meeting with the groom at the riverbank. They dressed her in a red silk wedding gown studded with pearls and embroidered with a gold and silver design of the traditional dragon and phoenix. May Ling wore a red fringed, beaded veil over her face, and her mother sprinkled a few drops of May Ling's favorite lily-scented perfume on her daughter's neck and handkerchief."

"Did May Ling marry the banker?" I asked eagerly.

Master Wong raised his eyebrows to pique my curiosity even more, then continued with his story.

"Two maids helped May Ling into the decorated sedan seat of an elaborate carriage. Double happiness symbols were painted in gold on the four sides of the carriage, while red silk curtains provided a degree of privacy for the young bride. She, of course, acted obediently so that she wouldn't be caged and padlocked, a remedy for many reluctant brides en route to their wedding. Four strong gentlemen carried her, their hands tightly gripping the bamboo rods threaded through the bottom of the veiled box. An additional attendant shielded May Ling with a parasol during those times when she was exposed to the sun, while another tossed rice at the sedan to ensure that there would be plenty of food in her future household.

"May Ling's parents had even hired a 'dajin,' a woman who would serve as a good luck charm and traditionally look after the bride before the ceremony.

"A group of musicians playing wedding tunes preceded the procession, which began from the Zhous' home. Firecrackers were set into the air to ward off evil spirits as the wedding sedan departed. Behind the carriage, several foot servants carried May Ling's dowry trunk. It took five hours of walking to reach the river where she was to be received by the groom's family boat, which would then cross to the other side.

"During the final mile along the river path, a violent thunderstorm struck, and the sky turned dark as a winter night. The rain was so intense that it quickly made the mud path unsuitable for further traveling. With no visibility whatsoever on the pathway, the caravan took shelter under a cluster of large trees. Finally, after two hours, the thunderstorm passed and the chambermaids peeled away the silk veil of the box seat to check on the bride. To their astonishment, only May Ling's red wedding gown and veil lay inside on the seat.

"All of the servants began yelling loudly and searching the woods for her. Not only were they concerned for May Ling's safety, but also for their own. If somehow they had lost her along the way, Mr. Zhou surely would have dealt with them severely, perhaps even putting them in physical danger.

"Soon one of the servants standing beside the riverbank screamed for the others, who then scrambled down the bank. They suddenly stopped in their tracks, frozen by the sight of May Ling, dangling from a silk cord strung over the largest branch of a huge willow tree. Still wearing her white inner gown, she apparently had climbed the tree and used her undergarment robe's sash to end her life.

"For her funeral, the Zhou family placed dozens of white lanterns on the willow tree so that her spirit would be able to see at night while in the other world."

Brother Lee had replenished the teapot with fresh water and set it over the fire for brewing moments before. Now he poured the steaming tea into Master Wong's empty cup.

"The spirit of May Ling remained around that large willow tree for as long as I know," said Master Wong. "Some people claim to see the white lanterns on the tree during rainy nights. Many travelers have sworn to have seen her ghostly image as they were passing through at night, although it's never really been confirmed."

The very thought of that sent shivers up my neck. I was sure she had been a very nice young lady, but the less contact with the spirit world, the better as far as I was concerned.

I couldn't help but ask, "What happened to the Zhous' servants? Did Mr. Zhou kill them?"

"Oh, no, no. It was an unfortunate tragedy. But the foreman and the chambermaid were fired without any recommendation letter, making it difficult for them to find employment elsewhere."

After a long pause, Master Wong looked at me and said, in a serious tone, "My dear child, your ancestors have given you a lot of Yang Chi to make you much stronger than the Ying Chi. When you were running, you ran through May Ling's spirit, and her perfume fragrance was released by your impact. You were very lucky that you did not see her image! It would not have been a pleasant sight! Now, we will burn some incense to ask for her forgiveness for intruding into her space."

All I could do was breathe deeply. Home by the fire never felt so good.

Chapter Fourteen
Staying with the Tao family

The day had slipped away much more quickly than I had anticipated. It would be difficult to get much work done at the office, but I needed to at least make a show of some type of effort. Besides, in these unsettling times, I could be asked to run a clandestine mission at a moment's notice, so preparation was a priority.

Equally concerning was Minister Tao's rather alarming version of our meeting with Admiral Saka. While I honestly couldn't refute most of his impressions of the events, I wanted to convey a more calming tone to Department Chief Lin. There was no point in heightening tensions at this time.

My transceiver research work was continuing, with excellent progress on improving the quality of the transmission, and all of the parts were now being made in China. By eliminating the long wait for German-made parts, we could repair and test the equipment much more quickly. So I felt like our communications were vastly improved, and we had intercepted many important Japanese transmissions defining many of their battlefield strategies.

With that technology at our disposal, the best course of action right now was prudent observation and a level-headed awareness of the potential threat. So it was my intention to speak to Lin alone and offer a more subdued assessment.

Driving back into town, I remembered how much the story of May Ling had touched Che Yu as we sat by the willow tree on the evening of my mother's funeral. When I told her that I had asked Master Wong if we could burn some money in a special ritual so that May Ling could afford a train ride to meet her tutor in the other world, she smiled and spoke admiringly of my "compassion." Whether because of Master Wong's ritual or some other force at work, I never encountered May Yee's spirit again.

Helping Che Yu up from the rock by the willow that night, it amazed me how elegantly she moved, even in those final stages of her pregnancy. She wouldn't leave the spot by the riverbank until both of us had bowed to May Ling's willow tree, even though the maiden's spirit had long since vanished.

Three weeks after my mother's death, Che Yu gave birth to our first child, a treasured baby girl whom we named Khan Kay. Due to the complications of the infant's breeched position, Dr. Chang assisted our midwife with the delivery. Wiping the sweat from Che Yu's face, I discovered a newfound appreciation for the difficulties of childbirth and, with it, an even greater recognition of my wife's love and commitment.

=====================

My discussion with the department chief later in the afternoon was well-timed for, as I had feared, Minister Tao had created a firestorm of apprehension, as well as targeted anger toward Admiral Saka within the department. While I, too, shared a real concern for the ambitions of the Japanese, I didn't believe this was the time to be rattling sabers. And I knew that, if all hell broke loose, Admiral Saka could well be my most valuable resource.

On the way home, I thought about spending the evening with Che Yu. After preparing our two young children for bed, we would retire once again to the parlor where I would resume my story of the night before about my life after mama left for Japan. Che Yu had been totally engrossed with my recounting of those events until sleep overtook her. And it was a period of my life that shaped so much of my later adult experiences. Even now, the memories were vivid.

After mama returned to Japan, I stayed at the temple for a few more weeks. On another hot evening in that summer of 1918, the temple was crowded with worshippers bringing their offerings to their ancestors' spirit world during the annual July holiday known as Ch'ing Ming Gee. The festival held during that time signified purification of the dead, achieved through good works and displays of light.

Tao Yee, the son of the man whose family would raise me for the next few years, arrived at the temple with his parents. An eight-year-old boy like me, he was arguably my best friend. Not only was he clever and kind-hearted, but he was also well-groomed and exhibited excellent manners. Tao Yee was wearing a light blue western jacket and yellow shorts that day. When I saw him, I thought to myself, "What a smart look. I like that yellow bow tie on him."

Tao Yee went on to follow the elders for part of the ceremony, but later I took him to my room and showed him my prized mountain bunny.

"Tao Yee, her name is Sunshine. I found her when she was wounded in the forest. She is completely healed now and follows me everywhere."

Yee stroked Sunshine on her head and the rabbit licked his face, which made him giggle.

"Sunshine likes you," I said. "Would you like to take her out for a walk and I'll show you my secret cave? We could also go to the waterfall basin to play."

Tao Yee eagerly took off his jacket and shorts and put on some of my casual clothes and a pair of old shoes. I held Sunshine in my arms and Tao Yee followed me to the woods. We climbed down the cliff barefooted to the waterfall basin and I showed him my cave wall paintings.

"Did you paint that?" He was truly impressed. "It is beautiful. You have many talents, Ling."

"Come on, let's go walk in the water," I suggested.

It was so cool and refreshing to walk under the waterfall. The basin was filled with river rocks, their smooth surfaces softly caressing our feet in the water, which was only about two feet deep. Our toes gripped the rocks and pebbles, providing us with plenty of traction against slipping or falling.

I placed Sunshine in the cave and started throwing rocks across the basin, eager to demonstrate my strength and prowess to Yee. The airy mist from the waterfall cooled our faces and mingled with our warm beads of sweat. For me, that day was like a gift from the gods. It was so gratifying to have a playmate, one who admired me and found me to be witty and interesting. I could tell that Yee felt that same sense of companionship, and I threw the rocks harder to show off my skills. With my father now dead and my mother away in distant Japan, Yee was my one reliable link to a life of normalcy. For wasn't that what young boys did…played and laughed and dreamed of one day becoming, in some sense, heroes to those we loved. But that required more than a solitary life, and so Yee filled a tremendous void that I tried not to directly acknowledge. To do so would be too overwhelming.

As the setting sun cast an expanding shadow on the temple, Brother Lee disrupted our reverie, his voice rising across the temple grounds.

"Ling, where are you? Tao Yee, are you with Ling? You must come back to the temple now."

With Sunshine in tow, we both climbed back up, taking the more challenging rocky hill instead of the gravel path.

Uncle Tao and his wife, standing alongside Superior Master Lou Ming and Brother Lee, greeted us in a friendly, outgoing fashion.

"How are you, Ling? It is so good to see you," said Uncle Tao.

I bowed and answered in an out-of-breath voice, "Yes, I am very well and I am so happy to spend time playing with Tao Yee. Didn't we have fun down there?" I turned my head to my friend.

Tao Yee looked at his parents and said, "Yes, I haven't had so much fun in a long time. Papa…mama…can I stay longer and play with Ling?"

Uncle Tao studied both of us. We had water stains and mud on our clothes.

"Yee, I am glad that you had the good sense to change clothes before playing with Ling. You two can play some more, but come back before the temple closes. We are staying here for supper with Superior Master Lou Ming because I have something to discuss with him."

After I placed Sunshine back in her cage, we raced into the woods where we hoped to see a wild animal, perhaps a mountain lion or a jackal. But instead, we gathered strangely shaped leaves and turned them into a natural mosaic on the ground. Like seasoned artisans we deftly blended the subtly different colors and adjusted the disparate shapes into interesting patterns resembling a natural painting. Tao Yee had many good ideas, but he always deferred to my judgment except for once when he respectfully, and wisely, replaced one of my leaves with another of a lighter, more complementary hue.

Time passed too quickly, and we heard the sounding gongs of the temple. Both of us were exceedingly hungry by then, so we turned and ran back to join the adults.

Uncle Pigtail outdid himself with the cooking that night. Set out on the table was eggplant with garlic sauce, ginger squash with mung bean clear noodles, bean curd with black bean paste and spicy hot pepper, winter melon soup and brown rice. Yee and I ate ravenously that night, both of us suppressing giggles about our good fortune of each having the company of an interesting playmate as well as a feast fit for royalty.

Once dinner was cleared from the table and Superior Master and Uncle Tao left for another room to talk privately, Tao Yee and I scampered up to my bedroom where we played with the half-dozen crickets I had collected during my stay at the temple. I had put them into a cool clay bowl with a flat bottom and covered it with a perforated lid for ventilation. It was popular sport in this region for young boys to stage cricket fights for amusement. Using a feather or a small wheat branch, the boys would tease both crickets in an enclosed miniature arena and entice them to fight. The insects would begin fluttering their wings in rapid cadence, then charge their opponents and engage in a certain type of wrestling motion. When the stronger cricket overcame the weaker one, it would stand on top of its defeated foe and emit a victory song with its loudly vibrating wings.

On this particular evening, I had several crickets contained in different bowls and showed my prizewinner to Tao Yee.

"This is Skull. I found him in the graveyard. He was chirping so loudly like he was calling to me. I figured that he must be a brave cricket to live in the graveyard. And you know what? He has been a champion ever since I got him!"

One of the monks peeked into my room and asked us to join Superior Master Lou Ming, Uncle Tao and his wife. When we arrived, they were sitting comfortably in the temple parlor with teacups in their hands.

Uncle Tao was the first to speak, telling me, "Ling, as you know, this Fall I will be your guardian and you will go to a private school in Nanjing. We will see to it that you go to Waseda University in Tokyo, along with Tao Yee, when you get older. In the meantime, you will be living with us and you can still visit the temple in the summer. How does that sound to you?"

I answered jubilantly, "Uncle Tao, does that mean I get to live in the city and play with Tao Yee all the time? Yes, yes...I would like that very much. Thank you, Uncle Tao."

Mr. Tao sipped his tea, looked me straight in the eyes

and said, "My dear Ling, you have no idea how close your father and I were. We were like brothers. While you are under my care, I will bring you to meet the Chows. Mr. Chow is the president of the Nanjing Chamber of Commence and also your future father–in–law to be."

I blinked, not sure how I felt about a betrothal at eight. Uncle Tao continued.

"Your father had many shares of the stocks at the bank. I was sorry that I could not repay the debts I owed to him before he passed away. Today, the bank is very successful. So I can assure you of an excellent education, through my debt to your father and his own funding. I will return any remaining amount, plus interest, back to you when you receive your diploma from Waseda University."

All of this talk about stocks and shares, repayments and interest was a bit much for me to comprehend. All I really knew was that Tao Yee would be my trusted friend and playmate for years to come. And, of course, there was the small matter of the wife-to-be. But I wouldn't worry about that for now.

As one of the monks added more hot water into the teapot, I turned my attention toward Mrs. Tao, who was wearing a pale pink Chee Pou with a mandarin collar and a fancy knotted button of the same fabric. Double-wrapped silk maroon trim decorated her collar, sleeves and hemline. A pretty lady with graceful gestures, she wore her hair braided and displayed a fresh red rose on one side behind her ear. Her long, dangling earrings sparkled under the soft lantern light as she moved her head. I was sure that Tao Yee considered himself to have an extremely beautiful mother, though it was difficult for me to acknowledge that she would be acting that part toward me. My own mother was miles away in Japan, and Mrs. Tao would assume her mantel.

Sensing my stare, she reached out her hand to touch my shoulder.

"You are such a fine boy. Did you know that your engagement was formalized when the young lady was still in her mother's womb?"

Uncle Tao told his wife, "Go ahead and tell Ling the story. He will find it fascinating!"

Uncle Tao repositioned himself into a comfortable posture in his chair and took a sip of the jasmine tea as he waited for Mrs. Tao to begin. I looked over at Yee to bail me out, but he merely stood there and smirked.

"During the civil war between Sun Yat-sen's government in Nanjing and the warlords, looting and gunfire were rampant in the city," said Mrs. Tao. "Your father was the very close friend of a Mr. Chow who owned several successful hotels and the bank in which we have some shares. He also owned quite a few commercial and residential properties in prime locations of the city.

"One evening, violence was worsening in the city. Your father took your mother and you, a baby barely a few months at the time, in a horse drawn carriage. He urged the driver to rush the carriage to Mr. Chow's residence. Once there, your father knocked hurriedly at their door and insisted that Mr. Chow bring his wife and join the three of you in the carriage. They needed to leave Nanjing immediately to avoid injury or worse in the riots.

"Your father explained to Mr. Chow that there was a retreat house just outside of Nanjing that was owned by the Japanese Embassy. The embassy officials had agreed that your family could stay there for safety until the city was orderly once again.

"While the carriage was trotting through the stone-paved streets, one could hear gunfire everywhere, as well as people crying and even screaming in their fear and loss. As the carriage passed the city gate, things grew quieter. Your father looked at the pregnant Mrs. Chow and asked, 'You are with child. When is the baby due?'

"Mr. Chow answered for her, 'In about five more months, that would be January next year.'

"Your father looked at his tiny baby boy. You were lying contentedly in your mother's arms. It was then that he reminded Mr. Chow of their long history of friendship and declared that if the Chows' baby were a boy, he would become a blood brother to you, Ling. If the baby were a girl, she would be engaged to marry you."

"Why did my father do that?" I asked.

"It was customary for those who shared a very rich friendship," said

Uncle Tao. "In response, Mr. Chow took off his long chain with a red jade pendant bearing a silver cast dragon, put it into your father's hands and clasped them with his own hands. The matter was settled and the agreement sealed before they even arrived at the Japanese mansion retreat."

Mrs. Tao smiled and I could see her red lipstick now smeared on parts of her bright white teeth.

"You will be able to meet Mr. Chow's family while you are living with us," she said encouragingly. "Incidentally, the young girl is very beautiful. When you see her, treat her gently because one day you will marry her as your father had promised the Chows."

The hour was growing late, and so the Taos prepared to leave. But before they did, Superior Master Lou Ming went to his room and carried a small package out with him. Taking Mrs. Tao aside and speaking privately with her, he handed her the package. Upon their departure, I kept waving to Yee until the Taos' images and their lighted lanterns disappeared into the woods.

Chapter Fifteen
Evacuation

When I returned to the office, I immediately regretted my decision to schedule some meeting time with the Department Chief. He was embroiled in a heated closed door discussion with several bureaucrats from the accounting department. I could only guess what kind of endless maze of red tape they were either sorting through or creating for others to untangle. I knew that his thoughts would be elsewhere, his mood irritable. But after more than an hour of waiting, I engaged him in a conversation that was cordial and succinct. He listened politely to my concerns, and my conclusions even elicited a nod of approval. While emphasizing the seriousness of the matter and the potential for grave consequences to occur, I was able to impress upon him the need for delicate statesmanship. This was not a time to be loud and accusatory with the Japanese.

Barely had I arrived home, still congratulating myself for my successful meeting with Lin, when I was met at the door by my wife's distraught half-brother, Che Ming.

"Hurry, mama is having a heart attack. She fainted and fell on the stone floor."

I rushed with him into Chow Papa's room where Dr. Chang and a nurse were administering oxygen to Che Yu's mother.

"What happened, Dr. Chang?" I asked.

"Apparently, she has had some pain in her stomach and chest for the past few days, but assumed it was only indigestion. Most likely, she has a clotted artery and the blood is not circulating well, though she is breathing now. When she lost consciousness, she fell onto the floor and also bruised her shoulder and head."

Che Ming chimed in. "The ambulance is on its way."

Chow Papa was crying at his wife's bedside and clinging to her hand, which he kept rubbing while calling her name.

"Wake up, Chow Lou Wah, my wife, Chow Mama, wake up!"

He repeated the words over and over again because he had been told that the hearing was one of the last things to go if a person was dying. If you called out your loved one's name, you might stir up the spirit to where the person could be revived. At least Chow Papa was holding onto that hope.

He and I joined Dr. Chang and Chow Mama in the ambulance. The remainder of the family left for the hospital in sedan cars driven by the chauffeurs.

The shrill, exceedingly loud siren sent my heart racing. Both Chow Papa and I kept calling Chow Mama's name and rubbing her hand to keep her blood circulating...more than likely a useless gesture at her stage of cardiac arrest.

In the waiting room, our large, extended family of 20 or more stood around anxiously for the updated news about Chow Mama who was undergoing numerous tests and treatments in the intensive care unit. Che Yu, as the eldest daughter, put her arms around Chow Papa and tried to comfort him.

Waiting for more news was excruciating. My mind conjured up all types of outcomes, most of which were poor prognoses. I didn't have a good feeling about this one.

Three hours later, Dr. Chang and another physician walked into the small area where we had gathered. The other doctor spoke.

"She is stabilized and is half-conscious. It was a massive heart attack, so we don't know the full extent of the damage yet. If you wish, I will allow two of your family members to go in at a time to see her."

Chow Papa and Che Yu went in first and stayed for what seemed like a long time. Later, after some of the others had ventured in, I paid my respects with Che Yu. Chow Mama was hooked up to a respirator, reminding me of my papa. Her eyes barely open, she was unable to speak.

That same feeling of the wind being jolted from my chest took hold once more, as when I saw my own father withering away. Tears gushed from Che Yu's eyes, only compounding my sense of depression. As Che Yu leaned over her mother and embraced her, I gave Chow Mama my hand and she latched onto it with a surprisingly strong grip. We stayed with her for what seemed to be a half-hour. Finally, when she appeared to be sleeping, we left the room and took up our watch in the waiting room with the others.

I never heard Chow Mama utter another word. She died that night with Che Yu and Chow Papa at her bedside. I had just finished reading a magazine article about ancient Chinese wood carvings while seated in the waiting area.

With the awkward uncertainties that accompany an impending war, family tragedies become even more cumbersome to manage. The funeral was simple, due to this instability and the spontaneous riots that were occurring with increasing frequency in the city.

Afterward, Chow Papa retreated into his room and hardly spoke or ate. His eyes became hollow and he seemed to age 10 years over a period of several weeks. At night he would complain about being cold, even with three layers of silk blankets on his bed.

Concerned about Chow Papa's health, we summoned Dr. Chang to perform a physical exam. It was then that we discovered that Che Yu's father also had suffered a heart attack, probably shortly after his wife's death. He got progressively weaker over the course of the next month or so and soon could barely move his legs. But he refused to go to the hospital and insisted on remaining in his own familiar bed.

Dr. Chang asked Che Yu's permission to hire a lady to sleep with him at night to keep his body warm. At first, Chow Papa tried to push the poor woman off the bed. If it had not been so sad, it probably would have been quite comical, like watching an old couple fighting over the covers.

Eventually, however, he submitted to this arrangement. She was a retired nurse, overweight with plenty of body fat to keep Chow Papa warm at night. Though extremely nearsighted, her nursing care didn't require her eyes to be sharp since Chow Papa could still feed himself.

This had been a particularly trying time for me because, not only was I expected to provide the male strength in the family due to Chow Papa's slow demise, but I was also grappling with troubling news on the political front. Skirmishes between Japanese troops and the Kuomintang had escalated into full-scale battles. My initial recommendation of caution and restraint was now being replaced with the depressing view that war was inevitable. Not long ago, Hirohito had ratified an amendment to remove the guidelines of international law regarding the humane treatment of Japan's growing number of Chinese prisoners. Staff officers had been advised to quit using the term "prisoner of war," indicating Japan's toughening stance toward its enemy.

Now, with my increasing influence and growing rank within the military echelon itself, I was urging the most extensive preparations possible to ward off a full-scale invasion. In a matter of months, my mindset had changed from conciliator to strategy coordinator. It was still my hope that negotiations and respectful compromise could help my countrymen avoid an all-out war, but in any case I wanted to assure that planning could be converted into fast action should circumstances deteriorate further.

Weak as he was, all of this was not lost on Chow Papa. One day as I was passing by his room, Che Yu was seated at his bedside and she signaled for me. Once I had bowed to Chow Papa and greeted him, he asked me to sit by his bed.

In a waning, ragged voice he said, "Ling, it is God's will that I die before the Japanese capture our country. It is up to you to take care of my family. Che Yu already knows what to do with the estate and she will divide the portions according to my will. As for my funeral, please keep it private and simple. I am due to join my wife in the other world, but I will be with my family in spirit."

Two weeks later, Chow Papa completely gave up the will to live and he passed away at dusk, alone, while one of the servants prepared his dinner and his nurse was tending to business in the bathroom. I had taken Che Yu onto the grounds for an evening walk because by now she was utterly exhausted, both physically and mentally.

Sadness filled the entire estate and white banners draped all of the buildings. But Chow Papa had accomplished his objective. He had died before the Japanese invasion, which was drawing inexorably closer.

It took only two weeks to settle all of the affairs of the estate. I watched as Che Yu single-handedly managed the sales of properties, dividing them according to her father's will. There was no attorney involved. She oversaw everything in a calm and sensible manner. Something that struck me then was that she was the unquestionable anchor of the Chow family and she would be our family's anchor as well.

I was scheduled to fly to Hong Kong in several days to oversee the purchase of a fleet of American-made Jeeps and German trucks designed for immediate battlefield use. It was a trip that I was hesitant to make, in light of the huge burden placed upon Che Yu in recent weeks. Her unending strength was the one thing that buoyed me and led me to believe that I could reasonably leave town at this time. Still, I hoped for some sort of reprieve.

Though not wanting to alarm Che Yu or her relatives, I had been secretly making plans to evacuate my family, should the Japanese army enter the city. I wasn't sure for how many people I could secure passage, especially since most all of the commercial and private ships in the area had been either reserved or already appropriated by the government. The most practical destination seemed to be Wuhan, located along the Yangtze River, several hundred miles west of Nanjing. I had secured a medium-size house there for Che Yu, our children and much of our extended family. Wuhan should be safe, at least for awhile, because the Japanese had already bombed the area several weeks ago.

I would have to stay behind, at first. With talk of me soon being promoted to General, loyalty to my country would be paramount. I might also be a prime target, considering the Japanese military elite's knowledge of me. My relationship with Admiral Saka could prove to be a two-edged sword.

The few conversations I had had with Che Yu concerning the possible invasion were enough to convince her to make some preparations of her own. When the estate was divided, Che Yu left much of her share of the compound to Che Ming and instead kept many of the family heirlooms, such as easy-to-transport jewelry, for herself. She hired a seamstress to sew a second layer of lining in an old, worn leather suitcase, and she stored the precious jewels in specially designed cotton padded pouches that would fit snugly behind the lining.

Resourceful in so many ways, Che Yu also visited her late father's jewelry store and instructed the staff to design at least a hundred sheets of gold leaves in four-inch squares, each 1/32" thick. In addition to the suitcase lining, the seamstress sewed a garment for Che Yu and for both of our children. These insulated jackets featured plain blue and brown cotton that had been boiled with tea leaves and buried in the soil for a week, giving them an old, worn appearance after washing. A lightweight silk filler served as padding between the jacket's top surface and inner lining while providing excellent insulation against the cold winter air.   Another layer of rough sackcloth cotton cut into multi- quilted squares served as secret storage compartments for the gold leaves. The idea was that if Che Yu needed money to pay for lodging or food, she would open one of the padded pockets and use the gold leaves to pay for the necessities.

Most of the relatives moved out of the estate several weeks after the will's assets were dispersed, though Che Ming and a few others elected to stay for awhile. Unbeknownst to me at the time, in just two days I would bid farewell to Che Yu and my family as they boarded a freighter to evacuate Nanjing. Then I would board another vessel taking me to Whampoa Academy and wouldn't see my family for quite some time.

In our room on this particular night, the candles were dim, flickering occasionally as a cool breeze wafted in through the window. Though it was now December, the weather was still reasonably comfortable. We lay in bed, fully clothed, but caressing each other tenderly. I was the first to speak.

"I feel so guilty that I may have to leave you at some time in the not too distant future. Things are unraveling more quickly by the moment and I may even have to spend nights at the ministry office."

"Ling, I married you because we are destined to be mates," Che Yu answered. "You have a mission guided by God. I respect and support your wish and your career. Now, let's not be sad. We need to treasure our moments together."

Che Yu's nursemaid knocked on the door, then brought in our Second Treasure baby boy, named Bing, now about two years old. I watched contentedly as my lovely young wife cooed sweet words into his ear. Then I leaned back, my hands folded behind my head, and stared at the ceiling.

Chapter Sixteen
Temple birth

Alone again in our room, after Bing had been returned to the nursery, Che Yu asked me to tell her once more about the day I met her. But first, for context, I told her about another day that had been ingrained in my memory for nearly 20 years...the day I left the temple and bid good-bye to my cherished friends and mentors, especially Master Lou Ming. He had already packed my belongings, including the bronze Quan Yin, and placed them in two baskets. I felt the tears in my eyes as Superior Master lifted me up close to his chest.

"Master Lou Ming, thank you for taking care of me and telling me all the stories and teaching me," I said, my lower lip quivering.

With a brilliant smile and a heartfelt hug, Superior Master replied, "I am so glad you were able to spend time with us these few years. You have been a delight for us, Ling, and you will always have a special place in our hearts. Don't be a stranger. Will you come back and visit me whenever you can?"

I nodded enthusiastically, as one of the monks ran a thick bamboo rod through the braided straw woven rope that was tied to the baskets.

As Uncle Pigtail and I began trudging down the trail, I kept looking back to wave goodbye to the group of monks standing at the ledge bidding me farewell.

At the foothill temple stood Master Wong who had also packed a small bundle of my belongings, which he then added to one of the baskets. Brother Lee, also down at the foothill temple at that time, smiled as he slipped a lollipop into my hand.

Quietly, he bent down and said, "I saved this especially for you."

At that moment, a large black automobile kicked up a whirlwind of dust, which gusted for several hundred feet behind the vehicle. "Beep! Beep!" It was Tao Yee vigorously pressing the horn on the steering wheel. He had come along with Uncle Tao's chauffeur, Li Zhong, to help move me to the city.

My eyes again swelling up with tears, I bid another farewell to my caretakers at the temple. Once Li Zhong, a small, proper man with a lazy eye, placed my belongings in the trunk, I climbed into the back seat and we pulled away from the main gate.

I had selected my best outfit for the occasion: a crisp white shirt and navy trousers, red suspenders and a blue baseball cap given to me by a foreign traveler who had once visited the temple. Pulling my favorite smooth pebbles from my pocket, I showed them proudly to Tao Yee. We played with the rocks for entertainment during the hour-long ride…hiding them in our hands, flipping them and rubbing them together in the hopes of drawing smoke. Only once did Li Zhong reprimand us, when Tao Yee accidentally banged one of the pebbles against the window.

As the car rumbled through the crowded city streets, one could see many exhilarating activities and bustling establishments, from colorful food stores and quaint rug markets to demonstrative merchants, haggling shoppers and the general hubbub of bicycles, rickshaws and a few scattered automobiles. Women in Chinese dresses or sleek western clothing, old men in hats and young dandies in modern suits all vied for their individual pieces of space in an atmosphere that was deliciously chaotic.

It was an amazing world for a little boy like me to absorb as our car passed through this rich tapestry of sights and sounds. It seemed as if I were watching a movie, one of a particularly surreal nature.

Finally, Li Zhong slowed the car in front of a large, red brick wall accentuated with green and yellow roof tiles laid in orderly fashion. The wall was nearly the length of a city block. Li turned back to me.

"This is the Chows' residence. Mr. Tao will bring you up to visit them soon."

Several yards further, the car stopped at a white stucco wall topped with brilliant scarlet red bougainvillea. The gate was opened by the Chows' personal guard, and we drove in and parked in front of a modern stucco house with large glass blocks at the entrance. Mrs. Tao and several servants had already come out to greet me.

Tao Yee hopped out of the car first and ran to his mother's arms. She smiled at him, then looked over at me.

"Dear Ling, how was your car ride? I know this is a new place for you, but you will enjoy living here with us."

She stroked my head with her nicely manicured hand as I arrived at her side and examined my new surroundings.

"Oh, I am sure I will like it here, Mrs. Tao."

"Ling, why don't you call me Auntie Tao from now on. You are one of our family. Is that all right with you?"

Before I could nod my answer, Tao Yee grabbed my hand and ran with me into the house, followed by Auntie Tao and the servants. Leading me up the curved stairway, covered with soft carpet, he eagerly showed me my room on the second floor in the west wing, right next to Tao Yee's room. Mr. and Mrs. Tao lived in the east wing, so we would have an entire section of the house in which to pursue our adventures without being underfoot of the parents. This was beginning to seem like an endless vacation to me.

The servants came in moments later to place my belongings into a dresser and hang some of my clothing in the sliding door closet. Up until now, I had remained respectfully silent. But compared to my room at the temple, this new abode felt almost opulent. So I began to merrily jump on the small twin bed with its brass headboard. Tao Yee happily joined me and we made the kinds of screaming, laughing noises that little boys make when they're playing with their best friend in the whole world.

Through the windows, the sun's rays slipped into one corner where it shined a warm, golden light on the freshly painted yellow wall. A white ceiling fan in the middle of the room turned slowly in a gently cooling fashion. Barely had I had time to observe the fan when Auntie Tao called up to us, instructing Tao Yee to leave me alone so that I could comfortably situate myself in my new environment.

I got up and eagerly investigated the rest of the room and its nearby surrounds.

"What's in here?" I thought, peering through a door. There, in front of me, was a glistening bathroom with a porcelain free-standing lavatory, a white porcelain tub and a western-style flushing toilet! I dropped a piece of toilet paper into the toilet bowl and pulled the chain hanging from the tank. Whoosh! The paper quickly disappeared, bringing a satisfied smile to my face.

Tao Yee and I had many opportunities to romp and play during this joyous two-week period of reunion before school started. We ran around the garden area and played war games with toy guns, bows and arrows. Sometimes we would slurp nectar from the honeysuckle flowers, then fall flat on our backs as if we'd been poisoned. Other times, we would pick up clods of dirt, not too big or too small, and hurl them at one another in a variety of elaborately choreographed ambush scenarios. One of our favorite games was a form of hide 'n seek, in which we would leave small markings such as leaves, pebbles and strands of straw for the other to follow. Then, just as the pursuer would close in on the hidden lair, the one being hunted would leap out into the open, roaring like a wild animal. It was a uniquely boyish game, that sense of wanting to find the other, yet knowing that a somewhat terrifying surprise would soon greet you.

Uncle Tao worked late most of the time and sometimes he had to take the train to Shanghai for business. So we often ate dinner without him. The food was scrumptious. I remember keeping a small journal, in which I wrote after several weeks at the Tao's, "I love the taste of the meat here… chicken, beef, pork, fish and even unusual foods like sea cucumber and eels from the lake when Uncle Tao is in town!"

I easily adjusted my palate from that of a vegetarian at the temple to savoring the delicacies of fine meats and gourmet cuisine. Being trained as a polite boy, I always complimented Auntie Tao after dinner. A common congratulatory theme might be, "Thank you Auntie Tao, I loved the steamed fish today. It was cooked just right."

To which she would reply, "Dear Ling, you are becoming a food connoisseur. And you are right, the fish tonight was cooked perfectly. If they had steamed it one minute longer, it would have been overcooked or one minute sooner, it would have been raw and fleshy."

I could sense that Uncle and Auntie Tao enjoyed my comments, and they seemed to like me quite well. As a result, they made me feel welcome in their home.

At the same time, they appeared intent on molding me into the proper little urban gentleman, much like their son, Tao Yee. Auntie Tao bought me uniforms for school: navy jackets, white shirts, khaki shorts along with white cotton socks, probably the softest I had ever had the pleasure of putting on my feet. A pair of black leather shoes and a navy short-billed cap sporting the school emblem rounded out my dapper school attire. Uncle Tao also brought me western clothing that he had purchased from Shanghai, China's most cosmopolitan city and its unchallenged high-fashion and economic center.

As for me, I did well in school and even excelled above my class in most subjects. Tao Yee was in the same class with me and, while I had a competitive spirit and secretly wanted to best him in all of the subjects, he seemed content to share information without any hint of competitiveness. The teachers, knowing of our relationship, allowed us to sit next to each other in class, which enabled us to work quite often as a team.

I had a better knack for many of the subjects, however, and whatever rivalry there might have been was considerably cooled by this undeniable truth. So when Yee asked if I could help him with his math homework during the first week of school, I was happy to oblige. In fact, the idea of acting as a tutor of sorts to Yee gave me a sense of importance and certainly did nothing to lessen his parents' growing admiration of me.

The school was not far from our house, and we normally met other classmates along the way as we walked. One of the kids was a bully named Xiang Ning. We always tried to avoid him, even crossing the street to the other side when we saw him coming our way.

One day at lunchtime, while we were in the cafeteria, Xiang Ning squeezed his large, overweight body onto the bench where Tao Yee and I were sitting. Immediately, he eyed our inviting lunch of steamed dumplings with meat and vegetables. With a combination of menace and longing, Xiang Ning grabbed the bamboo container sitting in front of Tao Yee and stuffed the dumplings into his month in one fell swoop. Without even thinking, I jumped up and pulled the fat thief off our bench.

"Xiang Ning, you shouldn't have done that. That is Tao Yee's lunch. You have your own. Don't your parents teach you any manners?"

Instead of responding, Xiang Ning started to kick me in the stomach. Knowing a small amount of elementary martial arts taught to me by Brother Lee at the temple, I pinned the would-be bully face-down to the table, with his arms secured firmly behind his back. Just for good measure, I raised his head once and slammed it back onto the table. Even Tao Yee winced.

"Help! You are hurting me!" Xiang Ning yelled.

Feeling a surge of adrenaline and the confidence that comes with pinning the school bully's face against a smashed dumpling, I exaggerated, "Quiet. I could break your arm if I wanted. I know martial arts."

Finally, after Xiang Ning swore that he would no longer terrorize the younger, smaller kids, I let him go, though I kept my guard up since I wasn't sure if he would strike back. But instead, he ran crying to one of the teachers and accused me of attacking him without provocation.

By then, word had traveled throughout the lunchroom that I was a martial arts specialist, and I had become an instant hero of sorts. Not wishing to dispel the myth and, at the same time, hoping that I wasn't challenged to another fight, I tried to quickly change the subject. With so many people speaking in my defense, it was soon determined by the teachers that Xiang Ning had been the perpetrator. From then on, whenever Tao Yee would ask me to demonstrate my prowess at martial arts, I would beg off with the excuse that my hands were registered as weapons and that it wouldn't be wise to use them. Kind of like playing with a loaded gun in the house.

Che Yu laughed gently as I related my story to her. I still had not reached the part where I met her for the first time. Che Yu remembered much of the story, but loved hearing my version. She leaned her head on my shoulder. We were both tired, but before we retired for the night, we rose from the bed and walked together to the window where we looked out on the familiar landscape. For the past few days, the Japanese army had dropped leaflets on Nanjing, urging a surrender. But their troops were still camped beyond the protective walls of the city, and the feeling was that they might still be dissuaded. I thought differently. The candles flickering behind us, we surveyed our outdoor surroundings with the shared knowledge that Nanjing, as we knew it that night, might soon never be the same again.

Chapter Seventeen
Dangerous time

Two days later, I awoke to see my personal maid, Ahma, standing before me in her nightgown. Slowly I rubbed my eyes to make sure it wasn't a vision, the remnants of some bizarre dream. But the look in Ahma's eyes was that of pure fear. Normally, she would never have approached me in this way, due to the strict decorum usually practiced between reputable families and their domestic help.

"Honorable Mr. Khan," she said, almost whispering.

I sat up in bed. Before I could answer, she spoke again.

"The Japanese have entered Nanjing. They are approaching the City Centre as we speak. What shall we do? We are all so frightened."

Quickly, I jumped from my bed.

"Gather everyone in the main kitchen, Ahma! I will be there right away."

I shook Che Yu from her slumber, then ran toward the nursery. In the hallway, I encountered Ming Ming, dragging a bleary-eyed child with each arm. Together we walked briskly toward our gathering place.

In the kitchen, I quickly turned on the radio for the latest news of the invasion. So far, there had been few casualties. The Japanese had moved with sudden swiftness, encountering very little resistance. But that was soon to change, and I knew it. It was imperative to move everyone in our estate to a safe place of refuge. I quickly decided that I would transport Che Yu and our two young children by vessel, if possible, to Wuhan as originally planned.

After eating breakfast standing up and frantically grabbing vital clothes and documents, we loaded as many people as possible into the large sedans parked side by side on the estate grounds. I remember counting 12 people and myself, which made 13. A few people had determined to wait it out, while Che Yu's half-brother, Che Ming, decided he would try to reach the temple at Purple Golden Mountain where he could stay with the monks in relative safety. Of course, with the reports we had heard about Japanese atrocities in recent days and the strategic importance of the observatory, nothing was certain.

The roads were already jammed when we headed into the direction of the city. Just as many cars, trucks, bicycles and carts were entering the main area of Nanjing as those leaving. From the instant we arrived by the docks at the river, I could sense that this wouldn't be a smooth evacuation. Only a few vessels had any kind of space available, and the lines of apprehensive evacuees had been growing steadily by the hour. Most of the private boats and commercial ships were filled fore and aft with soldiers, ammunition and small artillery.

I tried to push my way to the front, flashing my credentials, cajoling and even threatening a few of the more obstinate boat hustlers. My biggest regret was that I hadn't worn my military uniform, which clearly would have changed the complexion of my circumstances. If it had been merely myself to think about, perhaps I wouldn't have been so aggressive, but my family's lives were at stake and I knew that virtually none of these people before me had any chance of securing passage on one of the watercraft.

Finally stumbling to the front of the line, I was met by a shrill-voiced lieutenant who demanded that I back away. Shouting back and forth, neither of us was willing to surrender ground. After a brief struggle over my documents, I at last pulled out an official paper and handed it to him. Clearly, I had struck a chord and his confidence faded like a winter sunset. Outranked and overworked, he waved me through but warned that helping me find available passage was out of his hands.

For the next hour, I searched vainly for a familiar face and then finally turned away from the lines and walked back toward my family, which now had grown by four with the addition of the teenaged sons of an office cohort. In desperate straits, they had wandered into our group and immediately recognized Che Yu. I felt duty-bound to arrange for their departure from the city as well.

Hope was almost lost when my old friend General Lee, from my earlier days of training at the military academy, bumped into me and inquired as to my mission. After I told him that I was to report to Whampoa Academy where my command post was to evacuate the artillery units to Hankow, he offered to transport my family aboard a vessel belonging to the Supreme Commander of the Chinese forces.

It didn't take long for me to accept his generous offer. In fact, I said "yes" practically before he finished his sentence. As I had suspected, the uniform carried a lot of weight around here. Crowds moved aside as General Lee and I passed through the noisy throngs. Within a few minutes, we returned to where I had left my family and I reported the good news.

Unfortunately, General Lee explained that he couldn't take everyone in our group. There were just too many. My mind raced as I tried to determine who would go and who would stay. How could I leave any of our group behind?

"General, with all due respect, there must be some solution."

A pained expression spread across the general's face. He deliberated his next move.

"Okay, here is what we can do. Select the group that you wish to leave on the commander's vessel. Then I will arrange passage on several smaller boats going to the same destination. There may be a slight delay for those boats, but it is the best I can do. As you can see, there is bedlam here. I assure you, Khan Chi Yuen, I will see to it that they are all reunited."

I knew that General Lee would do his best, and I couldn't afford to quibble, now that I had an exit strategy for my family. We followed him to the large freighter and, before we boarded, the general asked to have a moment first to talk with the ship captain.

Minutes later, General Lee returned and led us onto the busy vessel. Soldiers vied for every available space on the deck. Packed in like canned fish, they wore the look of bewildered country boys unsure of their fate that lay ahead and somewhat numbed by the enormity of the experience. General Lee had handed us off to a Lieutenant Commander Tang, who led us past the uniformed troops, down a deep stairwell and into the bowels of the ship where we walked into a large room filled with rudimentary bunkbeds. Che Yu helped her elderly aunt Zeepou down the stairs as the old woman hobbled on her small bound feet.

Commander Tang spoke. "General Lee has instructed us to screen off this part of the space for you with sheets for your family's privacy. We will do that right away. Anything else that you need, please let me know."

I kissed my children and held on to my wife who was choking back her tears.

"Che Yu, the house in Wuhan should be safe for awhile. I have thoroughly investigated the situation there and it is stable at the moment. In case there is danger, you need to pack up and leave for the next safe place. I feel so much a failure because I have not been able to plan beyond Wuhan for you. Be sure to wire me where you are moving. I love you."

Che Yu was terrified that she may never see me again, that I would be swallowed up in the humanity outside and the capricious whims of this horrible war.

"But where are you going? Tell me again."

"For the moment, I will be at Whampoa Academy. But from there I leave for Hankow and wherever this military struggle takes me. You will be safe. I will find you."

Trying to put on my bravest, most self-assured face for Che Yu, I grabbed her close so she couldn't see me when my eyes began to moisten and give me away.

Clinging to my shoulders, her head nestled in my chest, she whispered, "I believe I am pregnant, dear Ling. This will be our third treasure."

I couldn't speak. My legs grew weak as if I had been slammed with a fifty-pound truncheon. Looking at her expressive, gentle face, I squeezed her arms, then turned and ran back up the stairs.

Several minutes later, as I pushed my way through the large and increasingly hostile crowd, I chastised myself for saying nothing to Che Yu. Did she understand how overwhelmed I was? Did she think I was uncaring because I didn't respond? The thoughts haunted me and churned in my mind, even as I stepped around people being pushed to the ground and stomped like smoldering fire embers.

Once I reached the pier, a jeep was waiting for me, my duffle bag already sitting on the floor board. We drove, some would say barged, through hordes of people to another pier where we transferred to a large military vehicle for the ride to Whampoa.

My heart was heavy and sorrowful. I lamented why I was here, when my place should be with my wife and family during these dangerous hours. I had left her to do a man's job, transporting and evacuating an entourage of twelve people, old and young. I was ashamed of myself, yet at the same time I knew that China needed me. My military training would be of incalculable value. And I was now a general, with all of the prestige and, yes, encumbering responsibilities that that carried with it.

For the next few weeks, we continued to receive ominous reports out of my home city. Accounts were at times sickening and nearly impossible to digest. The Rape of Nanjing had begun.

Japanese soldiers left a trail of utter carnage wherever they went. Looting, rape, arson and point-blank executions of war prisoners and civilians were commonplace horrors, often carried out under the pretext of eradicating Chinese soldiers disguised as part of the general populace. But the killings extended to women, children as young as a year-old and elderly as old as 80 years or more. Teenage girls were taken at random from their homes, raped in public, then disemboweled at the edge of a bayonet. Some of the women were mutilated in other creative ways...their breasts hacked off or their vaginas penetrated with long, knife-sharp bamboo sticks. Other citizens were tied up, dragged along the street and beheaded with butcher's knives.

Men had it no better than the women. Some had their testicles cut off, while others were forced to eat the severed remains. Farmers were often forced at gunpoint and knifepoint to commit intercourse with their livestock. Within the first three weeks, more than 100,000 Nanjing residents had been slaughtered, and this didn't take into account the many missing people who had had their hands and feet bound before being tossed into the Yangtze.

One group of Chinese soldiers and civilians was killed in a particularly heinous act next to the Taiping Gate. As many as 1,200 of them were doused with gasoline, set on fire, then blown up with landmines. An excavation known as the Ten Thousand Corpse Ditch served as the final resting place for at least 15,000 other victims of the Nanjing massacre.

Chinese civilians fled by the thousands during those first few weeks of what was to become a two-month onslaught. At the same time, the Chinese military instituted a scorched earth policy in which anything perceived of value to the marauding Japanese troops was burned to the ground. This included everything from military barracks and private homes to farms, communications facilities, woodlands and even whole neighborhoods, villages and common areas.

Consequently, the food supply quickly became a desperate situation for most. Some of the city's people abandoned their old and feeble parents, sold their own children or forced them into prostitution to secure food for the family. Others ate tree barks and roots, even their own beloved pets, to avoid starvation. Nor was it uncommon to find dead bodies stripped of their clothing by neighbors looking for garments to keep them warm as they searched the cold streets and alleyways for food.

One of the only places somewhat spared during the invasion was the western quarter of the city where many westerners and international businesses were located. This district, which became known as the Nanjing Safety Zone, escaped shelling and various atrocities visited on other areas of the city. Because the Japanese had agreed to ignore this area as long as the Chinese military didn't enter there, it served as a haven or sanctuary of sorts where tens of thousands of Chinese citizens were able to find refuge.

The Chinese had been ill-prepared for war. Feuding warlords as well as the fissure between Chiang Kai-shek and Mao Tse-tung had focused the military's efforts elsewhere. What's more, China had no real industrial strength…at least not on the level of the Japanese. Our army's mechanized divisions and armored forces were practically non-existent. So it was a rag-tag group of soldiers that I led, a general in name only with a paper army. Still, I was determined to make the most of my position, to wield it like a true leader and to instill some sense of resolve among the men with whom I'd been encharged.

Chapter Eighteen
Meeting my child bride

When we arrived at Whampoa, I was surprised at the steady, well-orchestrated pace of the evacuation procedures. It was still a monumental task, however, moving occupants of the school, its key files and documents, training equipment and whole artillery units downriver to Hankow, a challenging journey even under the best of conditions.

Exhausted after a full day of not only directing the mass exodus, but also providing a significant amount of physical labor, I curled up on a sleeping pad in one of the Academy's classrooms. It was well past midnight, and we hoped to have everything loaded and ready to go by late the next afternoon. The plan was to leave as soon as nightfall arrived.

I wanted to sleep, but found it exceedingly difficult. My mind kept wandering back to Che Yu, the possible pregnancy, my quick retreat up the stairs of the vessel after learning the news.

I thought about that Friday night, years ago, when Uncle Tao sat with Tao Yee, Auntie Tao and myself beside the fireplace in the black lacquered frame chair that he liked so well. Crisply pressed, white imported linen covers draped over the chair arms, yet never seemed to soil from his own arms resting there. Holding a newspaper in his hands, he lifted his head above it and spoke directly to me.

"Ling, it is time for you to meet Mr. Chow's family and your fiancée."

Tao Yee giggled and made a playful gesture toward me.

"Ling is going to get married," he teased. "You can't wait to see your bride-to-be."

I looked at Tao Yee with embarrassment and scorn, then turned to Uncle Tao.

"Do I have to? We have a lot of homework assignments this weekend, sir."

Uncle Tao scolded his son.

"Yee, that is not the right way to speak to your best friend. Besides, it is none of your business. You can go to your room now."

Looking back at me, he continued, "Tomorrow, we will pay the Chows a visit. They have invited us for afternoon tea, so we will leave here in the mid-afternoon. This will be your first time to meet with the Chow family members and see their home. Mind you, it is a very big house, even larger than the hotel where I took you to dinner last week."

Reluctantly I nodded my head and took my place by the fire. I remembered the hotel. It was one of the fanciest in the city, recently updated with imported furnishings. We dined in an intimate room dimly lit with a crystal chandelier that hovered gracefully above the round dining table. A beaded curtain separated this room from the main dining room, bringing back memories of when I ate in that very hotel with my father several years earlier when he was still lively and vibrant.

Sitting near the foot of Auntie Tao's chair and mesmerized by the fire pit flames licking at the cedar wood, I recalled once more how my father had often dined in that hotel with many pretty ladies and a few select uncles who served as his drinking buddies. I hated how the women touched my hair and face, and told my father what a handsome boy I was. They had long red-painted fingernails, colorful rouge on their faces, tiny eyes, and they laughed much too quickly and often at anything my father said.

One of the women, leaning toward my father's shoulder, told him, "Master Khan, you are so funny, you always cheer us up with your jokes. I was showing off the ring you gave me, and my cousins were so envious of me."

These women would help father fill the opium in his pipe while they chain-smoked long cigarettes. The smoke mingled nauseatingly with their excessive perfume, so I would make excuses to leave for the toilet where I could gasp for fresh air, away from their painted faces, affected giggles and bright gowns dripping with bangles and dazzling jewelry.

My mother, on the other hand, always dressed in a refined, understated way. She would often wear her long black hair tied in a bun on top of her head, and her exquisite taste in clothing deftly blended simplicity and elegance. It all seemed so long ago as I sat there, staring at the crackling logs in the Tao's yawning fireplace.

Saturday at the Taos' house arrived bright and early, with a knock at my bedroom door. It was the maid carrying an armload of fresh new clothing, which included a white dress shirt, a pullover white V-neck sweater with navy blue trim, a pair of navy blue trousers, white socks and a pair of shiny new patent leather shoes. As the crowning touch, I wore a yellow and red polka-dotted bow tie...quite dashing, indeed! Fortunately, Tao Yee was to stay home with his mother that day.

Before Uncle Tao and I drove off in the car, Auntie Tao handed me a wrapped present and said, "Ling, you are to give this gift to Mr. Chow when you see him. This is something your late father instructed Master Lou Ming to give to you for your meeting today."

The small, lightweight box was wrapped in a brown, silk handkerchief tied in a knot at the top. I wondered what could be inside and wanted to peek, but didn't dare with Uncle Tao sitting next to me.

It was a short drive to the Chows' home, too short as far as I was concerned. The chauffeur stopped at the gate in front of a long brick wall watched over by two uniformed guards wearing sabers on their waists. As the gate slowly opened, we drove into a large courtyard lined with rows of cypress trees and stopped in front of the columned main entrance to the inner house. Uncle Tao took my hand, then reassured me with a simple pat on the shoulder as we walked toward the front door. Being so young and innocent, I had no idea how important this day would be.

"Ling, when you meet Mr. and Mrs. Chow, bow to both of them to pay your respect."

"I know, Uncle Tao, I will be on my best behavior."

Gilded lanterns warmly lighted the inside of the structure, which featured a cavernous ceiling that must have been at least 20 feet high with carved, wooden rafters. Veined marble stone benches were placed sparingly in the hall, its walls covered in glazed tiles showcasing colorful designs and borders.

"This is the greeting hall, Ling," Uncle Tao whispered to me.

Two youthful-looking men, wearing black gowns and red-rimmed caps, approached us. After both bowed, one of them announced, "Our master, Chow, is waiting in the Great Room for you. Please follow me."

We turned slightly to face a stucco building with a green tile roof, just about 20 yards from the greeting hall. Yellow ceramic dragons at each corner of the tile roof rose in defensive posture as if they were guarding the building. Crossing through a red moon-shaped gate, we entered into a beautiful garden blanketed with water ponds filled with wild lily blossoms. Graceful willow trees bent their branches in greeting at each end of a small bridge, across which the fragrances of myriad flowers and plants wafted as if borne by the breath of heaven. We climbed several marbled steps at this point and entered through another bright red moon gate, made of wood, which led into the interior of the Great Room of the house.

Lifting my head up toward Uncle Tao I said, "This is such a big place. If Yee and I were playing here, no one could find us."

A muted funnel of sunlight still shone into the Great Room, and I watched as particles of dust glided and twisted amid the golden beams. The high ceilings and the carved wood rafters reminded me of the temple that I had recently left.

Sitting against a varied backdrop of tiger wood paneling, hanging painted landscape scrolls and a pale yellow embroidered silk banner was Mr. Chow, who occupied one of the room's two carved rosewood chairs. A slender man with gray hair and a distinguished, angular mien, he wore a traditional Chinese gown of navy silk, tone on tone, with double happiness symbols. A patterned navy blue silk hat trimmed in scarlet sat formally on his rather small head. Occupying the other chair beside him was his wife, a rather plump lady dressed in a red patterned silk che pou gown, contrasted with light pink trim and fancy knotted buttons. Expensive gold and jade jewelry adorned her fingers and wrist. But I noticed something else; her feet were smaller than mine. While in the sitting position, she revealed her embroidered shoes with wooden heels supporting her tightly bound feet.

Mr. Tao greeted both of them and introduced me to the Chows.

"Come closer to me, Ling," said Mr. Chow. "Let me take a good look at you."

Donning his spectacles, Mr. Chow remarked approvingly, "Ah! You look so much like your father."

He stroked my head and said, "I heard that you are doing very well in school. We are very proud of you."

I stepped forward, bowed and presented the brown silk box to Mr. Chow. This is the moment for which I'd been waiting. My eyes gazed at the box eagerly, my anticipation mounting to find out what lay inside. Without hesitation, Mr. Chow opened the container and pulled out a graceful red jade pendant, bearing the engraving of a silver dragon on one side, and a proud phoenix on the other. Intricately patterned silver-casted borders surrounded the pendant, the very one that Mr. Chow and my father held when they made their vow during the carriage ride out of Nanjing before the birth of the Chows' daughter. It was a symbol of commitment to the pre-arranged engagement of their children, and ultimate to their children's intertwining fate.

I remembered the story Auntie Tao told me back at the temple about the significance of this pendant, and I was to finally see its grand design after all these years…or at least what seemed like a lifetime to a young child.

Mrs. Chow reached out and touched my left hand, turned my palms up and looked intensely at the lines in the hand for almost a full minute.

Finally she said to Mr. Chow, "He is going to be a great man just like his father and his grandfather. And what a handsome boy you are!"

The Chows offered tea, rice cakes, sesame wrapped sticks and dried fruit candies, which I especially liked. While eating, I could feel all eyes upon me so that it was actually a relief when Mr. Chow finally offered to introduce me to their daughter, Chow Che Yu.

In the west wing of the house, men were forbidden to enter the ladies' quarters. The women wore a tiny bell on their shoes to signal that they were passing through, at which point any men in the area would bow their heads or turn away to let them pass without directly observing them.

Mrs. Chow rang the bell, and within a minute or two there appeared three female servants accompanying a beautiful, young rosy-cheeked girl. She was dressed in western-style attire, a pink dress with a big bow tied in the back and a white collar embroidered with small blue flowers. Che Yu's pink leotard socks and white patent leather shoes set off the dress perfectly, even to the point that a young fellow like me found it to be quite fetching (though I would never admit it to Tao Yee).

Mrs. Chow lifted up her daughter by her tiny arms and placed Che Yu on her lap, then introduced her in the formal manner typical of our customs of the day.

"This is Che Yu, our first-born daughter. She is eight years old. We do not send our children to school outside, but they have private tutors to teach them in our home. She is already quite good in poetry and math."

With those formalities out of the way, I followed Che Yu into the garden. I immediately liked her long black hair, which reflected dancing sparkles of sunlight. She also had a perfectly oval face, considered the best kind of feature for a beautiful lady. Just as importantly, I noticed to my relief that her feet were unbound…just normal-sized kids' feet hopping over stones and rocks in the garden as she showed off the many different flowers to which she'd given special names.

When she asked me what I liked best about school, I proudly proclaimed, "Math and Playtime." And when she scooped up a smooth rock from the lily pond and pointed out its polished, curving shapes, a bond was formed. I found another, with a deep purple cast to it, and proffered it to her, causing her to giggle shyly. For the coup de grace, I reached into my pocket and pulled out the smooth jade-like oval stone that I had found some time ago by the waterfall basin at the temple. I could still remember her high girlish voice that, as I now lay on the mattress pad in the corner of a Whampoa classroom, seemed like the sweetest music to my ears.

"Oh, it is the most beautiful stone I have ever seen!" she trilled. "It is a perfect oval shape and you can almost see completely through it when you hold it to the light."

If I had been telling this story to my wife, she would squeeze my arm and laugh at my teasing imitation of her little girl voice. As I lay wide-eyed there at the Academy on the night before our evacuation, I was sure of two things. I loved my wife madly and she still had that rock.

Chapter Nineteen
Che Yu on the Yangtze

Leaving just before nightfall in a flotilla of ships, we staggered their departure so as not to arouse too much suspicion from enemy fighters possibly stationed along the route. One of the vessels struck high ground south of Wuhan, just below the Han River cutoff, so we had to deploy another to help wrest it from the ground's muddy grip. During the ensuing effort to dislodge the boat, a military mechanic named Woo somehow became submerged while working near the stern, his head ultimately crushed by the large hull.

We traversed the remainder of the river without any more loss of life, though there was some cause for alarm when we pulled into Hankow, known as the "Mouth of the Han." The city extends for roughly a mile along the Yangtze River banks and for two-and-a-half miles along the Han, while afforded the protection of an 18-foot high wall. Across the river sits the city of Wuchang. As we passed beside a portion of the wall, at the half-mile point, we noticed a series of scaffolds that appeared to have been quickly abandoned. Scattered weapons such as high-powered rifles and even the occasional grenade could be seen either lying on the scaffolding or on the ground below. Whatever had transpired earlier had been scuttled by some sort of surprise. Whether the weaponry belonged to Chinese or Japanese troops, or even perhaps civilian citizens, was unknown to us.

I made contact with one of our forward officers, but he also claimed bewilderment by what he had seen. Only later did we learn that a local citizens group, hearing that an attack was imminent, had set the scaffolding up as a trap of sorts. They had hoped that any Japanese in boats along the riverbank might mistake the scaffolding for a construction site and attempt to scale the wall at that point. A civilian militia would then be conveniently waiting for them on the other side. But the men raising the scaffolding were frightened off by a false air raid siren. Many had dropped their weapons at that point and run for cover…not the most reassuring scenario for someone who might want to depend on the citizenry for help.

I remained in Hankow for several months, though I was sent on a series of missions to nearby provinces. There was very little contact between myself and my family, which would soon grow to five. On rare occasions, we communicated through telegram from my headquarters. In the stoic Chinese way, Che Yu told very little of her ordeals and misfortunes. It was only later that I would learn the true extent of her difficulties.

During the course of the evacuation, she had instructed our two children in the ways of survival by deception.

"My dear little ones," she would say, "you must listen to me and to all the elders. This is a very dangerous time and we cannot afford to let people know about our family background. You are to act like poor peasants; you have my permission to wipe your dripping noses on your sleeves to make the pretense authentic, but don't make a habit of it. All of your sleeves were made longer than your arms so that you could hide your wristwatches and gold bracelets within the sleeves. In case anything bad happens, both of you have your auntie's address and papa's headquarters information sewn into your britches."

Che Yu informed Uncle Woo and Auntie Zeepou that they were to take care of our children, should my wife be killed or disabled. Though quite elderly, they would know how to soothe and nurture our son and daughter until other family support assisted them. Our children, though very young, were instructed on how to be brave and to stay close to family members at all times.

Che Yu would tell the children, "I want you to remember to behave properly because, when the war is over, we want your father to be proud of your upbringing, even through these hardships."

After spending the first few weeks in Wuhan somewhat uneventfully with her family, Che Yu learned that the Japanese were coming back to use the town as a regional fort. Within hours, she and the entire entourage had packed their belongings. Che Yu purchased two oxen carts to carry the children, her elderly aunt and uncle, and assorted food supplies.

During the evacuation, she moved her family along the Yangtze River, toward Hankow, finally arriving in the city after a sluggish journey, slowed by Uncle Woo's sudden attack of colitis. Hankow itself was not much better than their traveling stops along the river. I had left the walled city by then, headed for Chengdu where Whampoa was being temporarily moved. Sirens blared day and night in Hankow, rousting citizens and refugees from their sleep and their chores with maddening regularity. It was not uncommon for Japanese planes to make five or six different sorties over the city on any given day. People leaving or entering the city would encounter fires and burned-out buildings in their path, from one end of the town to the other. Every morning would bring a new roll of the dice.

The smell of fresh gunfire and burning debris was rampant, and smoke filled the air and clouded the eyes. Tiny lost children, many no more than a meter high, cried longingly and wandered aimlessly in search of their parents who, most likely, had been riddled by machine gun fire, ripped apart by shrapnel or buried underneath a deluge of tumbling bricks and mortar.

Elderly men and women, wounded by the gunfire, were left behind under shade trees to die while some men carried their little ones or their sick mothers on their backs, each step a near stumble along the rocky, uneven paths. The stench of dead corpses along the roadside tested the mettle of even the most hardened. Only the flies and maggots seemed to move with any sense of purpose.

Che Yu couldn't bear to let our children see the sadness and horror of the scenes she was witnessing, so she covered them with a hemp blanket in the oxen cart. The elders rode inside the cart with them, and Che Yu and two subtly disguised bodyguards walked alongside on the road. The journey was difficult to navigate, but simple to analyze… merely follow the path into the mountains, away from further air strikes.

Their group hid behind rocky hills at night, and cooked potatoes and taro roots for sustenance. Occasionally, Che Yu could hear women screaming in the distance, possibly victims of rape from bandits roaming the hills and preying on innocent refugees. In the early mornings, Che Yu would pack up again and try to move on to the next small village before daybreak. Many of the villages had already been bombed by the Japanese, yet they still offered their own unique set of dangers.

Never did Che Yu see any of the Chinese fighters defending the cities. Only scattered gunshots from the ground could be heard, and they were sporadic at best. These shells had no chance whatsoever of reaching the Japanese bombers, so the enemy came and went as it pleased.

Che Yu's pregnancy was becomingly increasingly visible, and she was tiring noticeably quicker than in the past. It was important to find some sort of semi-permanent shelter.

Finally, their group settled into a rented cottage, nestled into a rock-strewn hillside near Huangshi. They stayed under cover for three months, never leaving the house other than to collect fresh water and to inquire among certain trusted villagers as to the movement of the Japanese troops in the area. Che Yu and her elderly relatives grew some of their own herbs and vegetables, and an old widowed man who had lost an arm in the bombings would bring fresh rice cakes and goat milk every week or so. After two months he never showed again, and it was rumored that he had had his throat slashed by poachers.

By staying relatively close to the Yangtze, Che Yu had been fortunate enough to keep track of my locales of operation from time to time, and she was able to notify me through messengers about her latest whereabouts. So when I was transferred to the first regiment of the Signal Corps as a two-star general, I sent for her and our two children to live with me in my new post, in Changteh. Ming Ming also accompanied Che Yu, but Ahma and the relatives stayed with Che Yu's sister, Che Ying, in a "safe house" located in a small village on the upper reaches of the Yangtze River.

Several months later our third child, a beautiful baby girl, was born to Che Yu and me. But I was there just long enough for the birth before having to leave suddenly on another mission.

This particular assignment was to use my influence as a businessman who had demonstrated particular success in dealing with the Japanese. I contacted a merchant by the name of Haro Ichiniro under the guise of purchasing a vessel for a new fishing enterprise. Per the arrangement, Ichiniro's company was to receive a sizable percentage of the profits. My real intent, however, was to track the source of the boat being supplied to me. My commander's hope was that we could isolate the shipyard factory, scout it for military activity and possibly even destroy the facility. It was imperative to slow the Japanese's increasing control of the waterways, which was making it very difficult for us to transport munitions and troops.

Ichiniro, however, proved to be corrupt, raising my risk of becoming ensnared in an internal Japanese investigation. This made it necessary to scuttle the mission during its early negotiations.

While I was away on the aborted mission, I received tragic news. Our infant girl had died of meningitis. My wife first suspected something wasn't right by the weakness of the child's suck when feeding. This was followed by extreme lethargy, accompanied by stiffness in the neck and upper body. Our little angel ran a high fever for several days and became increasingly irritable and difficult to comfort. Che Yu called in a doctor who gave the infant some medication, but the baby's skin became jaundiced on the third or fourth day and, within hours, she was dead.

Che Yu was so grief-stricken that she cried inconsolably for days. Writing to me, she was remarkably blunt.

"Ling," she wrote, "I cannot take this any longer. I am sick of this war and the constant moving and hiding. I do not have a home, nor do I have a family. I understand that it is your duty to serve the country, but it is taking every bit of strength in my body to stay the course. All I can do is pray to the Goddess of Mercy to smile on us and unite us soon."

I managed to take leave to visit Che Yu and comfort her, but I was also devastated by the loss. When faced with my wife's convulsive moans, it was all I could do not to yell at her and chastise her for her weakness. At times, I felt as if it were the only way I could deal with my own profound sense of grief. But I remained silent, other than to offer her my unwavering support in the face of my own slowly crumbling defense mechanisms. Most days, Che Yu wouldn't speak to me or eat. I was a singular tree in an open meadow…twisting in the wind with each passing hour.

Whenever I could, I would try to console her with stories from our past. I reminded her of how, after that first meeting with her as a child, I became a frequent visitor at the Chows. Che Yu and I would play together, often with her younger sister, Che Ying, tagging along. We often would begin with a game of hide-and-seek, but then I would get bored with the young girls and I would devise new games that entertained me as well as the girls. Often, those games had some relation to the concept of war. But, after all, I was a young boy growing up in an increasingly volatile country.

One day I had a particularly mischievous idea. I brought three long bamboo sticks, their inner pulp removed to create a hollow tube. Briefly soaking old newspapers in the pond, I then tore a small part of the wet paper. Putting it between my hands, I started rolling the paper into tiny balls, just small enough to fit into the bamboo tube. Then I placed the wet paper ball inside the front tip of the bamboo tube and blew hard from the other end. The ball shot out of the tube and flew just above the water line where it landed with a tiny splat on a flower by the pond. Satisfied with my creativity and prowess, I showed Che Yu and her sister how to play this game, which I called, rather unceremoniously, "hitting the enemy with paper cannons." Somehow, the girls blew hard enough that their faces turned blue, but they lacked the lung strength to blow the paper cannon ball out of the tube.

Che Yu laughed as she remembered that day long ago.

"And I said to you, Ling, we are not strong enough to blow the paper out of the bamboo. Why don't my sister and I become your assistants and make the ammunition instead. You grinned when I said we would watch you fire the cannon balls and see how much farther they would land."

"Yes, I remember it well. You took a small bowl with your dainty hands and dipped it into the lily pond for some water and then went back to our firing station. I was so delighted to have you girls as my own private assistants."

Chapter Twenty
Young love

After a short while in Changteh, we sent for Ahma, in the hopes that that would further stabilize our life there. I was able to arrange for her transport through a military associate who was traveling near the "safe house" on the Yangtze. He merely stopped by and picked her up, then accompanied her on a Chinese freighter.

While this offered a certain degree of comfort to Che Yu, it didn't do much for my state of mind. After the death of our child, we went through a period of mourning when our sex life became abbreviated at best. Che Yu, though still desiring my presence and strength as a man, was often preoccupied with grieving. So I found myself to be cranky and easily annoyed, traits that required even more restraint now that another adult was in our presence. Besides, I didn't want to outwardly show my frustration to Ahma who had always been easygoing and quite fond of me.

I must say, however, that as the days wore on Che Yu became more engaged in the rhythm of life once more. While still prone to spells of depression, she looked forward to our chats together and the tender reminiscences that we shared.

One night, as the children slept and Che Yu and I prepared for bed, I watched her brush out her long raven hair. Marveling at her graceful movement, I walked over to her and caressed her soft, long neck. It was easy to remember why I loved her, and soon we were reclining on the bed in each other's arms. After a pleasant turn at lovemaking, we remained in an embrace and remembered those high school years when Che Yu had blossomed into a beautiful, beguiling young lady.

Now that she had reached a certain age, I was no longer permitted to see Che Yu alone anymore. She would be present only when there were family members in attendance.

But I never felt a sense of overprotection. I always reveled in the knowledge that everyone in the Chow family adored me. They talked about how my features looked so distinctive…the deep double-folded eyelids, the straight, high bridge of my nose, the full lips and the healthy white, smooth skin. In addition, the Chows said that I possessed the mannerisms of a prince. Many of the Chows' cousins and friends, especially the females, would come by just to get a glimpse of me. Those times I spent with the Chows gave me a real sense of warmth, a feeling of family, for which I had longed my entire life.

There in bed that night, I reminded Che Yu about a funny dinner incident at the Chows during those teenage years. In China, the chicken's tail was considered to be the pre-eminent delicacy of the fowl's entire body. When chicken was served, one would only present the tail to the master of the house.

One evening, during dinner, Mrs. Chow picked out the fat chicken tail with her chopsticks and placed it on my plate.

"Go ahead, taste it," she instructed. "I have saved the best part for you."

I looked at this greasy triangular piece of flesh, skin still attached and a few stray hairs left on for good measure, in the dining room light. Completely horrified, I tried to stifle my look of disdain. According to Chinese custom, one must never refuse food set on the plate. So, with all eyes upon me, I managed to force it into my mouth and pretend to chew it. Actually, I swallowed the entire tail in one gulp, coughing so hard that my face turned flaming red.

Everyone asked if I was all right and Mrs. Chow told someone to get water for me. After I eagerly inhaled the water, the rogue piece of chicken finally passed down to my stomach, giving me some semblance of relief.

Mrs. Chow asked, "How was it, Ling? Isn't it the best tasting chicken in the world? The tail is the juiciest part!"

I answered respectfully, "Yes, Chow Mama, it tasted great!" (As a way of expressing her affection for me, she had asked me to call her Chow Mama.)

Then Mrs. Chow instructed the servants, "From now on, we will save a double portion of the chicken tails for Master Khan so that he can thoroughly enjoy his meal!"

Che Yu couldn't keep from laughing. It was infectious and I joined her.

"That night I prayed to Quan Yin, the Goddess of Mercy, to spare me the ordeal of ever eating another chicken tail," I reminded her.

Then Che Yu became serious. She stroked my hair.

"Do you remember when it was time for you and Tao Yee to travel to Tokyo for your college education? My father had agreed that, upon your return after receiving a degree from Waseda University, you could marry me and we could start a family."

She recalled the day I came to say goodbye.

"I remember that you wore a white suit, a pink and white pin-striped shirt with a white bow tie, white and tan leather shoes and a beige straw hat. You were also wearing a pair of imported sunglasses from Italy. You thought you were looking so handsome and dashing, like a movie star walking into our living parlor. And you did."

"Yes, and I presented your parents with a Quan Yin statue. I guess I didn't need it anymore for the chicken."

Smiling, Che Yu went on.

"You told my mother and father that you were leaving the next day for college in Tokyo. And you asked if you could leave the Quan Yin statue with them so that I could burn incense for you while you were away. They smiled and said yes, and then you asked my mother if I could walk you to the greeting hall to say good-bye."

I remembered how my heart skipped a beat when both of Che Yu's parents nodded their heads affirmatively. She then asked me to wait in the garden while she went into her room.

"From one of my dresser drawers, I took out a small bundle, wrapped in a red embroidered handkerchief, and hid it in my pocket," Che Yu recalled. "I walked with you side-by-side at enough distance so as not to have our clothing touch.

"Then, at the greeting hall, I glanced around to make sure no one was following us. Taking a deep breath to draw up the courage, I reached my hand over yours, and our skin touched for the first time since we were little children."

"Yes, you had tears in your eyes," I chimed in. "You whispered softly in my ear that you were going to miss me terribly and you said, 'Here, this is for you,' and handed me the red handkerchief."

"I couldn't wait for you to open it. It was something I had saved up for several years, knowing that that day would come. I told you that you might need it, especially in faraway places without friends to help you."

I remembered the moment like it was yesterday and marveled at how little Che Yu's soft, smooth skin had changed over the years. Now it was my turn to speak.

"When I opened the silk pouch, I found a pile of gold nuggets, at least ten to twelve ounces in weight. I told you that I couldn't take it, that I already had enough money to live at the university. But you insisted that it would make you feel better if I accepted your gift. You kept looking at me with pearls of tears running down your cheeks." that moment, years ago, I looked around the room again to make sure we were alone. Putting my arms around Che Yu, I embraced her for the first time and, my heart fluttering like a rabbit, bent down and kissed her on her cheek. I used my white handkerchief to wipe her tears and tucked the cloth into her hand. When Mr. Tao's chauffeur honked twice outside the gate, I gave her one last, deep embrace and said

"I will write to you."

We paused a moment to let the memories simmer, then Che Yu spoke.

"You had no idea how sad I was feeling. As you walked out through the gate, I sat down on a marble bench and noticed your handkerchief still in my hand. Your special fragrance, a famous German cologne.."

"Number 4711," I intoned.

"Yes, it was there on the handkerchief, which I folded carefully and tucked into my pocket before heading back to my chamber."

I closed my eyes. It felt good that Che Yu remembered all of the little details important to no one but us.

Chapter Twenty-One
The family secrets

By now, the war had pretty much numbed the entire populace, and there were signs that what had been primarily an Asian confrontation was widening into a full-scale world reckoning. Still, we were thankful for the moments we had together, even though I was often sent on assignments of one type or another, usually associated with procuring munitions and other equipment for the war effort. I had become one of Chiang Kai-shek's most reliable operatives. And, remarkably, I was still trusted by influential Japanese business interests.

My wife's birthday was coming and, at the Chows, birthday celebrations had been very important. They would invite friends to the house for a large feast, which typically lasted for hours. Guests would play mahjong before dinner and, afterward, opera singers would perform their favorite arias. For some of these events, the Chows would even hire professional masseuses who would roam throughout the rooms and give brief massages to whomever looked in need of relaxation.

While nothing so elaborate was in my plans this time, I did want to make this a memorable occasion for Che Yu since it was the first time in several years that we would be celebrating this event together.

I quietly contacted a local floral shop to custom make several flower arrangements, according to a photo from a Vogue magazine that Che Yu admired. Though she didn't read English, she enjoyed leafing through this particular magazine, which she had found at a book store several years back. Many of the pages were now finger-stained and wrinkled from the many times she had perused the photos of charming homes, place settings and furniture displays.

On the night of her birthday, we enjoyed a fine beef dinner that Ahma had prepared while Ming Ming cared for the children in the back room. Though red meat was difficult to purchase in the markets at this time, I had paid a premium to secure a particularly nice cut from a local food merchant.

When Che Yu and I retired from the table, I led her into our bedroom, where she was met by the custom-made flower arrangements.

"Oh, Ling, the flowers are beautiful! Are they all mine? They are just like the ones in my magazine!"

She moved gracefully around the room, leaning over to soak up the aroma of each arrangement.

"White Casablanca, ginger lilies," she gushed. "Red roses, pink roses, they are all so fragrant!"

The room looked like a floral shop…a bit overdone, I thought. But I knew this would make her happy. I had told Ming Ming to light all of the scented candles ahead of time.

The soft candlelight brought back cherished memories of our wedding night, and the flower fragrances were thoroughly intoxicating.

After changing into our silk robes, which she had hidden in the suitcase lining during the evacuation, I handed Che Yu a glass of champagne and a burgundy-colored velvet box.

"Open it, it is for you."

Che Yu delicately undid the silver ribbon tied around the box and carefully opened it. A noticeable gasp followed, as she stared into the sparkle of a three-karat diamond pendant drop with Imperial jade clustering.

"Oh, my," was all she could think to say. She seemed out of breath.

"Here, let me put it on you," I offered.

Che Yu still had the softest baby skin and a long, slender neck of the kind usually found on fashion models. I clasped the chain behind her, and she turned to display the diamond, which twinkled under the dim candlelight. Her smile was even more radiant than the precious stone.

We sipped champagne and even danced a spontaneous waltz for a moment. Che Yu's birthday celebration had been everything I had envisioned.

When we finally walked over to the bed and lay down, I stroked Che Yu's neck again. She was in a talkative mood this night, however.

"You always tell me such fascinating things," she began. "Now it is my turn. I want to tell you something you've never known before. It will be my gift to you, my show of trust in you."

This piqued my interest, and I encouraged her to continue.

"As the first-born daughter of the Chow family, I was greatly trusted by my father. Being reliable, mature and home schooled by excellent private tutors, I was quickly given certain responsibilities in the home. One of these was to take care of our family's household finances at the age of seventeen. As you were leaving for college, I was assuming a unique role under my father's tutelage.

"Soon I was managing the estate and paying all of the bills, including the staff's salaries. There were nearly 30 people on the payroll of the Chow estate, including tutors, servants and seamstresses, messengers, gardeners, bodyguards and chauffeurs. Others also received monthly amounts. Living at my parents' estate were my father and my mother, my sister and I and our half brother, as well as my mother's spinster sister, Zeepou. Two of my father's younger brothers, who were unmarried and smoked opium all of the time, the widower Uncle Woo and his daughter, my father's sister and her family of four also resided with us."

"Yes, I remember there was always a full house when I came to visit. And at times, your adopted brother would also be there when he wasn't away at school. Besides looking forward to seeing you, I must admit that I also enjoyed the warmth of such a big family. It was something I never had." Che Yu continued with her story.

"If you recall, our estate compound was designed with several buildings. There was the front building for receiving guests, one center building for the Chow family and separate houses on each side of the central building that were built for the relatives from both of our families."

"That's right...and the servants' quarters were placed at the back of each house where they had their own kitchen and dining areas. I remember it almost as if it were my own family's place."

"I loved the courtyards with their lush greenery and flower gardens that separated the individual quarters because it gave each family its own privacy. Do you remember, they all could enter the mansion through the main gate on Nanjing Road or through the back gate, which was facing the river?"

"Yes, yes. The first time I saw your estate, I was awe-struck. It was built on an entire city block with a ten-foot brick wall surrounding it, and the front gate was so massive, with plenty of room to allow automobiles and horse-drawn carriages to pass. I remember the covered parking area on the right side and the stable on the left side of the front gate, with street frontages on three sides of the property. And one of my favorite things was the Yangtze River at the back of your estate where you had your own pier. We threw hundreds of pebbles from there, didn't we?"

"My father, as you know, had acquired many properties that he had to manage. So it was difficult for him to also tend to the finances of the home. He owned a jewelry store, a hotel and, of course, one of the largest banks in the city."

"And don't forget, he also served as Chairman of the Chamber of Commerce of Nanjing City for many years," I added, eager to prop up her father's image, for I could tell she was relishing her remembrances of him.

"He had many successes in life," Che Yu conceded. "But my mother was never able to bear him a son."

"I never asked about your half-brother...I just assumed," I said, trailing off without finishing my thought.

"When I was only six years old," Che Yu continued, "I remembered mother had a visitor on a hot, summer day. It was a plainly dressed woman who was brought into mother's chamber by a servant. The woman was holding two baby boys, one of which was an infant. My mother asked the woman to come forward and hand the youngest baby over to her. She tapped her puffy fingers on the baby's wrist and listened to the pulse.

"In just two minutes, she said to the woman, 'This baby boy is my husband's child. The mark of a skipping heartbeat is the sign of the Chow family. My dear lady, you bore a son for my husband, and I will accept you as my husband's mistress.'"

I was shocked by the bluntness of Che Yu's admission, and she paused for my reaction. I merely smiled and said, "Go on."

"Just like that, she knew. My mother held the baby boy closer to her chest and touched his little cheek. He returned a sweet smile to her with his moist little glistening lips. She announced, 'Young lady, you will move in with us with your babies and I will prepare a room for you. Your older one is weaned, isn't he?' The woman nodded her head.

"Mother instructed her that she would continue to nurse baby Chow, and told her that the Chow family would care for her and her children."

"I was too young to know how these little boys had come to live with you," I told Che Yu. "Later, as I grew older, I felt that it was none of my business. I had no idea that Chow Papa had fathered one of them."

"The woman was most grateful. She promised that mother would always be my father's number one wife and she would treat her with the utmost respect.

"My mother had her servants prepare a room in the west wing of the house for the mistress. They bought her new furniture, linens and clothes. Mother even ordered the cook to prepare special nutritious meals for the mistress since she was nursing baby Chow."

All I could do was shake my head in wonderment. The always proper Chow Papa must have had another side to him. I could easily imagine it with my father, but Che Yu's pater familias was another story entirely.

"It had all begun to transpire a little more than a year earlier," said Che Yu. "One day a banking official named Mr. Lee came into my father's office to discuss some business matters. He told him, 'Mr. Chow, I have been working for you in this bank for the past 20 years. You know how loyal I am to you. Today, I would like to bring up a sensitive matter, if you would allow me to present it to you.'"

According to Che Yu's story, Mr. Lee spoke about a friend who had married a woman the previous year who had borne him a baby boy. Unfortunately, Mr. Lee's friend died shortly thereafter in a train accident, leaving no money for his newly widowed wife and baby child. At the time of Mr. Lee's conversation with Chow Papa, the woman was nursing the eight-month-old baby. Working as a seamstress, she barely earned enough to make ends meet.

Knowing that Chow Papa was a prominent man in the city, yet had no heirs to carry on his legacy, Mr. Lee thought it might be a good idea for him to take on this widow by providing her with food and lodging. Now here's where it gets a bit more problematical.

Mr. Lee suggested that, while the widow's womb was still warm, it might be possible for her to have a child with Mr. Chow. Perhaps, with some good fortune, that child might turn out to be a son, especially considering that she had already borne one of that gender. He went on to say that Mrs. Chow would not need to know about this.

"Mr. Lee told my father what a charitable man he was and that the gesture would be good for both him and the woman. Of course, my father being an honorable man, he was shocked by the suggestion of taking on a mistress. Nevertheless, when Mr. Lee asked if he would consider meeting her, my father replied that he would need some time to consider the proposal.

"After two weeks, Mr. Lee arranged for my father to meet the woman. My father immediately took pity on her and told her that he would provide her with a monthly allowance to take care of her lodging and food. If she bore him a son, he promised to give the boy a portion of his estate. In return, the son would carry on the Chow name."

I turned in the bed, the trace of a smile betraying my thoughts. Chow Papa, with his own paramour!

"Two months later, the woman was with child," said Che Yu. "The secret of the arranged affair was kept silent. Father never brought this subject up to our family.

"But then, through various rumors, my mother heard about the newborn baby boy. Being a gracious lady, she never confronted my father. Instead, she arranged to meet the woman and the baby first. Since she could not bear a son for father, this would be a great opportunity for her to act as the mother of a boy and raise him as an heir for the Chow family.

"After that initial meeting, all was settled. Father never entered the mistress's room once she moved into his house. The baby boy was named Chow Che Ming and, as you know, he has been the center of everything for the Chow family. After only a year, the mistress became ill and passed away at a very early age.

"Che Ming and our adopted brother, Che Wen, were both sent to the best private schools for their education while my sister and I remained in the mansion for home schooling. But remember how, on weekends and holidays, all of us would go to plays, concerts and picnics together? My sister and I were happy to have two brothers who, even though they were younger than us, always acted protectively toward us whenever we went out in public with them."

"And your mother never resented your father for his indiscretion?"

"Not to my knowledge, anyway. She seemed to take it all in with stoic resignation. If she could not bear my father a son, she reasoned, then why not someone else. And she admired the way that my father had adopted the other son. To this day, I don't remember my parents treating him any differently than my sister or me. But I know that Che Ming was the apple of my father's eye."

"And you were mine," I reminded her. "I treasured your letters…and, of course, the shoes."

"Oh, yes. The shoes. Every fall, after you left for college, I would take my sister to the market to buy fabric and material for shoe making projects that benefited the poor. It was a tradition that my mother had started years ago. All the ladies and servants were assigned to hand make these shoes out of the various fabrics. We invested hours of our time using silver thimbles and, stitch by stitch, preparing the shoes with thick, waterproof inner soles.

"By wintertime, we usually had completed more than a hundred pairs of all different sizes, which we packaged in sackcloth bags, along with kilos of rice and flour. Just before the New Year, we would load them onto carriages and drop them off anonymously on doorsteps in the poorer districts of town.

"I always saved the best fabric for the shoes that I sent to you. Maybe it was selfish of me, I don't know. But I got so much pleasure imagining you wearing them in the snow, your feet warm and snug inside."

"I did wear them…all the time. After the first pair you sent me, which was too small, every one thereafter left plenty of room for the thick socks that I liked to wear."

"Each day when the mailman came," Che Yu interjected, "the servants ran to check and see if I had received a letter from my fiancé in Japan."

She pinched me lovingly on the shoulder when she said the word "fiancé."

"My sister could not contain herself and tried to read along with me. One of the postcards you sent us, we giggled and laughed when you wrote about the Japanese customs in the public bathhouses. Do you remember… the postcard photo was of naked women standing half covered by the hot spring, their bodies and faces painted white. And all in fancy hairdos, too.

"And don't forget the naked men," I teased her.

"Those too, standing among the ladies in the bathhouse, so proud of their manhood."

"It wasn't like that," I corrected her. "There was no sense of self-consciousness. It was an age-old tradition that was just a way of life."

"I always replied to your mail right away. Remember, I would tell you about everything that was happening in the Chow family that week and how much I missed you. I often opened my bedroom drawer where I had hidden your handkerchief among my silk garments. Did you know that I also bought a bottle of your favorite cologne, #4711? When the fragrance on the handkerchief started to fade away, I would put a few drops of the cologne on it to keep it freshly scented. This always brought back the memories of how you touched my face and kissed my cheek when we first embraced."

She allowed that hundred-watt smile of hers to escape, and I quietly congratulated myself for arranging such a satisfying birthday celebration for her. I wouldn't see a smile of that magnitude from Che Yu for quite some time again, as the next months were filled with clandestine assignments. I was rarely home, and Che Yu once more fell into a gloomy malaise.

Chapter Twenty-Two
Children of war

In the winter, I received an order to transfer to Kwangsi province, which would act as my home base for a temporary period. This area, where many wild rivers flow into the Gulf of Tonkin, provided excellent access to nearby Hong Kong, where I was beginning to oversee the manufacture of another improved design of the transceiver I had created several years earlier.

I couldn't take Che Yu and our children with me, but Changteh City was no longer safe. So it would be up to Che Yu to begin evacuating the family. She arranged to meet up with her sister, Che Ying, and the relatives who were currently staying with her. While their rendezvous point was no more than several days' journey from Changteh, no place was particularly safe in this area because China was not only fighting the Japanese, but at the same time Mao Tse-tung's Communists were engaged in skirmishes with the Kuomingtang.

Che Yu covered her two oxen-driven carts with canvas cloth, both as a means of shielding the children from view and also providing shade, though the winter sun was not overly strong. Ahma, Ming Ming and several other foot servants carried bags on their backs while walking behind or in front of the carts. They and two new bodyguards hired in Changteh acted like independent villagers, concealing any ties with Che Yu's family.

When they neared the southern edge of Hubei Province, Che Yu's traveling party met up with my older half-sister, Gooma. A petite and very graceful lady, she had been the school beauty queen in Hubei Province before marrying the Governor of Hubei and bearing him a son. Communist bandits had captured the Governor and seized family treasures, clothing and furniture. For the past few weeks, Gooma and her young son had been in hiding in one of her servant's houses.

Through word of mouth, we had learned of Gooma's plight and, because Che Yu would be traveling through the area, she assimilated them into their group. After all, as long as food rations didn't create problems, there was strength in numbers.

Bandits and local warlords had surrounded many of the roads leading in and out of the area, however. Rumors were rampant about all types of thuggery, from robberies to rapes and even scattered killings. One night Che Yu's caravan parked to rest in a wooded area behind the main road. Several from their group had scouted the surroundings first, to make sure that it was relatively safe for overnight camping.

Everyone had settled in without incident and Che Yu had just finished feeding our children when she heard a rustling sound from deep within the bamboo forest. As the sound drew closer, the cadence of galloping horses was unmistakable. Quickly, Che Yu and Ming Ming put the children back into the cart and covered them with one of the blankets.

Moments later, three horsemen stopped in front of the camping party, the dust from the horses' hooves still swirling in the air. The half moon provided enough light to discern the features of the group's leader, still mounted on his dark horse. Short and chubby with several days of unshaven stubble on his face, he wore a turban wrapped loosely around his head. Positioned on his waist was a holstered gun and a belt full of bullets. In his right hand, he held an old Chinese government-issue rifle, which he pointed off to the side. He was fooling no one, however. The rifle was loaded, and he was prepared to use it if given any cause.

Che Yu's adrenaline had kicked in, and she rose quickly, tin plate in hand, to face the horsemen.

"Woman, what brings you to this forest outpost? The road is nearly a half-kilometer to the east."

He spoke in a clumsy local Chinese dialect, but one that Che Yu somewhat understood. She chose her words carefully.

"My lord, I can see that you are Chinese and clearly the leader of your group. How should I address you, my lord?"

The warlord laughed, showing a full mouth of gold-crowned teeth. "I am the warlord, Chun Ming, Commander in Chief of Hunan Province. We're fighting a just war for you against Imperial Japan. It's important for the people to support us."

"Oh, but we do, Lord Chun Ming." ChunMing hunched down in his saddle, his smile fading.

"But you don't show it. Where are the tithes for our war effort? We're short on ammunition, food…money."

Che Yu bowed to him and said, "Lord Chun Ming, my husband is also fighting the Japanese in the southern province. He is risking his life, leaving his family so he can engage our enemies. I know how hard it is to find the funding to support your troops."

At the corner of her eyes, Che Yu noticed her bodyguards standing discreetly amid the bushes. She took off her jade bracelets, her gold ring and pearl earrings, then offered up the jewelry in her hand to the warlord.

"Lord, I am saving these for an emergency to feed my family. You seem to need them more than I, so please take them."

The moonlight illuminated Chun Ming's craggy face, allowing Che Yu to note the wrinkles of a middle-aged man. His skin was like leather, but the eyes betrayed his bullying voice with a certain compassion that she hoped was more than just wistful thinking on her part.

"You are most considerate," he said, lifting the jewelry from Che Yu's hand. "Your manners show the upbringing of a good family. Since your husband is fighting the war, I'll let you go in peace. Where are you heading?"

"We are trying to get to Chongching to meet my husband," she lied.

The warlord's horse was getting restless. He turned it around and scanned the woods.

"Woman, there are many bandits along the road. It is a long and rough journey. I will send two of my men to accompany your oxen cart for the first day. They are supposed to pick up some ammunition in the next town west of here."

"Thank you, but that will not be necessary, sir."

"Oh, but I insist."

Che Yu bowed to the man and replied, "I am eternally grateful for your kindness."

Without warning, Chun Ming turned his horse around again and began galloping into the woods with his entourage. Turning his head back to Che Yu, he yelled, "Be ready first thing in the morning before sunrise. My men will be here to escort you!"

Che Yu waited silently until the men had disappeared into the forest. Then she sighed a long, deep breath as her bodyguards approached her.

"Mrs. Khan, you are very lucky," said Gong-shi, the taller of the two. "We need to separate ourselves with some distance," he added as he lit up a cigarette.

Che Yu immediately assessed the situation, evaluating the general fitness of those in her caravan. The group included her sister, Che Ying, her elderly aunt Zeepou who could barely walk on her bound feet and the former nurse companion who had cared for her late father and now tended to Zeepou. In addition, there were Che Yu's children, Ling's half sister Gooma and her son, the two maids Ming Ming and Ahma, the tutor Mr. Li, a family cook and Uncle Woo. The two bodyguards, both proficient in the martial arts and packing pistols inside their clothing, rounded out the group of 16.

The two oxen carts could carry the children as well as several of the more feeble in the group, such as Uncle Woo, Zeepou and even her overweight, nearsighted nurse.

With any luck, they would be able to meet up with a train in Wuhan, load the oxen carts onto one of the cars and skirt some of the province's trouble spots. But Wuhan was several days away.

After barely an hour, Che Yu and her fellow travelers had extinguished the campfires, packed up the supplies and quietly stolen out of the forest toward Wuhan. By sunrise they had put nearly eight hours between them and Chun Ming's horsemen, but they tried to blend in with other travelers along the road because the danger was still acute.

Several evenings later, after the caravan had parked near a mountain roadside for the night, Ahma went to the woods by the creek to wash some tin plates. Humming a traditional folk song, she scrubbed the plates clean and stacked them for her return journey to the campsite. Suddenly, she heard a rustling in the bushes behind her. Before she could turn around, a pair of strong arms grabbed her by the waist and swung her around.

Ahma tried to scream, but the burly stranger stuffed his turban cloth into her mouth. Under the moonlight, which had been growing progressively stronger for several nights, she could see the attacker's pock-marked face, his bushy eyebrows, grayish untrimmed beard and dirty yellowish teeth.

As he clutched at her clothes, she kicked his shinbone hard, but it didn't seem to faze him. If he were going to rape her, though, Ahma had determined to make him work for it. She craned her neck and tried to bite his hairy arm as he grabbed for her pants. The attacker's face was sweaty and crusted from the trail. Most likely a roadside bandit, he was used to grabbing whatever he wanted, and Ahma was overmatched. Grappling to keep the upper hand, he pulled her back toward the denser brush and thrust his body closer. All the while, he tugged on her pants and maneuvered her backward.

Suddenly, a voice from behind spoke up.

"Stop! Or I will kill you."

Mr. Chu, one of the two bodyguards from Che Yu's caravan, stepped forward, his pistol held high and pointed directly at the bandit's head.

"Now take the cloth out of the lady's mouth, slowly," Chu instructed.

Next, he ordered the man to lie flat on the ground, with his face down and his hands at his back.

"Thank God, Mr. Chu!" was all Ahma could think to say. "What should I do?"

"You can put that cloth back into our visitor's mouth. Snugly, please."

As Mr. Chu held the gun firmly to the man's head, he instructed Ahma to remove her attacker's belt and tie his hands behind him. Then he pulled a piece of twine from his pocket and gave it to her.

"This will have to do. We will have to tie down the blankets on the oxen carts with something else."

Ahma accepted the twine and asked, "His legs?"

Mr. Chu nodded and watched as Ahma adeptly tied his legs and finished it off with a particularly tight knot.

"Now what do you want to do with this man?" he asked.

"He is better off dead than alive. Otherwise, he is going to hurt and rape other women."

Mr. Chu thought for a moment.

"I don't want to use the pistol. He's probably not alone, and we don't want to arouse his friends. Let us drag him to the cliff and throw him down. Are you up to it, Ahma?"

The bandit's eyes displayed sheer terror. He tried to move from where he lay, but it was no use.

"With pleasure!" Ahma replied. "Let's do it. No one would find his body down there."

With the bandit fighting for his wretched life every inch of the way, they managed to drag him to the edge of the cliff. Beads of sweat dripped from Ahma's face onto the bandit, who emitted several raw grunts and groans once he realized how serious they were about completing their mission.

Peering down at a deep gully carved from the formation of sheer rock cliffs, Chu and Ahma turned and looked at each other, then reached down and slowly, arduously, lifted their catch.

"One, two," they swung the bandit's body back and forth, but before they could toss him on the count of three, he twisted free. Unfortunately for the bandit, he had nowhere to go but down. Sailing from the high cliff, he descended at lightning speed to the rugged brambles and scrub in the wilderness pit some 300 feet below, where he landed with a muffled thud, followed by a sharp popping sound.

Back at camp, a clearly shaken Ahma breathlessly told her story, and it was decided that it would be best to leave as quickly as possible from the area. Once again they followed a ritual that was becoming commonplace, the quick, efficient dismantling of their campsite. It was agreed that they would travel along the train route and hope to board their ox carts on a freight car at the next junction, some 20 miles or so to the west.

Che Yu realized that she was virtually going around in circles at this point, but the lesson of survival was to merely find safe residency, no matter where, until the depressing war was over. The most important thing was to stay somewhat close to the river and the larger cities so that Che Yu and I could transport messages back and forth. They would be sent primarily by telegraph to Whampoa Academy, and the officials there could inform me as to her latest whereabouts. I would try to meet up with her and the family when my missions allowed it, though I was always on call and the visits were way too short.

Whenever Che Yu found a safe village outside of a city, she would rent a small house from a villager and settle our family for awhile. The maids would draw water from the well, and they would cook mainly vegetables and rice for the meals

During these months of hardship and separation, Che Yu became a pillar of strength for everyone around her. Sadly, her porcelain hands became rough and calloused, and she lost a considerable amount of weight, to the point that it was sometimes alarming when I would see her after a particularly long absence. Through it all, she remained calm and capable, always ready to take charge of any dangerous or difficult situation. She had prepared well with her own family money, so that keeping everyone in her group alive and safe was a reasonable goal. Because I was so involved with the war effort and moved constantly from town to town, Che Yu suggested that I not even try to send any support money since it could very likely become lost in transit.

Despite all of the moving from town to town and the infrequency of our visits together, I managed to impregnate Che Yu once again. I actually felt some remorse, knowing that I might not be there to see her through much of the pregnancy. But Che Yu seemed genuinely pleased, and she assured me that she would have plenty of able assistance from the extended family.

Our fourth baby and third surviving child, a girl, our forth treasure named Khan Ching, was born in a small hillside village near Chengdu in Sichuan province. I was, naturally, on assignment at the time. Che Yu had rented a small cottage several months prior from a local innkeeper, Mr. Ying. His wife had been a teacher who was killed by a Japanese bombing at her school.

Mr. Ying located a midwife to deliver our baby girl, though Che Yu had to endure the ordeal without sedation or pain medication of any kind. My wife was so weak in the beginning that Khan Ching had to be fed with goat's milk for the first month or two before they could find a local nursemaid.

Che Yu and the family stayed at the inn for almost six months. Though the climate was often gray and gloomy, the temperature was relatively mild and the location was near a fertile basin. Moreover, Mr. Li, our children's tutor, was glad that the youngsters finally had a relatively peaceful place in which to study.

He had to teach Khan Kay and Khan Bing at different levels because of their age differences. Sometimes, however, he would have Kay and Bing sit together for a lesson, especially when he told stories about the histories of foreign countries. The children especially liked the time he showed them a picture of an American Indian chief."His name is 'Running Fox'," Mr. Li had explained. "The American Indians often took an animal's name as their own because they believed that the animal's instincts for self-preservation and their bravery were good omens for an honorable and successful life."

The children also liked the fact that the chief always wore a headdress made of different bird feathers embellished with colorful beads. Soon they were referring to me as Sleeping Eagle because often I would be worn out when I came home to visit, and Che Yu and I would retire to the bedroom. They also came to associate me with the eagle paperweight that graced my small work desk at home. I, for one, enjoyed the moniker because it seemed to hold positive connotations for my children, and who was going to argue if someone wished an honorable and successful existence for them?

Sometimes when I came home, I would find Kay and Bing playing by the creek near the rice fields where they acted out their perceptions of Running Fox and Sleeping Eagle.

Ming Ming handled most of the washing chores for our family since Ahma had become somewhat traumatized by her ordeal with the bandits some months earlier. Ming Ming would walk to the creek where she would use a stout, gnarled stick to beat the clothing, which she would lay on top of a flat rock. Next, she would rinse each garment with creek water, then bring the pile back up to the house and hang the clothes to dry on a thin rope line by the back of the kitchen.

One day Ming Ming was taking a break after finishing her chores. Walking along by the creek and picking wild flowers as she went, she saw Mr. Ying, the innkeeper, reading under a large shade tree. Ming Ming's bashfulness instilled in her the desire to turn around and walk quickly back to the house.

"Ming Ming, please don't go!"

She heard the voice of Mr. Ying behind her and turned to face him.

"Ming Ming, if you have a moment," he said in a pleasant tone, "I would like to talk to you."

Gathering her courage, Ming Ming walked slowly toward Mr. Ying and asked, "What are you reading?"

"I am reading the history of China. It is immensely fascinating. And I have plenty of books in my library that you are welcome to borrow anytime. By the way, I have been watching you since you moved in along with Mrs. Khan's family. I like your mannerisms...where did you learn to walk so gracefully?"

Ming Ming began to blush, but dutifully answered, "I have been serving Mrs. Khan since I was nine years old. The Chow family took me in when I was in an orphanage. Mrs. Khan has treated me just like a sister. She is the one who taught me how to walk this way and how to talk in a civilized fashion."

Ming Ming continued, "Mr. Ying, thank you for your offer about the books, but I can only read a few words because I never went to school."

Mr. Ying closed his book and studied her face.

"I would be happy to teach you how to read and write if you would allow me."

Ming Ming's eyes sparkled and she spoke excitedly, "Really? Mr. Ying, I would love to learn after I have finished my chores."

Chapter Twenty-Three
Life in village

One day as Mr. Ying was giving Ming Ming one of her increasingly frequent reading lessons, Che Yu wandered down by the stream to watch her children play their favorite games. But as soon as she reached the stream bank, Khan Kay and Khan Bing rushed past her toward the front of the field by the house. Soon a car horn began beeping loudly, and Che Yu turned to see what was causing all of the commotion. She watched as a uniformed driver opened the door of a jeep, and another uniformed man stepped out.

Dressed proudly in my two-star general's jacket and trousers, I strode purposefully toward the front of the house. The children ran squealing up to me and I joyfully picked them up, one by one, followed by enthusiastic hugging and kissing. Che Yu also ran toward me in her soft peasant shirt and pants, her long hair flying to one side, caressed by the wind. When our bodies touched, I hugged her close to me. She felt strong yet vulnerable, perhaps a bit thinner than before the war, but as beautiful and enchanting as ever.

"I can't believe you are actually here," she gushed. "How did you get away from work?"

"I asked for a short leave of absence. They really couldn't deny me, considering how much of value I have been to them lately."

Without any prompting, Uncle Woo went to the nearby neighbors and bought a chicken and fish to cook for a dinner celebration. While I rested in the bedroom with Che Yu, Kay and Bing watched transfixed in the kitchen as Uncle Woo gave them a primer in the fine art of undressing and cooking a live chicken.

"Now you will see how we prepare this fine bird for the pot. Here, you two, sit on this bail of straw and watch me."

He began to describe the necessary steps as he gave them a firsthand demonstration.

"I am boiling a big pot of water to be used later," he said, sharpening his large knife.

Next, he described in great detail as he grabbed the squawking chicken from its cage and held onto its neck firmly. Expertly, he plucked several feathers from the underside of the fowl's neck and, without warning, slit the bird's jugular vein.

The kids winced and let out two sharp little squawks of their own as Uncle Woo turned the chicken downward and drained its blood into a bowl below.

"We save the blood and make bean curd soup for the servants," he noted.

Kay turned to her brother. "Yecch, I don't want chicken for dinner."

Uncle Woo, however, was clearly proud of his exhibition and continued with a running monologue.

"The next thing to do is hold the chicken's head and dip the entire body into the boiling water for a few seconds. Then you place it on the table, on top of these newspapers, and begin plucking the feathers out. See how much easier it is when you dip it into hot water first. Do you want to try to help me?"

Kay and Bing shook their heads emphatically, but Kay had an idea.

"Uncle Woo, can we have some of the feathers now? We want to make an Indian's headdress like the picture we saw of an American Indian Chief."

"Yes, little one, but don't do it outside. The wind would blow it away."

By now, Uncle Woo was happy that the children were leaving his kitchen so that he could begin doing some serious cooking.

One afternoon, I received a message from headquarters that I had to leave for Vietnam and Hong Kong to purchase military items. I decided to take my wife with me, though Che Yu said we would have to bring along our five-month-old child because she was nursing her. We arranged for Che Yu's sister, Che Ying, to take care of the household.

The night before we were to leave, Mr. Ying came to visit us and brought a gift box with him.

"Mr. and Mrs. Khan, I have enjoyed getting to know your family since you rented my cottage," he began. "Here are some dried fruits that my staff cured for your traveling. I will also keep watch for the safety of your family."

Mr. Ying then looked at Che Yu. Without hesitating, he spoke again.

"Mrs. Khan, you know that I have been a widower for three years now. I have been teaching Ming Ming to read and write for the past two months and I have grown to be very fond of her."

He smiled and swallowed.

"May I have your permission to marry her? I know she belongs to you and I will be happy to pay whatever price you might want, in order to buy her freedom."

Che Yu looked over at Ming Ming, standing over in the corner of the room. Her servant's face had turned a bright crimson.

"Do you want to marry Mr. Ying? "

"Yes, I do and I would be very happy to stay with Mr. Ying and start a family."

Che Yu took a jade bracelet from her wrist and a gold ring from her finger and put them into Ming Ming's hand.

"This is a small token of your wedding dowry," said Che Yu. "If that is what the two of you want, then Mr. Ying, you may have my permission to marry Ming Ming. Promise that you will always treat her with aforethought and kindness. And there are to be no payments. Ming Ming, you are free to go with our blessing!"

"A thousand thanks for your kindness and generosity."

Ming Ming dropped to her knees and bowed three times to Che Yu and me, but Che Yu quickly took her hand and helped her up.

"I am happy for both of you."

The next morning, a driver arrived early at our door and we stowed two pieces of luggage in the jeep, before driving away from the cottage with Khan Jing and a wave to our two older children.

I felt relaxed and optimistic, confident that the vacation would be good for Che Yu. After all, she had been through tremendous hardships during the evacuations, and the loss of our third child still left us fighting considerable bouts of depression.

We met up with 20 military staff members who were to accompany us, the next night, to a nearby town to purchase more trucks that would ship ammunition to Kumming, a two-day drive in rough terrain.

A nondescript room in a small village inn served as accommodations for Che Yu, our baby and myself, while my staff stayed in a dining hall, with knapsacks laid wall-to-wall on the floor. In the middle of the night the first round of sirens went off and, seconds later, bombing commenced from what seemed to be every direction. In our room, Che Yu and I could hear the buzz of the airplanes flying low over the roof, while little baby Ching nursed at her mother's side.

When the sirens sounded, I was writing orders at a small desk, by the light of an oil lamp. I moved over next to Che Yu and Ching once the rumble of the planes grew near. Suddenly, a Japanese bomber dropped a payload just a short distance from our hotel. As the blast went off, our building shook and jolted for a few seconds and a portion of the ceiling collapsed above the bed in our room. Loose plaster and concrete blocks fell onto the bed, just a few inches from where Che Yu was nursing our baby. By some miracle or quirk of fate they were unhurt, though Ching began wailing in fear from the horrific impact.

It was then that Che Yu told me of a brief premonition she had just had, and she suggested that we divide our traveling party into two groups, leaving at different times.

We should leave later than the first group, at least an hour or more, she advised.

I deferred to my wife's instincts and, as soon as the bombing passed, quickly made my way to the dining hall where I instructed 10 of the men to leave in their jeeps immediately. Three hours later, around two in the morning, my family and the other 10 staff members fled the inn in a truck, with the intention of meeting up with the first group at our next destination.

When we arrived at sub-headquarters, we learned that the Japanese had ambushed the first group. Only six of the staff members had arrived, with three already wounded. After huddling with advisors for a quick, impromptu meeting, I left my wife and baby Ching at the headquarters and set off again with one of my lieutenants to rendezvous with two French arms dealers and a Cambodian equipment broker to pick up our purchases. Included in the transaction were three trucks, two jeeps, two German tanks and 300 cases of guns and firearms. The tanks and many of the ammunition cases would be picked up and transported several days later.

The Cambodian, a young, wiry guy with fire in his eyes, but who always seemed to be smiling at a private joke that only he knew, questioned the amount of money that I lay on the table for him. He swore that we had agreed to at least a thousand more silver coins. The Cambodians were famous for this, so I produced a document that outlined the payout. He still wasn't satisfied and moved his shirt to the side slightly to reveal a pistol holstered at his belt. With my lieutenant sitting beside me and several bodyguards and drivers waiting just outside, either the man was crazy or… well, that could be the problem. He was crazy.

When he began shouting in some type of Cambodian dialect, one of the Frenchmen addressed him harshly in French, which he seemed to understand. He pushed himself away from the table abruptly and nodded. The deal was done.

Warily, we loaded the goods and covered the trucks and jeeps with a large canvas top. After securing the canvas with ropes wound through a series of grommet holes, we boarded the vehicles and drove them back to the headquarters where they would be re-routed for delivery to Kumming. Che Yu, baby Jing and I would board a transport plane traveling south to Vietnam.

Relieved that my portion of this particular mission was complete, I could finally relax once our plane was airborne. I clasped Che Yu's hand and determined that we would emotionally reconnect during these next few days spent together.

In Vietnam, Che Yu finally felt alive again. I took her shopping for some new clothing, jewelry and perfume. While I perused the offerings at a nearby tobacco shop, she had her hair styled at a popular beauty salon. Even baby Jing seemed to sense that a cloud had lifted, at least temporarily.

That night, in bed, Che Yu leafed through an American fashion magazine. She reminded me how, as a young lady, she had always kept up with the latest trends featured in popular periodicals from the U.S., France and Italy. There was no doubt about Che Yu's good taste. Her ancestors used to operated a silk factory, raising the finest breed of silk worms from Honchow, weaving the most exquisite fabric for the Royal Palace and made the Emperor and Empress's garments, silk blankets and tapestries. They were not allowed to sell the goods to anyone else except exclusively for the royal families. Che Yu began speaking,

"Before each season started, my sister and I would take the train to Shanghai to shop for a new wardrobe. We would buy the most beautiful imported lace and velvet floral-on- silk fabrics by the bolts, in addition to many French trims. The shops would ship the goods to Nanjing and, when they arrived, I would design my own clothes and have our seamstress make the garments for Che Ying, my mother and myself.

"In my bedroom chamber, there was a carved redwood jewelry chest, about the size of a small night stand. The inside was lined with a padding of red silk. Several layers of drawers contained the family heirlooms: the finest Imperial jade, pearls and 24 karat gold rings, pendants and earrings. Hair combs set in pure gold and embellished with precious stones of emeralds, topaz, sapphire, rubies and ivory inlayed with mother of pearl and countless pure gold nuggets were all part of my dowry collection. I was saving all these treasures for my wedding. My papa gave me a good sum of allowance for my duty in managing his household finances. I used that portion of the money to shop with my sister and for charities."

Che Yu smiled slightly, then grimaced and gave me a look of uncertainty.

"Ling, I have a confession to make. I first ask for your forgiveness. If you don't forgive me, then I will not confess."

I was in a playful mood.

"You never told me that you have secrets, Che Yu. Have you been naughty? I know that you were a virgin when we consummated. You must tell me your confession."

She tugged at my shirt.

"Say that you will forgive me, then I will tell you my secret."

"OK, I forgive you."

I sat up, propped my pillows and waited anxiously for Che Yu to confess. Part of me was excited, part fearful of what I might hear.

"All right," she began. "One summer, my sister and I went shopping at a famous department store in Shanghai. Che Ying noticed a young man was following us, even to the ladies clothing department."

She smiled and searched my face for any signs of jealousy or curiosity.

"After shopping, we had Earl Grey tea in a lavishly decorated hotel lounge. While we were sipping our tea...by the way, I love the English high tea time."

"Go on, go on, Che Yu," I urged her.

"Well, my sister leaned forward and told me in a hushed tone, 'Don't turn your head, but that man is still following us. He cannot keep his eyes off of you!'

"I was very poised and said to Che Ying, 'Don't be silly, I am engaged to Ling and I am not interested in looking at any man.'

"But Che Ying was emphatic. She said that he was not like any other Chinese. Then she described him as looking like a movie star, with thick bushy eyebrows and deep-set eyes. He actually looked somewhat like Tyrone Power."

I forced a smile...fairly strong competition.

"Then my sister said excitedly, 'He is walking closer to our table!'

"I was becoming curious and asked what he was wearing. Che Ying described his outfit...a white shirt with the sleeves rolled up in a confident manner, his shirt collar loosely opened and a blue and gold striped tie hanging leisurely over the collar. He was wearing khaki-colored linen trousers and white and brown two-toned shoes. Oh, and did I mention a straw hat, slightly tilted?"

I was becoming slightly annoyed that Che Yu remembered so many details about this man, but I tried not to show it.

"He was extremely handsome. And as he walked past the table, he tipped his hat to us, smiled softly, then disappeared behind us."

"That sneaky man, who does he think he is!" I blurted out, without thinking. I was actually becoming jealous.

"Do you want to hear the rest of the story or not, Ling?"

"Tell me, yes tell me. What happened next?" I shook Che Yu's arm gently.

"On our train ride back to Nanjing, all Che Ying could talk about was the handsome gentleman who followed us. Then, two weeks later, my father came home and called us into the parlor. He said, 'I heard that you two stirred up the city of Shanghai a few weeks ago.' And we asked if he meant we had spent to much money shopping this time.

"He said no, that it was another matter…a man whose father had been a friend of his back in his high school days. My father's friend had later moved to Paris, started an import business and married a French lady. His son had just come back to China to look for a Chinese wife."

"He fancied Che Ying?" I asked hopefully, not wanting to hear that the man following them in the department store was interested in Che Yu. But her shy smile made clear the target of the man's affections.

"Evidently," she said, "he was attracted to me. And my father had just received a hand-delivered letter from the young man at his office. I was a bit taken aback that he had tried to track me down and came to my father's office, but father explained that he had given the letter to a messenger."

"What did it say?"

"It asked for permission to court me. But my father responded to him in writing that I was engaged to be married and that the Chow family would be obliged if he did not contact us again.

"That night, my sister and I could not sleep and she confided in me that she wished the handsome gentleman had wanted her instead. I put my arms around her and told her how beautiful she was and that she would find someone just as nice and attractive to marry one day.

"But I must admit, my heart was very tempted to find out about this strange admirer. I blushed every time I thought about him, and I made my sister promise not to tell you about this whole episode. You were the only man I loved and I couldn't wait for you to come back. It was just very flattering, though."

Che Yu studied my face and waited for a reaction.

"I forgive you for thinking about that man," I said. "I am just glad you had better sense than your sister. Whatever happened to him?"

"I don't know, we never kept up with the news about him. And my sister is still single."

Chapter Twenty-Four
Hong Kong

Once World War II began in full force in Europe, and the United States stepped in after the Japanese bombing of Pearl Harbor, all of the Chinese battle strategies were revamped to address the new realities.

Some months earlier, I had finally decided to move my family into the safer environment of Hong Kong, which was a British colony and, therefore, under the Crown's protection. Though with Japan's recent occupation of Canton, Hong Kong was effectively surrounded, there was still a sense that British defense strategies would delay an attack perhaps indefinitely. Sir Robert Brooke-Popham, the Commander in Chief of the British Far East Command, seemed to be gaining Churchill's ear about providing additional reinforcements for the area, for which everyone was waiting anxiously.

The British had also established the Gin Drinkers Line... no not some group of Brit expatriates sitting shoulder to shoulder at a Hong Kong drinking emporium, but actually a line of defense named after a bay in nearby Kwai Chung. This line, which was actually a series of defensive positions, included bunkers, trenches, fortified machine gun nests and even the mountains north of Kowloon Peninsula. Running about 18 or 20 kilometers in length, the Gin Drinkers Line was more of a stopgap measure than a true defense line. It was thought that it might prove beneficial as a way of delaying the Japanese invaders as the British continued to mobilize.

Was Hong Kong immune to the power of the Japanese forces? No one believed that to be the case, but with Chiang Kai-shek fighting on two fronts...against the Japanese and, more subtly, the Chinese Communists... there was no telling where the next threat would occur. At least with my growing family in Hong Kong, I felt some sense that they were relatively secure. My own safety was another matter.

While still working undercover for Chiang and the Kuomintang, I started a shipping company that navigated the South China Sea and served a variety of ports in mainland China. Our business plan was to transport rice, oil, beans and flour in exchange for electronics from Hong Kong and cement, salt and other products from other nearby cities. Though unwritten, my primary mission was to thwart Japanese shipping interests wherever possible, while maintaining a food line to the different remote villages around Hainan Island and its smaller neighboring islands.

At Hainan, I was known as Lord Khan, rather than General Khan, because they were aware that I had been funding some of the war against Japan with my own money. In the two years leading up to the establishment of my shipping company, South China Transport, I had thoroughly gained the trust of the islanders. They had allowed me to set up headquarters in HaiKou, the main port of Hainan island and a passageway from the South China Sea to the Gulf of Tonkin. Through my efforts, we had also built a lookout post on one of the strategic points of a nearby island so that I and my staff could monitor Japanese naval movements and assess the enemy's association with the local pirates. I personally owned, under a different name, several gunboats that regularly patrolled the islands and scouted Japanese positions there.

Because of my relationship with the Japanese Navy Admiral Hiro Saka, I became friends with many of the Navy fleet commanders. To the Japanese, I was a non-partisan soldier of fortune during the war, an independent businessman whose main loyalty was to the almighty dollar. I also happened to be quite an entertainer at parties, with my better-than-average dancing and singing of Japanese folk songs.

Though I had wisely invested my father's inheritance and amassed considerable wealth through my various commercial ventures, it cost a considerable sum to manage a fleet of ships and support boats, while purchasing ammunition and meeting a large payroll each month. Chiang Kai-shek had pledged that he and his government would reimburse me for all of my expanses. So I kept a running tab, which seemed to grow exponentially each month.

Soon I had settled down comfortably with my family in Hong Kong. My business front appeared quite convincing and my intelligence work seemed to be reaping noticeable benefits. The situation with the Communists was at the same time deteriorating, however.

While Chiang Kai-shek's troops were spread thin, Mao's Red Army had returned to concentrating primarily on the country's civil war. This led to some key victories in strategic towns that had previously sided with the Kuomingtang. Chiang's focus was becoming increasingly blurred, I thought, as he appeared to be preoccupied with the battle that seemingly lay ahead with Mao, rather than with the Japanese incursions. Either way, I was concerned about Chiang's ability to pay for the many services that South China Transport was providing.

My business was nevertheless flourishing. People who could afford to escape from China had settled in Hong Kong and, even during war time, were beginning to enjoy life again in this thriving British Colony offering a variety of business, cultural and recreational activities.

With the large amount of money that I was making from my shipping business, I could afford to buy blocks of different properties if I had wanted. But, because of the uncertainties brought on by the war, I chose instead to rent a house for my family and staff…a family that had recently welcomed a new addition, baby son Khan Long, fifth treasure, our first child to be born in a hospital.

Our rental house was located on Pan Long Tao Road, in the high rank district of Tong Law Wan. The area was known as Happy Valley, which in some ways it actually was when compared to the difficult, trying life that Che Yu and I had lived recently. Built in a Modern style, the house contained three stories, including two flats per story divided into an east and west wing. It was a comfortable size for the 16 people who lived there, including immediate family members and extended relatives, as well as staff members who lived in a separate section on the west side of the house. My half-sister Gooma and her son were no longer with us as they had elected to remain in central China.

Community stairs featured large glass block windows at the landing area of the house, allowing a generous amount of natural light into the building. This especially pleased Che Yu, who always loved homes that were open and bright.

My staff members, among them bodyguards, chauffeurs, secret agents and even a couple of favorite informers, were extremely dedicated to me.

Most had left their families and followed me from the small villages where I had recruited them.

Che Yu and I made sure that our children attended private schools that stressed a bilingual education, and she hired a nanny for each child. Life was good, at least during those times when I was in Hong Kong, and my wife and I became involved in the city's social circles.

Some of my friends even convinced me to buy a soccer team from a British businessman who had been called back from Hong Kong to London. The team had a great history of success and its coach even felt that a championship was attainable the following year. But the turmoil of the war weighed heavily on everyone, and even the soccer league's schedule had been abbreviated, due to the need for young men in the army. At the last minute, I decided not to purchase the team, which was just as well... they lost nearly all of their games that next year.

My name was known among many different business entities, and I received invitations to a number of local events for executives and entrepreneurs. At one such meeting, a local bankers' get-together, I saw a familiar face across the room. Politely begging off from a conversation with a Macau investment manager, I strode over to the corner of the meeting hall where a lone figure stood smiling and watching the activity around him.

"My good friend, Tao Yee," I addressed him. The attractive, somewhat slender, bespectacled man turned to me and immediately broke into a wide grin.

"Ling, my dear Ling."

It had been nearly 10 years since I had seen Yee. Once we graduated from Waseda University, he stayed on in Japan for two more years, at which time he worked for a bank specializing in start-up business financing. He later returned to Nanjing, married a local girl and settled into life as a gentleman banker since he had been rejected by the military for minor health reasons. My course of life was much more haphazard and uncharted. Though I had been living in Nanjing, as well, my commitments to the military, my broadcast station and various other interests had kept me from staying in close contact with Yee. As we stood there reminiscing, I felt a tinge of guilt. Clearly, he had tried to maintain a continuing relationship with me, but I had not reciprocated.

"Yes, my two daughters are now in grade school," Yee said, smiling politely. "No boys yet, but we are still trying."

We shook hands and promised to stay in touch, especially now that Yee had been transferred by his company to the outskirts of Hong Kong. I could tell by the wistfulness in his eyes that he hoped he could trust my promise to call, but it was just as obvious that he expected I would not.

In my defense, I barely had enough time for my own family as I tried to juggle the shipping business and my ever widening role in subverting the Japanese. It was a strange dance that I was doing with Chiang Kai-shek during this time. While trying to distance myself from his increasingly disjointed operation, I had to maintain the semblance of undivided loyalty because by now his organization owed me millions of dollars. I was more and more convinced, however, that if I were going to fight the Japanese and have any success with it, I would have to do so in a more independent manner. Chiang's attention span toward what I felt was the ultimate struggle was being trumped by his intensely personal conflict with Mao.

It was necessary to work with Chiang directly on certain occasions, however, because I needed his support for air strikes if I happened to locate any Japanese fleets around Hong Kong and the surrounding islands. By now, I was not taking any pay from the government, in order to avoid any paper trails. So the Kuomintang's debts to me continued to rise.

Though I had not had the time for Tao Yee, I was clearly cultivating new relationships that could benefit me. One of these was Doug Yang, a native Chinese who had studied at Rutgers University in New Jersey and become westernized in every sense, even down to the structure of his name. Doug was an accomplished business broker, with whom I had worked many advantageous deals.

On a beautifully clear day, Doug and I rode in my car to a private horse stable in Repulse Bay. He had arranged for me to see several exquisite racehorses, which were available for sale.

Our car turned into a narrow cobblestone lane and moments later we pulled up to the freshly painted stables. Doug jumped out and started to walk toward the front of the barn.

"Stop, I want to see that gorgeous brown horse standing behind the white fence." I insisted.

"Ling, that one is not ready yet. He is still being broken in."

I ignored Doug and walked toward the horse. My friend followed me to the edge of the pasture, and we leaned forward across the fence. A beautiful chestnut stallion ran friskily back and forth, occasionally raising its front hoofs to show off its magnificent form and strength.

"How old is the stallion,?" I asked while gazing at the horse.

"He's approaching two years old. Guang Li, the best trainer in Hong Kong, is training him. Mr. Wu was the owner of the stallion as well as the rare collection of several esteemed racehorses in the stable. But since he passed away a few months ago, his wife has wanted to sell the business and move to America to be with her grown children."

One of the caretakers came to join us. A short, lean man of about 30, he climbed nimbly over the fence and put a bridle on the horse who at first shied away from him and even became agitated. Clearly the man knew what he was doing, however, and soon he led the chestnut stallion over toward the fence. It was love at first sight. I put my hand on the animal's forehead and stroked his shiny hair.

"What is his name?"

"Thunder, yes, he is a beauty!" answered the stable boy. "And you are Mr. Khan, no doubt. My name is Shorty."

I tried to suppress a smile. Someone had named him well.

Patting Thunder's head and glistening mane again, I studied the horse closely and his eyes locked with mine.

"The trainer is still working on him. He is quite temperamental. He won't be ready for racing for another six months.

Doug grabbed my arm impatiently.

"Come, Ling, let us go see the horses in the stable." Shorty led the way. There were at least ten stalls in the stable, but only a few were occupied.

"It is hard to find someone to buy out the whole stock," Doug said. "So Mrs. Wu is selling the horses individually to any interested buyer. Of course, she might entertain a special offer if you were to buy in volume."

I smiled playfully back at Doug, who was ever the shrewd business broker. Then I walked around several times in front of two horses that were somewhat attractive to me.

Suddenly, a loud kicking sound was heard in a distant stall. We scrambled over to see what was causing the commotion.

"Ah yes," said Shorty, admiringly. "It is China Pride. He is bored right now. Since Mr. Wu passed on, we have not entered him in any races. He had a few races last year, placing second and almost nose-to-nose with

Guardian Angel, the Happy Valley Cup champion. At three years of age, he has plenty of good racing left in him."

I lifted my hand and brushed China Pride's head and his long elegant nose. He was also a stallion, pitch black from mane to tail.

"He came from the thoroughbred blood line of the retired champion, Lightning Cross," Shorty said proudly. We have had him since he was a foal."

"Ling, you are an extremely wealthy man," Doug reminded me as he began to build his case for a lucrative sale. "You need a hobby that befits you, a good sporting interest for a pastime. Think of it, if you owned these horses, with Guang Li as trainer and Shorty here as the exercise rider and stable boy. That would surely be a winning combination."

My mind was churning with the possibilities.

"Are there any private stables at the Happy Valley racecourse? I would only consider owning the horse if it were kept near my residence."

"The arrangement could be made. Which ones are you interested in?" Doug asked anxiously. "Mrs. Wu is practically giving them away at the price she is asking. Selling against the trainer's advice, I might add."

Without any hesitation, I pointed at China Pride and then out to the pasture at Thunder.

"I like them both. See about getting them settled in at Happy Valley. If the price is anywhere close, then I'll take them. By the way, Shorty, tell me about yourself."

"Sir, my name is Show Han, but everyone calls me Shorty. I have been a stable boy since I was 12 years old. I've worked for Mr. Wu for almost 15 years."

"Would you be interested in being on my payroll and taking care of my horses?"

"Yes, sir…yes, sir, I would. Mrs. Wu told me to start looking for another position. She has been very nice to keep me around for the time being. I will take excellent care of Thunder and China Pride. Maybe with a little exercise and training, we could enter China Pride for the Happy Valley Cup again this fall."

I went back to the car and pulled a camera from the back seat. For the next few minutes I took photos of my new purchases. I felt like a kid opening birthday packages.

Motioning my bodyguard and chauffeur Chang Gore to start the car engine, I looked back once more at Thunder. He was my favorite. I smiled at him, and I could swear he smiled back.

When Che Yu saw me walk into our living room that evening, she sensed that something wonderful had happened.

"Don't tell me, you bought the horse."

"I bought two," I answered, grinning. "They are both stallions and magnificent animals. I will take you and the children to see them once they get settled in at Happy Valley."

It was particularly exciting to think about how the children would react to my newest purchase. Kay, our eldest, had been especially glum lately. Classmates at the prestigious school she attended often ridiculed her and accused me of being a traitor to the Chinese. Some days, she would come home in tears.

Che Yu couldn't tell her that I was actually spying against Imperial Japan, but she would say, "Your father has been very generous to the Chinese people. He has brought food to many of them so they could feed their families. In some instances, he has even provided them with money and medical supplies."

She had reminded Kay that people spread rumors all the time, without knowing the true facts.

"Just remember that your father is an honorable man who loves his country," Che Yu said, as little Kay sniffled quietly.

It hurt to think that many people in the city thought of me as a turncoat, especially since my high-level contacts had enabled me to save various Chinese doctors, businessmen and government officials through what the Japanese called cash "donations." Even more painful was the thought that my children had to suffer verbal barbs from their playmates because of me.

Today, still grinning from the euphoria of now owning two extraordinary racehorses, I envisioned more pleasant days ahead for our entire family.

The next morning, I took my wife to her favorite jewelry store.

"Darling, pick out anything you like. I got my new horses and it is your turn to treat yourself. I want you to be the happiest woman in the world."

Chapter Twenty-Five
The Unforgivable Sin

Because I was a man of wealth and power, everyone considered me to be a ladies' man. Many women would go out of their way to try to meet me. Hong Kong had become such an elixir for my confidence that temptation and ego soon got the better part of me. I started staying out late at night, drinking and partying with my new-found friends and the admiring ladies.

My generosity (not all of it altruistic) was legendary, making me a very popular figure. One time a banking officer saw me wearing a cashmere coat and commented, "Mr. Khan, that is such a fine coat, it would take me a year's salary to be able to own such a fine piece of workmanship."

Right there on the spot, I took off the coat and presented it to him.

"Now, you may have it," I told him. "It is yours."

Doug Yang always liked to hang around in my presence at parties. One night, while we were drinking in a private room, he pulled me aside.

"Ling, look to the far left by the window. There is a lady who would like to meet you. Her name is June Lee. She is the niece of the chairman of our Hong Kong Chamber of Commerce.

"How do you know she wants to meet me?"

"She has seen you many times at parties, and tonight she mentioned to me that she has really taken a liking to you. Come on. I will introduce you."

Being half drunk, I didn't see the harm in meeting a few pretty ladies. After all, it was known that I was happily married. And as a well-known Hong Kong civic leader, it was important to socialize. We walked to where June Lee was standing.

"This is Khan Ling, Miss Lee," Doug greeted her. "Could I get you a drink?"

"Sure, Champagne please. I love the bubbles."

June Lee turned to me with an enticing smile.

"How are you, Mr. Khan? I have heard so much about you. You are even much more handsome than what everyone told me."

Suddenly, I was feeling a bit unsteady. I had drunk too much, too fast.

"Excuse me, but I have had a bit much to drink. I need some fresh air. Would you care to walk out to the garden, Miss Lee?"

She nodded, then put her arm around my waist and steadied me as we walked toward the mansion's stone patio overlooking Repulse Bay. The ocean breezes felt cool to our skin. The wind was blowing a few strands of hair across her lovely face. After a few moments of casual, meaningless banter, she touched my arm softly.

"Mr. Khan, would you like to take a drive with me? The breeze will do you some good."

I followed her like a puppy dog to her convertible where she helped me into the passenger seat. Then we started our scenic tour of Repulse Bay, with its azure waters lapping the wide sandy beach, its sweeping views of the city, its luxurious colonial style hotel on the water's edge. At last, she stopped the car near one of the quietest areas of the beach. Staring into her rear view mirror, she touched up her lipstick and powdered her nose.

I was comfortably lounging in the seat, half asleep, when she walked around, opened the door and dragged me out of the car.

"Come on, let's go!"

"Where…are we going…pret..ty lady?"

"Let's go swimming."

As soon as we reached the sandy beach, she started to take off her shoes, then undressed herself in front of me. Though I was half-drunk and my vision was blurry, I could see a young and firm body silhouette that looked liked a goddess in the moonlight. She helped me to take off my shoes and socks and undressed me.

Holding my hand, she led me to the chilly ocean waves. The freezing saltwater awakened my senses and, though I could have turned back at this point, I found it difficult to refuse the young woman who was caressing me and touching my body in a most pleasant manner. Next, she placed my hand on one of her taut breasts, and we moved in a smooth, softly undulating cadence with the rushing waves.

The next afternoon, I woke up and found myself in a nicely furnished hotel room. Sleeping next to me was a beautiful young lady in her twenties, completely naked and her arms wrapped around my chest.

"My God, what have I done?" I thought.

But the temptation of my flesh was greater than my will. She reached her hand across and touched me between my legs, sending the blood rushing through my body. I was quickly aroused, surrendering once more as she mounted on top of me.

We spent two days and nights making love in the room and drinking wine and liquor ordered through room service. Occasionally, my bodyguard would knock on the door and ask if his boss wanted anything.

The liquor was a way to numb my senses and help me forget that I was a married man. This beguiling young woman had brought back my youth and made me feel like a privileged prince. I was totally bewitched.

On the third morning, as I washed my face with a warm towel and looked into the mirror at my unruly whiskers, the folly and tragic nature of my behavior struck me. I finally came to grips with who I was.

"What am I doing here?" I cried out silently in my mind.

I saw these images in my head of Quan Yin looking disapprovingly at me. How could the goddess of mercy have any compassion for an adulterer, for someone who had betrayed a loving wife and three beautiful children? No matter how I felt now, though, I knew that I could never have these past two days back. All I could do was make amends as quickly as possible.

Walking out of the bathroom, I called out to the hallway for my bodyguard to buy some shaving cream and blades for me. Then I quickly dressed and told Miss Lee that I had business matters that needed my attention.

"When are you coming back?" she asked, caught off guard by my new disposition.

"Please, don't trouble yourself with that."

"But remember that first night at the beach? I was so cold and you promised to buy me a mink coat. The furrier is going to deliver the coat to our room this afternoon. Don't you want to stay around and watch me put it on? I will wear the mink coat only…and nothing else."

I ignored her comments and continued to dress myself. But she was persistent.

"Come back and we will have room service again tonight." She rubbed her bare breasts against my chest while I was attempting to put on my shirt.

"Miss Lee, I should not be here. I won't be seeing you again. You can keep the mink coat."

"Thank you, but you are welcome to visit at any time. Just ask Doug, he knows where to find me."

She gave me a kiss on the mouth, but when she tried to use her tongue, I backed away. When would my shaving cream and blades arrive?

===================

While I had been away from home for the past several nights, daughter Kay stayed in her mother's room and saw her crying in the bathroom. When Che Yu signaled her to leave, Kay went back into the bedroom and noticed a piece of paper lying on her father's side of the pillow. My daughter read the note, a poem that my wife had written to me. A poem revealing a broken heart.

Kay carefully put down the paper where she had found it and left the room. But when I returned home, my daughter, only eight years old, asked me, "Papa, why did you make mama sad?"

Before returning to our house, though, my chauffeur drove me to a friend's home where I took another shower and put on new clothes that I had just picked up from the store. From the friend's house, we headed to my office.

My staff greeted me in a friendly manner, but I could tell by the eyes that followed me down the hall to my office that they knew what I had done. I buried myself in paperwork for the rest of the day, this brave military man and bold spy not even daring to venture into the reception area.

My mind was on Che Yu the entire time. I didn't think that I could lie to her about my indiscretions. Besides, it was clear by the reaction at my office that someone from my inner circle at the party had already spread the news.

A stack of messages from my wife lay on my desk. I wasn't yet ready to call her back. What should I say and what should I do? I had never been so ashamed and so afraid before. That afternoon at the office was the longest day of my life. Finally, I told my secretary to call Che Yu and tell her that I would be home for dinner. The rice would be cooked and I would have to face the consequences.

There was no welcome from Che Yu when I arrived at our home. We ate across the table from each other, alone in our thoughts. The children had already been put to bed since two of them had school in the morning and the other was so young. Che Yu's silence was more lethal than a bullet in my head.

After finishing a glass of wine, I walked wordlessly into our bedroom. Che Yu remained in the dining room, still seated in silence at her chair by the dinner table. I was the Invisible Man. I had expected that she might cry and throw me out of the house. At least that hadn't happened. My clothing still hung neatly on hangers in our closet, so she hadn't tossed them into the yard or packed them in suitcases.

Slowly I changed into my pajamas and crawled into bed, my face grazing the piece of paper on my pillow. I turned on the bedside table lamp and saw the poem my wife had written for me.

Stay with me, my love!

Stay with me, my love,

I am the fruit bearing tree in this garden,

Providing you with shade from the scorching sun

and the freezing rain,

I am the fruit that would quench your thirst

and satisfy your hunger.

Stay with me, my love.

The wild flowers outside the garden come and go according to their seasons.

My love, you are a resident in this garden,

The wild flowers send their fragrance

and full bloom blossoms.

They intoxicate you and lead you astray,

But my love, soon they will wither and die.

Stay with me, my love.

Let me be the mother whom you have missed so long ago,

Let me be the wife who bears your children to continue your legacy.

My roots are grounded in this fertile land,

You and your children will stay under my loving branch.

Stay with me, my love,

Stay with me, my love!

I was so ashamed of myself, especially since my wife is expecting our sixth treasure whom we will name Khan Fong if she turns out to be a girl.

Chapter Twenty-Six

Occupation

In 1943, Che Yu and I were blessed with another treasure, our fifth child. Little Fong grabbed my heart from the very beginning. She had my eyes, and there was an unmistakable twinkle there that said she was definitely "daddy's girl."

During this time, the inhabitants of Hong Kong lived in constant chaos and fear. Gunfire, bombings, collapsing buildings and wailing sirens could be seen and heard across the breadth of the entire city. Japanese naval fleets had put a stranglehold on Hong Kong harbor, while enemy soldiers marched in the streets with regularity, often looting the shops and homes. All of the residents locked their doors and kept their ears to the radio for news broadcasts about the occupation. Though Hong Kong had formally surrendered its territory to the Japanese on December 25, 1941, conditions had grown steadily worse.

Many of the famous Hong Kong streets had been renamed in the Japanese language. Food shortages were commonplace, with each Chinese family given a rationing license to buy necessities such as rice, oil, flour, salt and sugar.

Because of the scarcity of food and other supplies, the Japanese enforced a repatriation policy, deporting all unemployed people from Hong Kong island to the mainland. The city's population dwindled from 1.6 million to barely a million during this time. Even so, many died from starvation.

Simultaneously, the occupiers reconstructed government and private buildings for their own use, confiscating structures and even demolishing some. In order to expand the airport to accommodate Japanese planes, they destroyed the Kowloon Walled City and the Sung Wong Toi Monument.

The particular morning of the invasion more than a year ago, Hong Kong was bathed in warm sunshine. Aside from the presence of hundreds of Japanese flags filling the city, all appeared somewhat normal. The sporadic gunfire that often could be heard at all hours had ceased.

I was hunkered over a small desk, surrounded by a minimal staff, in my office hideout in the basement of our home. Weeks earlier, I had managed to set up the facility without drawing attention to the renovations I had put into place.

My trusted radio operator walked over and handed me a series of telegraphs he had just intercepted between the Japanese Army and Navy.

"General Khan, the Japanese are now in full control and in occupation mode of Hong Kong. Both the Japanese Navy and the Army are setting up their headquarters in the Tong Law Wan district near us. The Navy is poised to take over the racetrack clubhouse, and the Army is commandeering the Governor's mansion."

Wing Kwok, my on-duty operator, had been working for me since I started the broadcasting radio station in Nanjing. Whatever news he gave me, I could be sure of its veracity.

I maintained my silence for a moment. No one dared breathe or speak in the small room. Then I leaned forward and spoke softly.

"The fate of Hong Kong, at least for now, is sealed. But we remain steadfast and committed to the cause. The Japanese must never find this place. From now on, no one calls me General…not even inside these walls. I am a businessman only."

Everyone nodded solemnly.

"Our ship now docking in the harbor, if it hasn't yet been confiscated, will remain idle for several days," I said. "We must come and go as usual, though. If anyone at the harbor asks what you do, remember you merely work for me, a businessman with a shipping and transport company. As soon as the gunfire stops, I will try to make my way down to the dock. Brother Chan, I want you to come with me." One of our men knocked on the ceiling twice, and a household staff member opened a trap door installed into a tiled floor of the first floor kitchen, which was located at the backside of the west wing of the house. Another secret door in the basement led to a tunnel that opened up to a wooded area in the backyard.

After a mobile kitchen counter was rolled away and the trap door opened, a kitchen staff member dropped a flexible rope ladder. Two of my men and I climbed up immediately and everything was moved back to its original place.

I peeked though the curtain from my front living room. Across the vast yard, I could see two uniformed Japanese patrolling the street in front of our house, their weapons ready in their hands. I turned to Chan.

"Wait here while I change my clothes. We are going down to the racetrack to check on my horses."

Che Yu followed me to the stairwell when I appeared from the bedroom.

"Ling, be careful and come home as soon as you see danger."

She held out Admiral Saka's ring and slipped it onto my finger, then embraced me warmly.

Chan and I walked from the house, out onto the street where we observed some recent destruction of several nearby office buildings. The Japanese had been somewhat discriminative, minimizing the damage in this expensive residential district. Yet not every house or building had escaped unscathed. The longer I looked, the more I could see that Japanese soldiers and barricades were everywhere.

I asked, in Japanese, to speak to a sergeant in charge. The guards let us pass and handed us armbands to wear so we could walk freely around the district. We walked all eleven blocks to the Racetrack Clubhouse, of which I was a board member.

Passing the Navy guards, I flashed my board member card and we went upstairs to meet with the commander in charge of this district. Even in this time of war, the privileged on both sides enjoyed certain courtesies.

Chan and I bowed toward the new officer in charge, and I greeted him in Japanese.

"I am Commander Nikko for the Navy department," he said, reaching out his hand to shake mine. He recognized my ring.

"Where did you get this?"

I took off the ring and let him study it.

"Admiral Hiro Saka was my professor at Waseda University where I was a student. Years later I met the admiral in a more formal military setting. He has been somewhat like a father to me, and he respects both my Japanese and Chinese heritage."

Commander Nikko had also been a student of Admiral Saka, and he quickly warmed to me. Though Chan couldn't understand a word of our conversation, he was hopeful that all of the smiling was a good sign. When Commander Nikko slapped me on the back and pulled out a bottle of sake from his desk drawer, Chan became noticeably more relaxed. Two drinks later, Nikko and I were singing the Waseda University school songs.

Now in an amiable mood, the commander offered to help me as the Japanese were already rationing rice, salt and water to long lines of people. I quickly latched onto to his magnanimity.

"Yes, I have a big family and employees to feed. There is a large storage room in the hotel down the block. I used to throw large parties there. The kitchen has several coolers containing ham, meat and other food staples. There is an extensive wine cellar, as well. I would appreciate an official pass so that I may gather some of that food for my family and staff."

Commander Nikko scribbled a short note and stamped his seal on it.

"Here, use this as a pass to get anything in the district. I will invite you back for drinks another day after we settle in. Perhaps you could entertain us with some horse racing."

Chan and I saluted Commander Nikko and left the clubhouse. From there, we headed straight to the hotel lobby and had no problem passing through the cordon of guards stationed near the entrance. Once we had made generous "donations" to several well-placed officers, as well as to the hotel manager, several of the soldiers helped us to find large, empty flour bags in which to stuff the ham, steaks, fish, noodles and rice. The bags were so full that we needed a wheelbarrow to cart them home. A soldier followed us and posted a paper note on the front of our house, giving us immunity from military harassment.

When we returned to the house, Che Yu's sense of relief was palpable. That night our main chef, Dacifu, a Chinese culinary artist trained as a private chef for a Russian diplomat but under my employ for the past six months at our house here, created a spectacular meal for our entire group. After dinner, I retired to the backyard where I sipped a brandy and allowed myself the rare pleasure of a good cigar while chatting about the day's events with Chan. I marveled at the paradoxes of this great city. Hong Kong was indeed a place with a brittle psyche during this time, a city of big dreams and broken promises, of exquisite luxuries and unspeakable fears, all consuming one another with an unfettered passion that only Hong Kong could summon.

One thing was certain. It was wise to cultivate any relationships that could give you a decided edge, an "ace up the sleeve" as the Americans were fond of saying, in an environment such as this. So during the next few weeks, Commander Nikko and I became friends. I showed my prized thoroughbreds to him and, because he was so fond of horses, we often rode together. He particularly enjoyed exercising the racehorses.

I took this opportunity to ratchet up my business, sailing ships loaded with salt to China and transporting rice, oil and flour back to Hong Kong. My vessels flew a special flag that allowed me to sail in the open seas without threat from the Japanese Navy ships, though pirates still presented some prickly situations from time to time. To reduce this danger, I designed my own flag, which I flew alongside the one given to me by the Japanese. Set against a sky blue background, it featured a yellow eagle spreading its wings in full, its sharp talons clasping a black anchor. I made special deals with some of the pirate gangs, and my flag served as a signal that a deal had been struck. The fact that my ships sailed under protection from the Japanese Navy helped, too, because most of the pirates were wary of their strength and willingness to open fire at the least provocation.

Money, of course, also changed hands with the Japanese because I learned that there is no better protection than the kind secured with a generous monetary reward. The cash was transported in large potato sacks, and Che Yu would select expensive gifts to send to the Japanese Commander and his staff. At the same time, we continued to pay our own staff well and support various charity organizations and local orphanages.

Meanwhile, I was smuggling cannons and ammunition regularly on the ships and dropping them off at nearby islands for installation. We also equipped our vessels with cannons as a means of protection on the high seas. The Japanese were a bit uneasy with this arrangement, but they were quite pleased with the size and weight of the potato sacks.

Each time we sailed for business, my officers would veer slightly off course to the nearby islands where they would monitor Japanese naval activities and report back to Chinese headquarters about suspicious maneuvers or changes to their usually predictable schedules.

I also provided the people of the island villages with food and protection in exchange for vital information on any Japanese movements. In just a few months, South China Transport had secured their trust, and informants were as common as wood rats.

One day we received news from an informer that there was a small Japanese fleet biding its time in a small cove near the island of Peng Chau. My crew sailed out at night, approaching from the backside of Lantau Island. As we neared the cove, we spotted through our high-powered binoculars two small battleships. All was quiet except for the sound of a slight offshore wind.

Moving our main vessel out of the sight zone, we sent out two fishing boats that deftly maneuvered their way to a secured spot on the shore. Drawing a bead on the longitudinal and latitudinal positions of the Japanese fleet, we radioed Chiang Kai-shek's headquarters, then stole away into the night.

Early the next morning before sunrise, Chinese air strikes scored direct hits, destroying the two battleships. These were the kinds of periodic victories that kept my outlook positive, when there were so many other circumstances that could have easily shattered my optimism. These moments had to be well chosen, however, and extremely discreet. Too many of these successful strikes would draw suspicion and make future forays nearly impossible.

When I returned home after midmorning, I tried to act as normally as possible. I greeted the Japanese soldiers outside our gates in a friendly, yet not overly ingratiating way. A few business papers could be seen jutting out of my briefcase, and I alluded to working overnight in town, at the small dock shop that I kept by the pier.

That afternoon, I took what I felt was a well-earned nap, but was quickly awakened by frantic banging at the front door. When I opened it, a dozen Japanese soldiers entered without any formalities and began diligently searching the house.

Che Yu rushed over to the nannies.

"Hurry, take all the children and the dog downstairs through the back way and let them play in the garden. Don't come back in until I signal you. Take some snacks and drinks with you."

The nannies and our children left quietly, one by one, through the back entrance and remained in the yard, while inside there was chaos.

After a thorough ransacking of the house, the Japanese appeared frustrated that they hadn't located any kind of "smoking gun." No radio transceivers, no secret operations rooms or hidden caches of illegal weapons.

Nevertheless, they pointed their guns at me and eight of my assistants, then escorted us downstairs. Speaking slowly and clearly in Japanese so that there were no misunderstandings, I told them of the terrible mistake they were making. And remembering that the best defense is sometimes a strong offense, I threatened to take down their serial numbers and report them to Commander Nikko.

Standing beside me, Che Yu held my hand and tried to stifle her fears.

"Where are you taking my husband? He is innocent. Please ask your commanding officer to notify me when he will be released."

Chapter Twenty-Seven
Prisoner of War

At the Japanese Army compound, I was shoved into a single cell with a damp, stone floor and high ceilings. My mates were placed into adjoining, even smaller cells. I wanted desperately to communicate my instructions to them, but it was too risky. One couldn't be sure who else was on the cell block, whether other prisoners with loose tongues or Japanese guards who would be all to eager to report any incriminating conversation.

I was confident, at least to a point, that all of my men knew the drill. It was something we had discussed many times before; in the event of capture, their only answer would be that they worked for me in handling shipments. They were just following orders and knew nothing else. That was the standard refrain that had been drummed into their minds during training. They knew to leave it to me to deal with the officials.

For several days, the Japanese interrogated my men. I couldn't be sure how much torture was being applied or who, if anyone, was talking. Several of them appeared to be badly beaten, however, and their eyes expressed growing despair.

I had been spared so far, the strategy being to break down my subordinates first, then interrogate me with a keener knowledge of the truth they were seeking.

Finally, after the third day, I was taken to what appeared to be an "information room." I was left there for almost two hours by myself before being introduced to an army captain shaped somewhat like a pear with thin shoulders and a large, spreading rear end. He smoked a big, cheap Filipino cigar and spoke with a somewhat effeminate lisp. But he rarely smiled and, when he did, it almost always connoted bad news.

Bound by ropes, I was seated on a wooden chair while two young soldiers stood to either side of me, their guns strapped tightly to their waist holsters.

The Captain blew a few smoke rings, proud of this asinine trick that even a 15-year-old kid could master.

"For whom do you work? We know that you are a spy for the Chinese government. Names, please."

I remained silent throughout most of the questioning, other than to occasionally say that I didn't know what he was talking about. From time to time, I would remind him that I was a respected businessman with close ties to Commander Nikko and Admiral Saka.

His reply was always the same.

"We are not done with you yet. Our soldiers are going to comb through your house to find the evidence we need. You may be a rich and powerful man in Hong Kong, but all the money you have cannot buy your freedom."

By the tone of his interrogation, it seemed reasonable to surmise that none of my men in the cellblock had cracked. He still had nothing but strong hunches and the previous word of a possible informant, perhaps from within my own staff.

"Captain," I reiterated in my best Japanese, "I am only a businessman. My people earn their salary by working for me and they need to support their families. We are civilians, with no ties to the Chinese government."

"What are you asking of me, then?"

"Please let my workers go. They are just following my orders for loading shipments of rice and flour."

The captain blew a few more smoke rings and smiled at his handiwork.

"I know you are a good friend of the Navy Commander in the Tong Law Wan district, Commander Nikko. He has spoken of your innocence, but he has no jurisdiction in the Army. Let me give you one more chance."

My reply was succinct.

"I have nothing to confess."

The captain suddenly became enraged and yelled at the two soldiers, "Take him back to the cell. I don't want to see this pig face again!"

That night, the prison guard brought food to my cell, but not the usual stale roll and tea. The tin tray held a bowl of rice, steak and pickled cucumbers, radishes and a small tin cup of sake. I hoped this wasn't meant to be a "last supper" of sorts.

I walked to the front of the cell and peered through the bars. Hoping that my men could hear me, I spoke haltingly.

"Please forgive me if I have put you in this unbearable position. Because of me, we may all lose our lives tomorrow or in the very near future."

I silently cursed the trembling in my voice, which betrayed my fear and consternation…but most of all, my sadness.

One of my younger staff members, Kin Li whom we all simply called Butch, spoke up.

"Honorable Khan, we are proud to be here. We love our country and admire your courage as our leader. Fate will determine what will happen to us tomorrow. It is not for us to say."

I sat cross-legged on the hard stone floor and began reflecting on what I had done with my life…the neglect and disinterest I had shown many times for my wife, while pursuing my business and military ambitions. I wanted to cry out, "Che Yu, I am so sorry that I didn't love you as much as I should, that I failed you as a husband and a father to my children."

My mind turned to Quan Yin, the Goddess of Mercy. I asked her to understand that I was born and called for this mission for my country. But even in that, I had somehow failed. And now the suffering of my people would continue. The only difference would be that there would be no one to support my family and my dedicated men. South China Transport would become only a name that would soon lie in tatters just like the light blue flag with the screaming eagle.

The glow from a half-moon peeked into my cell window and danced on the cell bars, which cast a striped shadow that ran the length of the floor. Morning was sure to break calm and clear tomorrow, ideal for an outdoor execution. In my mind, I ran through the days that would follow this event and hoped that the information that might come forth wouldn't prevent Che Yu from accessing my funds. Once the Japanese learned the true extent of my spying activities, they might freeze a great deal of my assets and, God forbid, even inflict physical harm on my wife and family. Much of what was known, however, I would take to the grave, as would my loyal men. So hopefully the fallout would be minimal.

I sat back against the wall and dabbled with my food, as I stared in fascination at what appeared to be several rat droppings in the corner that hadn't been there earlier in the day. Even the rats had the good sense to leave this place after only a short time.

=====================

Che Yu had quickly sprung into action after my arrest. She rummaged through my closet and jewelry cabinet where, after some frantic searching, she found the ring given to me by Admiral Saka. When I had taken it off several weeks earlier, I had not returned it to its original place.

Afterward, she asked Chan to accompany her to a local shop of considerable renown where she selected an expensive gift for Commander Nikko. She and Chan tried fruitlessly to arrange an impromptu meeting with the commander, but were told that he was out of the office for the rest of the day. They were instructed to schedule an appointment for the next morning, but due to a fire at one of the Japanese security checkpoints in another part of the city, Che Yu was delayed in meeting with Nikko until the afternoon of the next day. By then she was frantic.

The commander graciously received Che Yu, who was wearing my ring at that point. But the news he gave to her in his almost flawless Chinese was less than optimistic.

"I first tried to convince the Army captain in charge to release your husband. He told me, quite correctly, that I did not have the authority to interfere with his department unless there was an order coming from the Imperial Emperor's high official. When I appealed to his sense of etiquette, after describing Khan Ling's many fine contributions to the city of Hong Kong, he merely sniffed and said he could not be bothered with trifling matters such as that."

"But Commander Nikko, you and my husband have had many fine moments together and you know of his integrity."

"True, true. But it is a time of war. And I must say that your husband has put himself into a very questionable position. This is not an easy case to resolve."

"I beg you, please find Admiral Hiro Saka," pleaded Che Yu, who was becoming increasingly desperate. "He might be the only person who could possibly save Ling. Here is the ring that he gave to my husband. Can I write a note for you to deliver to the Admiral?"

The commander rose from his desk and poured some green tea for Che Yu.

"Here, drink the tea. It will calm you down. I have already been tracking Admiral Saka. It is my understanding that he is in a mother fleet outside of Taiwan Island. So far we have not been able to make contact."

Commander Nikko might have left it at that, but he could see the resoluteness in Che Yu's eyes. Surely, she would take the matter further up, which could cause problems for Nikko. At the same time, if he could help her secure my release, he knew that it might benefit him greatly since he was keenly aware of my wealth and largesse. He handed her a piece of paper.

"Here, write your note on this. I will include the ring in a package with my notes also."

He sat down and wrote in Japanese with a brush. Che Yu wrote in Chinese and Commander Nikko instructed his translator to re-write her words in Japanese and then asked my wife to sign the paper.

"Go home now, wait for my news. I will send the package in one of our planes, about a three-hour flight time."

Once the translator finished the note, Nikko poured hot red wax on the envelope, sealed it and stamped it with an official mark, then rang the bell for the courier who would transport the letter to the plane. All Che Yu could do was wait and hope.

"Mrs. Khan, I suggest that you return home. I will notify you as soon as we have the Admiral's reply. In the meantime, I will warn the Army captain not to do anything he regrets."

Che Yu spent a second sleepless night, after no word was sent to her regarding contact with Admiral Saka. The next morning, she received news that Nikko still had not located him.

Determined to apply as much pressure as possible on Nikko, Che Yu dressed and had Chan drive her back to see the commander once more. A small crowd had gathered in front of the administration command building.

Members of the Japanese press and even a few family members of fallen sailors in another Chinese attack on a Japanese fleet were demanding an audience with the commander. This might help Che Yu's cause, she reasoned, because I was behind bars and couldn't have orchestrated the attack, at least not personally. At the same time, it could raise increasing pressure on Nikko and other naval brass to offer up a scapegoat as a way to appease the grieving families, not only the few here in Hong Kong but the many back in Japan who would be reading the articles written by the aggressive press corps gathered outside the building. In that case, I might be among the first to be sacrificed.

This time, it required brute force for Che Yu and Chan to push their way past the press contingent. One of the Japanese photographers landed a sharp blow with his camera to Chan's forehead, just above his left eye, drawing blood. Ironically, this provided Che Yu with the opening she needed because, when the crowd parted momentarily to make way for the stumbling Chan, she raced ahead. Chan quickly regained his feet and followed Che Yu to the top steps where she pleaded with a group of young soldiers guarding the front door. Fortunately, one of them spoke a fair amount of Chinese.

Finally she was admitted, though Chan was instructed to remain outside. Once in the building, though, Che Yu met more resistance from the naval bureaucracy. Now in tears, she began trembling and beseeching anyone within earshot.

"My husband is an important benefactor who is being held unjustly," she cried. "Has the whole world gone mad?"

She was being politely escorted toward a side exit when Nikko's assistant, a young naval attaché with close-cropped hair and a formal manner, recognized her. Sensing the sympathy that Nikko had shown for her, he motioned for her to follow him and led her to the commander's office.

Nikko seemed pleased to see Che Yu and invited her to sit down. He poured a cup of tea for her and leaned back against the edge of his desk.

"We are making progress. We know exactly where Admiral Saka is now."

Che Yu smiled politely, trying to hide her anxiety.

"But I have heard through sources that my husband is in grave danger. They may be…preparing to execute him."

She couldn't contain her emotions any longer, and she began silently crying. Nikko put a hand on her shoulder to comfort her.

"These things take time. So much official protocol. So many people to involve. Perhaps, just perhaps, it is possible to move the process more quickly."

Outside the administrative building, Chan nursed his head wound with a handkerchief spotted with his blood. Confusion still reigned among the press corps and scattered protesters. The soldiers had tried to create two straight lines of people, and it was almost comical watching them usher back into the line individuals who kept popping in and out like gophers in a hole. Chan, still a bit dazed, stood off to the side where the soldiers obviously thought he was no threat. At least, no one approached him either to shout orders or render aid.

Finally, Che Yu arrived back at the entrance. A bit flustered, but still resolute, she led Chan away from the crowd toward their automobile parked on the next street.

"We must get you home, Chan. That is an ugly cut."

"And Master Khan, what is to become of him?"

Che Yu merely shook her head without answering.

Chapter Twenty-Eight
The cost

The next morning, just after sunrise, three grim-faced guards walked up to my cell and brusquely told me to change into the garments they carried with them. They looked like civilian clothes, but of a very poor cloth and monotone beige in color. Was this to be my uniform for a date with the firing squad? I joked that they should have sewn in a red target at the chest, but no one laughed.

After I had changed into my khaki uniform and tried to comb my hair as best I could without a mirror, they led me down the hall, past the neighboring cells that now were vacant. Had they already executed my men? I had fallen asleep for an hour or two. Though I had tossed and turned, I had never been aware of movement in the cells next to me. Panic set in; I had let my loyal staff down, sleeping through their most trying ordeal.

But when I was pushed into a large, airy room with massive overhead fans, I came face to face with my men. Quickly I counted them. No one was missing.

The pear-shaped captain stood off to the side and, as soon as I entered, he stepped forward.

"You are so very lucky," he began. "I have here an order from Admiral Hiro Saka, acknowledged and authorized through the Army commandant's office, to release you and your men. He vouches for your good character and your support of the honorable Japanese cause. It is something that I neither endorse nor question. I have no opinion. You are free to go."

The visceral dislike and the distrust that the captain had for me simmered on the surface but, to his credit, he did a reasonable job of disguising it. Obviously, there were no handshakes, no "atta boys" or good-hearted ribbing. In fact, no more words were spoken at all. One of the guards simply nodded his head at us, and we all filed out of the room and walked toward the waiting jeeps outside.

As we wound our way through the streets, back toward the Tong Law Wan district, I told the good-natured driver, a young lieutenant, "Please tell Admiral Saka that I am eternally grateful to him."

The lieutenant smiled and said that he didn't know the Admiral. I knew that would probably be the case, but it just felt so good to say it.

Che Yu was at the door when I walked upstairs. She ran toward me and cried, "Thank god, you are safe. Are you okay? Did they hurt you?"

"I am fine, but send for the doctor to tend to my men in their quarters. Some of them have injuries that need attention."

Zeepou walked slowly toward me on her small bound feet and said, "We were sick with worry. When the children returned back to the house after your arrest, they found the entire house completely ransacked. The soldiers even used the blade tips on their rifles to cut up some of the sofas, chairs and mattresses. You can see some of the results."

She pointed to several of our expensive furnishings, which bore slash marks and openings from where the foam stuffing was pushing its way out.

"All your clothing on the floor, drawers opened, holes poked in walls, everything!" she added for emphasis.

Zeepou told of how Che Yu cried at first, but then had quickly composed herself and instructed the staff to begin cleaning up the mess.

"We are to live here as usual, just like any other day," Che Yu had said. "Tell Dacifu to prepare Russian beef goulash and bake a chestnut cake."

That was one of Che Yu's greatest strengths, to move steadily forward and take care of even the most mundane matters in the face of adversity. By maintaining some semblance of normalcy she could convey a sense of calm to those around her. She had shown those traits after the deaths of both of her parents and throughout that period when she moved our family from town to town. The only time when that talent seemed to desert her was after the death of our third child.

All of this talk about our chef Dacifu had made me hungry. A good meal was something for which I had been yearning, even though I had been gone less than four full days. After I cleaned up and ate a satisfying dinner, I savored my cup of green tea as never before. Getting up from the gouged sofa, I walked softly into each of my children's rooms and hugged them more purposefully than ever before. For what seemed the first time, I experienced the unequivocal joy of a father's love toward my little ones.

Walking into the garden, I said a silent prayer of thanks to Quan Yin, then went to check on the injuries to several of my men. Che Yu awaited me in the master bedroom, and I felt especially giddy this evening. This would most likely be a night for candlelight.

=================

The next day, I prepared a gift package with a thank you note for Admiral Hiro Saka, which I planned to deliver to Commander Nikko, who would know how to send it to him. I called ahead and invited the commander to the racetrack for tea. It was the least I could do.

We sat at a table in the nearly deserted clubhouse tea room and traded stories about past adventures as well as about several mutual friends that we discovered we both knew from Waseda University.

Afterward, we walked down by the stables and, finally, I broached the subject that was most important to me on this day.

"Nikko San, thank you from the bottom of my heart for tracking down Admiral Hiro Saka and getting my wife's message to him. We are forever grateful to you and your men."

The Commander bowed graciously and commented about how loyal and devoted my wife seemed to be. Then he turned his eyes back to the two priceless racehorses in the stalls next to him. My own eyes lit up, for I knew what I was to say next.

"Commander Nikko, in return for your kindness, you are now the official owner of a prized stallion. Please, be my guest and select one of these fine horses for yourself."

The commander was dumbstruck, looking back and forth from the horses to me. Finally, he said, "For me?"

I laughed. "Yes, for you. Which one do you fancy?"

Putting a hand to his chin, he studied the two exquisite stallions. Finally, after what seemed like nearly a minute, he pointed toward China Pride. I was relieved, for my favorite was the younger horse, Thunder.

"China Pride, please."

"Done."

"May I change his name to Nippon Pride?"

This request caught me off guard. It was tough enough to give up a famous stallion, but to name him in honor of the Japanese? That was almost too much.

"Why, of course," I said.

"Then I shall buy you a drink to celebrate this day. We will salute our two countries and our growing friendship."

That evening, in bed, I told Che Yu about my gift to Commander Nikko. She seemed troubled, and I immediately became defensive.

"It is only a horse, Che Yu. Remember, Commander Nikko took extreme measures to secure my release, expecting nothing in return. That is the way of our family…to be generous to those who bestow favors on us. And besides, Nikko San is quite fond of you."

Che Yu began to blush and, at the same time, frown. She hesitated, then moved in closer to me.

"That was part of the problem."

When she paused, I urged her to continue.

"On the final day that I went to visit Nikko, he was not very encouraging. He was still having trouble contacting Admiral Saka and admitted that it might not be possible to save you. But I would not take 'no' for an answer, and I pleaded with him to do more…"

Che Yu hesitated again, but this time I didn't push her. I merely waited and she picked up the story again several seconds later.

"It was then that he suggested there might be a way to move things forward more quickly."

"What are you saying?"

"Commander Nikko propositioned me. He asked if I would stay the night and said that most assuredly he would be able to reach Admiral Saka by that next day. But I refused in a polite, respectful way, and I reminded him that he was an honorable man and, most importantly, that you were a very close friend of Admiral Saka."

"What did he do next?"

"He asked if I was certain about my choice, and I said 'yes.' Then he quickly apologized and began acting as if nothing had ever been said between us. He told me to go home and that he would continue to monitor the situation."

Che Yu began to sob.

"Oh Ling, I did not know if I had thrown away my only chance to see you again. I was so utterly distraught until news came to us at the time of your release that you were being set free."

I stroked her hair and kissed her forehead.

"You did the right thing. You are my angel. My guardian angel."

I silently cursed Nikko, but knew that to challenge him on the matter might create immense problems for my family. At least he had apologized and had followed through with his pledge to contact Saka. But I also knew that, during this treacherous war, no Japanese was my friend. Perhaps not even Saka, I thought, when I realized he had not returned the ring to me. Maybe it was his way of saying the ring gives me one free pass, but after that, there are no more deals...no more compensations. At that moment, I felt my Chinese heritage more strongly than ever before in my life.

Chapter Twenty-Nine
Macau and China Sea

After my release from prison, I notified headquarters in Chongching that I needed to maintain a much lower profile, and I ceased my political activities in Hong Kong.

Several months passed, and I decided to relocate my operation and my family to Macau, a Portuguese territorial island on the western side of the Pearl River Delta facing the South China Sea.

Though more than 90% of those living on the island were of Chinese ancestry, the Portuguese influence had been significant for nearly 400 years, and it was the oldest European settlement in the Far East. Initially developed as a port for Chinese-Japanese trading, Macau was a peculiarity… governed by the Portuguese in a rental agreement with China, who still collected land and customs taxes. That arrangement held for nearly 200 years until the Portuguese declared Macau's "independence" in 1849. The Protocol of Lisbon, enacted nearly 40 years later, had created a sort of tenuous agreement between the two countries, with Portugal continuing to administer the island with China's interests in mind. As the only neutral port in South China during the war, Macau was enjoying relative prosperity at the time of our arrival.

We moved into a white stucco, two-story house with a huge backyard featuring a pair of almond trees and a wooded hill at the back. The home looked out in the front to a white sandy beach. Our children often walked down to the beach with us. By now we had five, ranging from a year old to nearly 10, and they loved to cavort in the water and the sand as mama and papa watched.

"Papa, look what I have found! A colorful rock. Look, there is more around this sand dune," exclaimed Bing, our older boy.

I bent down to pick up a charcoal rock and promised to show Bing my black diamond ring when we returned to the house.

"It is in the processing stage of becoming a diamond. "It would take hundreds of years to purify the charcoal into a clear diamond, but maybe you will live to see it," I kidded him.

Little 4-year-old Jing was fascinated with the small crabs that inhabited the cracks and rock crevices, while our eldest, Kay, would run back and forth in the shallow, ankle-deep water by the shore. The salt air breezes and rushing white sea foam waves had a calming effect on my family who welcomed this dramatic departure from the tense environment back in Hong Kong where the raids and rationing continued.

Our children loved to pick fruits from the trees we had planted in our garden, which included mangos, persimmons and pomegranates. Che Yu could always be seen wearing a large sun hat or carrying an umbrella to shade herself from the rays as she watched over the children playing outdoors. Laughter often filled the house and we remarked about how relaxed our life had become.

For me, it was a double-edged sword. I loved the sense of calm and security that Macau afforded my family. But I soon grew restless, knowing that a war was still being waged just across the channel.

I soon began acquiring more boats, which I outfitted as fishing vessels, but also equipped with the latest radar and sighting technology. My transport business once again became more active, and success came easily with all of my connections and resources. We employed three different chauffeurs and had amassed two Rolls-Royce and two Mercedes Benz automobiles, several jeeps and, for the company, a fleet of transport trucks. With the acceleration of my business came new dangers, so I kept three bodyguards on the payroll. No one knew which automobile I was going to use each time I went out and, on a couple of occasions, we had them re-painted.

One time, at a dinner party, I returned to our table after engaging in a conversation with one of the hosts and reached into Che Yu's handbag for a writing pencil. What I grabbed instead was a 32-caliber revolver.

"What is this all about, Che Yu?"

She quickly pushed my hand back down into the bag.

"Shhh...I always protect you, my love. Remember, at the shooting range you told me I was a good markswoman."

I smiled. Make that four bodyguards.

Though my wife sometimes complained about the growing realities of running a business such as mine, there was no disputing its lucrative nature. When it came time for the Chinese Lunar New Year, we decided to celebrate with a sumptuous feast. Our two chefs prepared our favorite dishes, including bird's nest soup, five-spice meat with taro roots, sweet and sour shrimp with hot red peppers and the main attraction of Beggar's Chicken, a famous dish of stuffed chicken with chestnuts, corn, garlic and onions, baked for eight hours in a covered wrap of clay and spices.

When we sat down at the table, I once again regaled the children with my tale of the Beggar's Chicken. It was a story they loved more, every time I told it.

"One day the Emperor was passing by a village with his guards. He was famished and smelled a delicious aroma emanating from the woods. Immediately, he sent his guards to find out the source of the aroma. They returned with a ragged beggar who was holding a wire rack with a steaming mud ball on it. The ball had begun to emit a tantalizing scent that enticed the Emperor's appetite. It turned out that the beggar had taken the chicken from a nearby farm, prepared the stuffing with vegetables picked from the farmer's field and seasoned it with his own mixture of spices and herbs. Then he had wrapped the chicken in a mixture of mud and stream water and roasted the chicken for hours over a campfire.

"The Emperor had arrived just as the ball encasing the chicken was about to be cracked open. When he tasted the well-seasoned bird, he was so satisfied with this unique and tasty dish that he told the beggar what a fine cook he was. Then he offered him a job in the royal kitchen as one of his personal chefs. Thus, the Beggar's Chicken became a royal dish."

Everyone clapped when I finished my story, though Che Yu had heard it many, many times before. The telling of it, like the dish itself, had become a New Year's tradition.

The feast lasted for three hours, topped off by Dacifu's acclaimed chestnut cake with fresh whipped cream. It was also customary to present the children with new clothes, and we added to their excitement with red envelopes filled with "lucky money" for them. Elderly Zeepou saved some of her Chinese coins throughout the year and gave them to the children, though we didn't have the heart to tell the old woman that the money was no longer usable.

On the following day, the doorbell at our rambling beachfront home rang incessantly. Friends and merchants made deliveries of all kinds. Not only were New Year's gifts still arriving, but it was Che Yu's birthday. Though her favorite peonies were out of season, I managed to fill the rest of the home with all types of exotic, blooming flowers. That evening, we sat around the fireplace as Che Yu opened her gifts, including imported perfumes and bolts of French silk that I had bought for her. Finally, I asked my wife to open a medium-size box wrapped in gold paper and topped with a bright red bow. Inside was a delicate jewelry box accented with French brocade. When Che Yu opened the box, there lay at least a dozen pairs of earrings, as well as rings, pure gold chains, pendants and precious stone necklaces, which flashed and sparkled under the light of the crystal chandelier above. Little Kay said that it reminded her of the treasure chest in the storybook, "Treasure Island."

I had spent the past months seeking out and purchasing some of the finest jewelry in Hong Kong and surrounding areas, to replace many of the previous gems and heirlooms that she had sold to keep our family safe and well-fed during the evacuations. Many jewels from that collection had also gone to support my wartime expeditions. So even though Che Yu hugged me and gasped in amazement, I felt these were not so much gifts as repayments that she richly deserved.

"You did not have to do all this, my dear Ling. All I really ask is that you promise to spend more time with us."

This was a promise that I was afraid I might not be able to keep. Rather than talk around the issue and defer it to another day, I felt it best to discuss my plans here and now.

"Unfortunately, that will have to wait. I will be gone for awhile...can't be helped. We will be returning a captured Communist ship to Chiang Kai-shek."

"But I thought you said you are trying to distance yourself from him."

"Yes, but if you recall, he had promised to reimburse me for all of my war expenses. So far, it has amounted to eight million dollars and continues to get larger.

"An opportunity presented itself two weeks ago. We captured a Communist freighter en route from Shanghai that was moving through the Haikou channel near Hainan Island. It was heading to Vietnam with gold to purchase armory from the French."

"How did you seize it?"

"Fifty of our shipmates approached it from under the water at night, then climbed on deck with weapons drawn. It was a complete surprise. After subduing several of the guards with a great deal of stealth, we were able to reach the machine gun mounts and turn the guns on the Communists. We captured those that we didn't kill and transported them to our Haikou prison compound."

I watched for some sort of smile of acknowledgment for this great feat, but was met instead with a stony silence. Che Yu had grown weary of war so that she greeted any news with ambivalence.

"We found over one thousand pounds of gold bullion under the rice bags in the belly of the ship. I contacted KMT headquarters and spoke to Chiang Kai-shek who told me to bring the freighter back up the coast. His forces are to meet us at the British concession on Shameen Island, near Guangzhou. The Japanese control the city, but we will be disguised as a commercial vessel. Once we get there, we will be escorted by Chiang's men to the navy dock to check inventory…at which time I will receive half of the gold payment for my expenses."

"It sounds very dangerous. What if you are double-crossed or even captured by the Japanese once more? Why must you accompany your men? Don't you trust them?"

So many questions…although I had to admit to myself that they were good ones. But it was settled, I would be on board that Communist freighter. There was too much at stake.

The journey itself, once we cleared the Hong Kong area, was relatively smooth. A Japanese patrol boat stopped us once, about 60 miles south of Guangzhou, but we were able to convince them that we were transporting rice and salt. I still flew the flag granting me passage by the Japanese, even despite my earlier imprisonment, and I had forged some very authentic-looking documents specifically for this trip.

When we arrived at the port on Shameen Island, Chiang's men met us and efficiently guided us through the bureaucratic maize. Since it would take a few days to get a full accounting of the bullion, I was wined and dined. Even my men were treated like dignitaries. Once or twice, I attempted to return to the dock, but was assured that matters were proceeding on schedule. The one time that I did manage to board the ship, I was satisfied that the operation was in good hands. Two of my trusted assistants continued to monitor the unloading, so I decided to remain patient and let the process takes its course. If I were too demanding, it might jeopardize my arrangement with Chiang.

After three days, however, I requested payment. The request became a demand once I realized that nobody was claiming to have any authority. Several of the people with whom I had dined and discussed the financial agreement were suddenly unavailable. I went directly to the freighter, which was now completely emptied out. Finally, I tracked down my two assistants who were equally perplexed. They had been trying to get answers for the past 12 hours.

At this point, I was no longer concerned about professional courtesies. I insisted on speaking with Chiang Kai-shek. One of the admirals told me that he was ill and had left the city. Then he weakly tried to pass blame.

"General Khan, I am very sorry. Someone has clearly misappropriated the gold shipments. We are trying to trace the source, but it could take months."

I angrily rebuked the man and claimed that the entire operation was a setup. Rather than argue, he sheepishly turned away.

Upon my return to Macau, I went directly to the secret operations room in our home basement without saying a word. Che Yu followed me, concern in her eyes.

"What has happened, Ling? What is wrong?

"They betrayed me. There will be no money!"

Reaching for my neatly wrapped military uniform, ripped the general's stars and bars right off the coat and threw it into a heap in the corner. Chiang Kai-shek would need to find another general to fight his war.

Chapter Thirty
Mercy for betrayal

Several weeks later, I woke up in the middle of the night after a fitful sleep. Che Yu also awoke when she heard me tossing in the bed. With a troubled expression, I looked at her.

"I must share a dream with you. It is so vivid, Che Yu, that it is quite troubling."

"By all means, tell me."

"My men and I had just completed a battle at sea. The boat had become crippled, so we landed it on a small, deserted island nearby. We were all so thirsty, but could not find a well or drinking water anywhere. Soon, I saw a light in a wooded area. We approached it and found a wooden shack with a straw roof. An old man with a hunchback and a long white beard greeted us from his door and asked if we needed anything. We asked for water, so he and his family went to their backyard and drew some water from the well to quench our thirst. He also filled our water containers before we left. Then the old man got down on his knees and bowed to me.

'General Khan, you do not remember me,' he said. 'But I am the one who betrayed you and your men, causing the Japanese to put all of you in the prison in Hong Kong. Today, I wanted to thank you. Your men wanted me dead, but you spared my life. Here is my family, both my daughters are married and I am a grandfather of five grandchildren. I am a bean farmer and we don't have much money. But, I am forever grateful, for I have the joy of watching my grandchildren grow up.'

"Then I woke up."

Che Yu put her arms around me and replied, "Ling, I think God is telling you to be merciful, even to your enemies. We were blessed because Admiral Hiro Saka and Commander Nikko were merciful to us. Remember Superior Master Lou Ming? He instructed you in the ways of being merciful!"

The next day, I rousted one of my bodyguards and we walked down to my warehouse by the Macau harbor. Once there I huddled with my executive team as we continued to discuss Hongzong, a former staffer who had worked under Captain Lou as a messenger. Though I had never formally met him, he was of keen interest to us now. For the past few weeks, we had been tracking his movements.

Hongzong had left the company shortly after the arrests of my staff members and me. No longer involved in any types of military operations, he was working as a commercial fisherman to support his wife and two children on one of Hong Kong's outlying islands.

The more we looked at the facts, it seemed increasingly likely that he had been the mole who had offered us up to the Japanese. Several suggestions were made to "take him" out during one of his excursions on the water. But today I felt strangely liberated from the entire war mentality. No doubt, my circumstances with Chiang Kai-shek's Kuomintang officers had hastened this feeling, but it was also due to my dream and my conversation with Che Yu. I longed to be sitting at the feet of Superior Master Lou Ming's elegant redwood chair once more as he smoked his bamboo pipe and drank his favorite green tea. He would surely have a story and a life lesson for me.

After each person in our group at the warehouse had his say, I spoke up.

"The greatest relief is to know that the betrayal came from no one within our inner circle. He was someone who had been with us less than six months, and Captain Lou has already been exonerated. So let us move on. He is a fisherman, he has a family, war can do strange things to people. Should he ever set foot on Macau with ill intent, we will make short work of him. But today is not the day for revenge. Let his family enjoy him. We have our own lives to live."

With that, I stood up, signaled to my bodyguard and walked back home without another word.

Noting their lucrative nature, I began operating shorter routes with my fleet, making supply runs along the eastern coast up toward Guangzhou. During this time, because I was still operating occasionally in a military intelligence capacity, I wanted to keep my business fluid and highly flexible. In keeping with this approach, I relocated our headquarters to Hainan Dao Island, southwest of Guangzhou province. Local warlords had terrorized the islanders for years, but the Japanese presence near the area had neutralized them to a point, and we negotiated agreements with them that further reduced their threat to the local people. Though it cost me a considerable sum of money, in the long run it would pay off since it gave our ships unobstructed access to the waters around the island and fostered an affectionate relationship with the villagers. We made it clear that any warlords who balked at our terms would face repercussions. It was a calculated risk but, as I expected, they were eager to accept our money.

One crystal clear summer night as I and a small crew patrolled several islands just off the coast, my radio operator received the news for which everybody had been anxiously waiting. It was no longer just a pipe dream, but a shot of reality that, in this case, was joyously welcome. He raised his voice and cried out, "The Japanese have just surrendered! The War is over!"

Despite the fact that we were technically on patrol, someone produced a case of rice wine, and the celebration began. Lieutenant Tang, one of my longest-tenured officers, approached me as we headed back to shore amid the revelry.

Drawing me aside, he said quietly, "The people of the Hainan Dao islands call you Lord Khan and they worship you because of your fairness and unselfish nature. In fact, you have devoted followers throughout the island chains as well as on the mainland."

It was true that I had become somewhat of a cult hero among the islanders. My exploits had been recounted so many times that the truth and the myth were difficult to separate. The bombing of the Japanese fleet, which had gotten me thrown into prison, only served to raise my exalted rank in the eyes of the villagers. And, granted, I had provided them with an enormous amount of food and building materials during the past few years. Much of that was offered with an ulterior motive as a great number of them served as valued spies. But I also felt a kinship with them and a sense of compassion for their plight. Whatever the reasons, they had even created a song about my deeds.

Song by the Villagers of Hainan Dao Islands

Lord Khan is our Guardian Knight,
He heard our sorrows and sensed our frights.
The pirates and Japs are the offenders,
Taking our wives and daughters and demanding surrender.
Our men are few; our defenses are weak,
Lord Khan heard our sorrows and our pleads.
He sailed his ships through the freezing night,
Lord Khan conquered our invaders and silenced our cry.
Lord Khan is our Guardian Knight,
Lord Khan is our Guardian Knight!

As Lieutenant Tang laid out his scenario, I suddenly realized what he was suggesting. Now that the war with Japan was over, we had plenty of surplus ammunition, gunboats and willing partners for a struggle of another type. He saw this as the perfect opportunity to capture Macau from the Portuguese and return it to China!

While at first I viewed the plan as radical and far-fetched, he made some strong points. The Portuguese Army and Navy were notoriously weak and stationed, for the most part, thousands of miles away. With our three main ships and several others that we could easily secure, we could effectively surround the island. Because of Macau's shielded location, the only logical way in by boat would be through the South China Sea, which I might be able to persuade the Chinese government to temporarily defend. Europe was still in a state of euphoria due to the Germans' surrender in May, so the Portuguese might not have any stomach for further conflict.

Still, the Chinese government had not expressed a burning desire to reclaim the island, though Mao's organization had vocally opposed the occupation. On the other hand, certainly my country would not be adverse to reacquiring a property of considerable worth, one that possessed a certain cachet for its mild weather, active port and thriving commercial development.

Tang kept repeating, "General Khan, you could be the hero who changes the history of China and the world!"

When one of my closest aides agreed with him, my ego took hold. Back on shore, I decided to test the water, so to speak. Not wanting to risk a telegraph message, I sent my most trusted messenger with a note to Che Yu. In the note, I suggested evacuating Che Yu and my family from Macau, in preparation for possible military action. I worded it in such a way that was purposefully vague, but Che Yu understood my intentions beyond any doubt.

The next day, I received a clear, straightforward reply.

"Ling, the war is over!" it began. "Your job is done. Now you want to shed more innocent blood? I will not, under any circumstances, move out of my house in Macau with our children and my relatives. If you and your men are crazy enough to want to capture this island, you might as well kill me and your children! You are not being a hero, you are being a fool! Come home, please!"

I was flabbergasted. Che Yu had never spoken to me in that tone before. But I knew she was right. The more I mulled over Tang's suggestion, the more foolhardy and irresponsible it seemed. I abandoned any thoughts of retaking Macau by force. That night, I telegraphed Che Yu with the news: "I'm coming home."

Chapter Thirty-One
Releasing the Japanese prisoners

My communications officer had another transmission waiting for me the next morning when I directed my captain to pull anchor and head back to Macau. It was a message from the Kuomintang, with a request to turn over all Japanese prisoners in my area to Chiang Kai-shek's jurisdiction. I was to gather them in my ships and sail northward to an arranged transfer area. Several locations where prisoners were now being held were included in the missive.

I mulled the request for several minutes, then made an executive decision. There would be no handing over of prisoners to Chiang Kai-shek. I had washed my hands of that organization after the bullion incident on Shameen Island in Guangzhou. The alternative, to merely leave all of them in captivity here and ignore the entire communiqué, would have been callous and inhumane as their fate would lie in the hands of untrained, lower level officers with grudges to avenge.

Instead, I pulled two older freighters from my fleet and stocked them with rice, water and other staples. After showing my papers to arrange the release of the Japanese prisoners, including rank-and-file and officers alike, I loaded them onto the two ships with proper navigational maps to help them chart their course homeward. My secret intention was to repatriate the captured soldiers with their native country. These men, who had endured their own hardships while following orders, would once again see their loved ones. My own risk was minimal since there was no clearly defined leadership in southern Asia at this time. Chiang Kai-shek had his hands full battling Mao's troops, and these additional prisoners would have proven cumbersome to him, at best. Besides, should he decide against executing them, Chiang must have known that I would have a legitimate claim on whatever compensation he could reasonably expect from the Japanese in exchange for the prisoners.

The three prison encampments, though relatively small, were nonetheless filled with soldiers with limitless futures ahead of them. It gave me a sense of satisfaction to know that many of these young men might one day become professors, doctors, politicians and athletic stars. Even those who would merely dig sewer lines, drive taxicabs or file documents in the corner of some bureaucrat's dark office would at least have a chance to raise families and pursue their dreams.

The next two days were spent in conversations with myriad military officers and government officials in an attempt to locate Admiral Saka. I felt it my moral duty to ensure his safety, in the event he had been captured by the Chinese or allied forces. Finally, at the end of a long, exhausting day filled with many dead-end searches that created more questions than answers, I learned that Admiral Saka had been killed during a sea battle, a few days prior to Japan's formal surrender. Reflecting on the course he had taken, from that of my college mentor to one of the respected leaders of the Japanese Navy, I felt that he had been one of those privileged few to live an extraordinary life. His spirit would surely be at peace with me. Still, I wondered what had happened to that very special ring that allowed me to see Che Yu and my family once again.

Knowing that I had fulfilled Superior Master's counsel to show mercy to others, now I could also face Che Yu with dignity and show proper respect to Quan Yin. My early years spent in the temple at Purple Golden Mountain had allowed me to lap up the nourishing philosophies of so many wise teachers, not only Superior Master, but also the other monks and brothers of the temple who by word and deed helped to define my past as well as my future. Most importantly, though, I learned that knowledge isn't something static that's passed on to others through mere words. It's a continuing dynamic in which the truth reveals itself in evolving layers.

So did I truly avenge my mother's cruel death or merely find other ways to make it seem less painful? Cruising westward within eyesight of the Hong Kong harbor and watching the celebratory fireworks filling the air, all I could really feel for sure was that it seemed so right this time to be going home.

I raised my company flag, the light silk background blending in with the sky, the proud eagle clutching the anchor with a tenacity that I had personally selected for the design, but had never really noticed until now. It flapped in the wind, poised to secure free passage for my vessel on the open sea. With such a short distance ahead, there would be no pirates today. I sat back and stared at the shore until it disappeared on the horizon, now just a fine, endless line of changing shades of blue.

 **THE END**

Rising Son
Reflections of a Chinese Gentleman Warrior

Illustrations

*All the following artifacts belong
to the author
Janita Lo's private collection*

THE ROYAL SCROLL

GIVEN TO MY GREAT GRAND FATHER KHAN GUNG SHUN, BY THE CH'ING DYNASTY EMPEROR, QUANGXU, SECOND YEAR OF HIS ASSENSION OF CHINA, DATED 1889

HAND ENGRAVED WRITING STAMPPED ON A SPECIAL WEAVE OF LINEN SCROLL IN SECTIONS OF BLUE, TERRA COTTA AND BEIGE BACKGROUND. THE CHINESE CHARACTERS WERE WRITTEN IN INK WITH EACH PARAGRAPH IN DIFFERENT COLORED MADE WITH VEGETABLE AND MINERAL DYE.

TITLE:
FROM THE ROYAL PALACE, THE LAW OF HEAVEN IS TO BE RESPECTED AND OBEYED

CONTENTS:

FIRST SECTION: WRITTEN IN HAN (CHINESE LANGUAGE) ROYAL IDIT DECLARING KHAN GUNG SHUN, COMMANDER OF THE ROYAL ARMY WITNESSED BY HEAVEN:

"HE IS A MAN OF INTEGRATY, HIS HIGH STANDARD VIRTUAL GLIZZENED IN THE LIGHT AND BRING BRIGHNESS AROUND OUR PLACE. IT ALL STARTED FROM THE VERY BEGINNING OF HIS ANCESTRY. HIS FAMILY TAUGHT HIM TO BECOME A SERVANT HEART, UNSHAKEN DETERMINATION FOR THE GOOD AND TRUTH, HIS DEDICATION AND HARD WORK ACCOMPANIED BY HIS ENORMOUS TALENTS AND GIFTS , WHICH WARRANTED THIS HONOR OF HIS REMARKABLE CHARACTER FROM THE EMPEROR.

THE GRAND FATHER OF KHAN TAUGHT HIS GRAND SON WITH THE HIGHEST STANDARD. TODAY, I, THE EMPEROR GIVE HONOR TO HIS GRAND FATHER WHO BROUGHT

HIM THE TRAITS OF INTEGRITY, WELL NATURE AND
A MAN WHO IS WELL LIKED AMONG HIS PEOPLE. HIS
ACCOMPLISHMENT IS CREDITED TO HIS GRAND FATHER
WHO SPARE NONE TO PROVIDE HIS HEIR THE BEST
EDUCATION AND MARTIAL ART TRAINING IN PREPARING
HIM BOTH IN HIGH LITERACY ACHIEVEMENT AS WELL AS A
FINE WORRIER WITH A MIND FILLED WITH INTELLIGENCE
AND WISDOM IN STRATEGY FOR OUR GOVERNMENT AND
ROYAL COURT MATTERS.
KHAN GUNG SHUN'S GRAND FATHER IS WORTHY OF A
NEW TITLE GRANTED BY THE EMPEROR, THE LAW OF
HEAVEN. HE SHALL BE GIVEN HONOR, WEALTH AND THE
ROYAL GARMENT WITH A FIVE SYMBOL AS AN HONORARY
KNIGHT.
THE THREE-GENERATION OF THE KHAN FAMILY SHALL
FLOURISH THROUGH OUT TIMES."

SECOND SECTION: WRITTEN IN HAN (CHINESE
LANGUAGE)

"TO THE CHA FAMILY, GRAND MOTHER OF KHAN GUNG
SHUN. THIS IS THE DAY OF CELEBRATION IN THE ROYAL
COURT. TRACE THE ANCESTRY OF THIS FAMILY FROM
ANN WHEY PROVINCE, A PRINCE WAS BROUGHT UP BY
THE WISDOM OF A GRAND MOTHER WHO PRACTICED
GOOD DEEDS. THE RELENTLESS NURTURING OF LOVE
AND LOYALTY PLANTED THE SEED FOR HER GRAND SON
TO REAP THE REWARD OF THIS PROMOTION IN OUR
ROYAL COURT. CREDITED TO CHA GRAND MOTHER'S
FINE CHARACTER AND GRACE, THE UPBRINGING OF A
VITURIOUS MAN. NOW THE MAJESTY AND THE HEAVEN
SHALL REWARD HER WITH BOUNTIFUL GIFTS, SPECIAL
FAVORS FROM THE EMPEROR AND THE EMPRESS,
ADORNING HER WITH THE RARE ROYAL SILK GARMENT.
LET HER FRAGRANCE SPREAD OUT TO ALL PLACES WHERE
EVER SHE SAT HER FOOT UPON; TO SHOW THE SPLENDID
GIFTS FROM THE EMPEROR AND THE EMPRESS.
LET PEOPLE PRAISE HER GRAND SON, KHAN GUNG SHUN

WHO GIVES HIS UTMOST OF HIS INTELLIGENCE, REFINED MIND OF LITERATURECY AND A MIGHTY SKILL OF A WARRIOR IN SERVING HIS MAJESTY THE EMPEROR. PROSPERITY SHALL FOLLOW WITH THE KHAN'S FAMILY FOR MANY GENERATIONS."

NEW TITLE OF KHAN KUNG SUN:
BLUE FEATHER ROYAL GUARD DIVISION, HIGHEST HONOR

EMPEROR QUANGXU, SECOND YEAR REIGN, JULY 4th
THE ROYAL SEAL

THE SECOND HALF OF THE SCROLL WAS WRITTEN IN MANCHURIAN LANGUAGE WITH THE SAME MESSAGE.

PAINTING BY EMPRESS CIXI DOWAGER

THE HAND PAINTED BLACK PEONY WAS PART OF THE GIFTS TO KHAN GONG SHUN.
HAND PAINTED BY EMPRESS CIXI DOWAGER

1.　Royal Scroll from Emperor Quangxu, Ch'ing Dynasty, 1876-1880. An award given to Khan Ling's grandfather, Khan Gong Shun

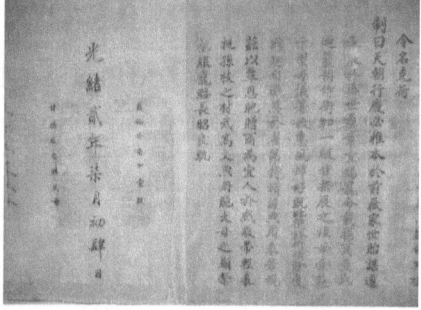

2. Detail: Title "Royal edit from the power given by heaven

3.　Detail: Script includes new title of Khan Gong Shun and the Emperor's name, date and the royal seal

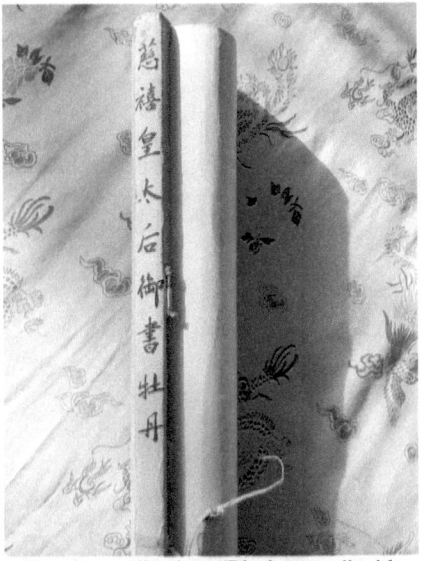

4. Royal art collection: "Black peony" with painted by Empress Cixi Dowager. This as part of the gifts to Khan Gong Shun at the celebration of the promotion of his rank at the royal palace

5. Detail: Black Peony painted on silk with Empress Cixi Dowager's seal (Signature)

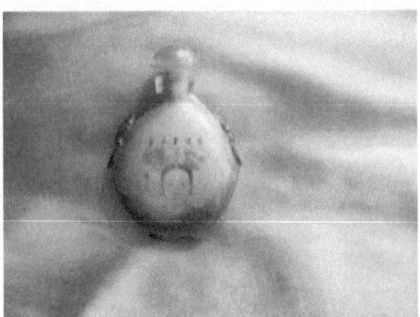

6. Snuff bottle with Empress Cixi dowager's portrait painted from the inside of the bottle

7. Opposite side of the snuff bottle with landscape painting and poem

8. Royal china collection: Bowl with the first Ch'ing Dynasty Emperor Qianglong, late 1780. The Emperor's portrait is painted inside the bowl with inscription of his earth ruling and heaven's blessing

9. Outer painting of the Emperor's bowl with writing of long life, prosperity and floral design

10. From the royal china collection: A shallow desert bowl for the Empress Cixi dowager with her portrait painted inside

11. Royal seal underneath the desert bowl with decorative designs and four charters: Good fortune, prosperity, long life and double happiness

12. Side view: Pure gold rim

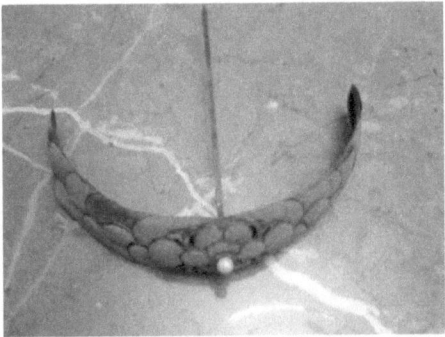

13. Kingfish feather hairpin, similar to the one of Empress Lou Yu and princess May Szee's possession

14. From the Royal china collection: A porcelain bowl with Empress Cixi's portrait painted inside. Writing of motherhood of everything under the heaven, prosperity of the country and powerful strength of the people

15. Outside of this bowl was painted with lotus blosoms and blessing charters. Royal seal At the bottom of the bowl

16. Emperor's bowl: Outside of the bowl with silver dragon and phoenix symbols over the Imperial yellow and painted designs. The silver trimming was to test if any poison food was in the bowl

17. An arranged engagement token (a red jade pendant with silver dragon and phoenix on each side, worn by Khan Bei) between Khan Bei and Chow papa, for Khan's 11-months boy   infant, who was to be engaged to Chow papa's first child if the child was a girl.. If it was a boy, they would be blood brothers. Chow Che Yu, who was still in her mother's womb, was destined to be Khan Ling's wife before she was born.

18. Red quartz bowl, laced with silver dragon and phoenix for the groom at Khan Ling's wedding

19. Green jade bowl laced with silver dragon and phoenix for the bride, Chow Che Yu's wedding

20. Emperor Quangxi and his aunt Empress Cixi dowager's royal court robes

21. Marble boat commissioned by Empress Cixi and the screen where she ruled behind two generations of the Emperor's throne

Note: Photos of #20 and #21 were from the book of Secrets Word of the Forbidden City, The Bowers Museum of Cultural Art

22. Khan Ling, Grandson of Khan Gong Shun

23. Wife, Chow Che Yu

24. Khan Ling and his wife, Chow Che Yu
Nanjing China, 1933

25. At Khan's broadcasting office
after marriage

26. Chow Che Yu's father, Chow papa

27. Left: Chow Mama, right, her sister

28. Khan Ling's Japanese mother, Namiko

29. Bamboo path to Temple at the Golden
Purple Mountain, Nanjing, China

30. Che Yu visiting the temple of the
Purple Golden Mountain by the waterfall

31. Che Yu with child being carried up in
Sadan chair to the temple

32. Eau de toilette made in Germany,
(Used by Khan Ling)

33. Khan Ling with half sister, Gooma

34. Chow Che Yu with sister Che Ying,
1933, Shanghai

35. Lower temple at foothill of Purple Golden Mountain

36. Winter scene of lower temple (Monks' lodgings and farmland)

38. Khan Ling's shipping freighter and disguised fisherman's boats

37. Khan Ling's invention of radio trans-receiver for KMT military use

39. Hai Nan Island-South China Sea, military base of commander Khan Ling ,1944

40. Khan Ling on roof terrace after riding at Happy Valley, Hong Kong

41 Khan Ling's private military (some were volunteers) sets up in Hai Nam Island

42. Khan Ling, wife, first daughter and son at Happy Valley Horse Race Track, Hong Kong. 1943

Appendix

XX

Ch'ing(Qing) Dynasty Royal Descendent:

First Emperor Jiajing:
1760-1820
5th son of Emperor Qianlong,
Accession 1796
Wife: Empress Xiao Yi,
Concubine, Empress Xiao Shu
5 Sons, 9 daughters

Emperor Daogung:
1782-1850
Accession 1821, mother: Empress Xiao Shu
Wife, 1st empress: Xiaom
2nd empress: Xiao Zguan (died 1840)
Children: 9 sons (2 died young),10 daughters

Emperor Xianfeng:
1831-1861,
4th son of Emperor Daogung
Accession:1851,mother Empress Xiao Zguan
Wife:1st empress: Niuhuru, Xiao Chen,
Dowager Ci An,died 1881
2nd empress: Xiao Qin, Yehonala family
Dowager empress Cixi, died 1908
Children:2 sons, 1 daughter

Emperor Tongzhi:
1856-1874
Accession: 1862 as Tonghi
Son of Emperor Xiafeng, mother: empress Cixi
Wife: Empress Xiao Che Alute
No children

Emperor Quangxu:
1871-1908
Accession: 1875, Second son of Prince Jun,
Mother: Cxi's younger sister
Wife: Empres Long Yu, died 1913
No children

Khan Family Descendent:

Princess May Zee: (Name changed)
1873-1909
Grand daughter of Emperor Xianfeng
Uncle: Quangxu Emperor, Aunt: Empress Long Yu
Wife to Khan Gong Shun, royal army commander

Khan Gong Shun:
1863-1898
Parent from Anhui Province,
Father and grandfather: Ginkis Khan's descendent.
Grandmother's surname: Cha
Children: One son, Khan Bei

Khan Bei:
1889-1916
First wife: No document (Deceased)
Second wife: A Japanese physician, Namiko (1892-1934)
Children: One daughter: Goo Ma, by first wife
              One son by Namiko: Khan Ling

Mr. & Mrs. Chow:
1886-1934
Children: 1st Daughter, Chow Che Yu, wife of Khan Ling
              2nd daughter Chow Che Ying
              Son by mistress: Chow Che Ming

Khan Ling:
1910-1998
Wife: Chow Che Yu, 1911-2000
Children: Daughter: Khan Chi(First Treasure)
         Son: Khan Bing (Second Treasure)
         Daughter: Khan Mai (Third Treasure,
         1938-1938, deceased in a small village west of Yangze river during
         evacuation)
         Daughter: Khan Ching (Fourth Treasure)
         Son: Khan Long (Fifth Treasure, 1942-1948, deceased
         in Shanghai)
         `Daughter: Khan Fong (Sixth Treasure)

Khan Ling Family History and Significant Dates of Events

1840-1842   Opium War

1864-1873   Prince Kong enlisted Western help against the Taiping bandits and Muslim power. Restored internal order for the Empire

1873-1909   Princess May Szee born to Emperor Xianfeng's 2nd son.

1863-1898   Khan Gong Shun was born in Anhui Province. He entered the Imperial Palace in 1887. From a peasant to a Royal Commander serving the Emperor Quangxu.

1889   Khan Gong Sun married the Princess May Szee in the second year of Emperor Quangxu's accession.

1889   Khan Bei was born in the Palace, son of Khan Gong Son and Princess May Szee

1899   Summer Palace partially restored Japan aggression to China, Sun Yes-Men founded the New Republic of China

1900   Boxer rebellion began, anti-Christian and foreigners. The hungry and poverty victims supported Rebellion group. Empress Dowager Cixi supported the Boxer movement, she declared war to eight foreign countries.

1898   Death of Khan Gong Shun. (Murdered)

1908   Death of Emperor Quangxi

1906   Khan Bei studied in Waseda University in Tokyo, Japan.

1909   Khan Bei married a Japanese nurse and settled in Nanjing. Khan Bei was a follower of Sun Yat-Sen, to form a new Republic China.

1910	Khan Ling was born in a Buddhist temple due to the riot in the city. Khan Bei died 1917 when his son was only seven years old.
1911	Che Yu was born to the Chow's family in Nanjing
1912	Republic of China was founded by Sun Yat-Sen
1914	World War I began in Europe.
1916-1919	Ling's father left funding for the monks to be Ling's caretakers, Superior Master Lou Ming who Shared the stories to Ling about his family background. Ling lived in the Temple until he was nine years old.
1917	Khan Gong Shun, ling's grand father died in Nanjing during official business, he was murdered by Empress Dowager Cixi's Enoch's scheme
1919	Conference of Versailles ending WWI
1919-1928	Mr. Tao became the caretakers for Ling. Mr. Tao was repaying the debts he owed to Ling's late father, Khan Bei.
1920	Khan met his fiancée Chow Che Yu. Khan Bei, Ling's father and Mr. Chow pre-arranged the marriage when Che Yu was still in her mother's womb in 1911.
1921	Sun Yet-Sen was elected as President of China. Communist party founded in Shanghai.
1921-1928	Khan Ling spent time with the Chow's family during holidays between the age of 11-18. He and Che Yu became great childhood friends. He was treated as part of the Chow's family members.
1929	New warlords rising in China. Stock market crashed in New York. Worldwide depression.

1929-1933   Khan studied Electrical Engineering at Waseda University, Tokyo, Japan. He stayed at his professor Hiro Saka's home in the summer. Hiro Saka later had been promoted as Admiral by The Imperial Emperor of Japan during the war between China and Japan.

1932   Japan bombed Shanghai and established Manchukuo.

1933-1935   After the wedding of Khan and Chow. Khan bought a broadcasting radio station as his cover up business. He was working with Chiang Kai-Shek fighting the Japanese underground. He often left for months on secrete missions. His wife Che Yu had to take care of a big family including their first born girl, Khan Chi, Second son Khan Bing. She single-handed took charge of the evacuation, fled from Nanjing with servants and relatives during the evacuation hardships. She took care of everyone all by herself and sold her dowry jewelry for food and transportation, she kept more than a dozen people alive and safe. Her determination for survival helped her escaping from the roadside bandits, Communist parties, Red Guards and Japanese soldiers along the Yangze River.

1934   Ling's mother Nemiko died

1937   Khan's rendezvous with the Japanese Admiral Hiro Saka and the Last Emperor Puyi in northern part of China. A significant ring of the Admiral ring was given to Ling.

1937-1938   Che Yu bored Khan Two more children. Khan Ching, the forth daughter was born two weeks after her 10-months older baby sister died of high fever during the bitter war.

1939   German invasion of Poland, WWII began in Europe.

1939   Khan was promoted to be a three star general and was in charge of the South China Sea war activities including Hong Kong, Macaw, Hainun Island and the surrounding islands.

1941   Japan bombed Pearl Harbor, US entered WWII in Asia

1943   Japan invasion of Hong Kong. Underground mission lead
         to Khan being captured by the Japanese army. His life was
         spared by the Japanese Admiral Hiro Saka. The youngest
         baby girl was born in Hong Kong, The sixth treasure,
         named Khan Fong.

1945   World war II ended, Japan surrendered. Khan released
         hundred's of Japanese prisoner of war back to Japan instead
         of tuning them in-to Chiang Kai-Shek's jurisdiction.
         Khan's family settled in Macaw.

www.janitalo.com

About the Author

Janita Lo was born in China and received her primary education in Hong Kong. Majoring in architecture at the Royal Melbourne Institute of Technology in Melbourne, Australia, she transferred to University of Houston and earned a Bachelor of Fine Arts degree in Interior Design, in 1965. She has been practicing as a professional interior designer in Houston, Texas, since 1965, with major clients such as Houston Astros Minute-Maid Park, Walt Disney World Company, Wyndham Hotel, Westin Hotel, George R. Brown Convention Center and more. Ms. Lo has been an award-winning professional interior designer in Houston, Texas since 1968. Publication and television programs of her honor award projects were both shown in trade journals and Discovery Channel.

Ms. Lo, who has always had an affinity for art and the written word, has also become established as a respected watercolor artist. Her work has won awards at a variety of exhibits and her commissioned artwork is part of various impressive private collections. It also can be publicly viewed throughout the U.S., London, Paris, Hong Kong and Malaysia.

Ms. Lo recently began writing a novel in which she regales readers with stories about her late father's extraordinary life. The significant place that Ms. Lo's family holds in both Chinese and Japanese history spurred her to produce a comprehensive account of her father's mercurial career as a military leader, adventurer, spy, inventor and successful business entrepreneur. She saw this retelling of her family's story as a way to nurture her love of writing and to recall the exploits of Khan Ling, the gentleman warrior. This remarkable narrative is based on true events, Ms. Lo has also did intensive research on historical and political archives to verify the authentication of the facts, timing, characters and locations.

Ms. Lo is planning on a sequel to "Rising Son," which follows the Khan family after the turmoil of World War II and its subsequent settling in America and became born again Christians. The author lives in Houston, Texas, surrounded by her artwork, her mementos from the Royal Chinese court and a beautiful canopy of trees viewed from the glass walls of her mid-rise home.

Collaborator Bio.

Randy Schultz is a writer "for all seasons," having established his credentials in a wide range of mediums. A Bachelor of Journalism graduate of The University of Texas at Austin, he has won more than 25 awards for his writing and creative conceptual work, which includes the full gamut of advertising and marketing, radio and television commercials, video scripts, TV, feature films, books and magazine articles.

His articles have been published in a number of respected national and international publications, regarding subjects as diverse as the Mayan culture, the Ku Klux Klan and the controversial Ash Robinson Murder Trial, to name just a few. Mr. Schultz's work has also appeared at the Atlanta Summer Olympics, the National Academy of Sciences Museum and exhibits for the World Trade Center and Sears Tower.

He currently is completing a comedy screenplay with a Hollywood director and working on a second script, based on a novel recently optioned by Mr. Schultz and his filmmaking partners.

Mr. Schultz currently lives in Los Angeles, at the foot of the Hollywood Hills, with his wife and their curious cat, Elliott.

www.ingramcontent.com/pod-product-compliance
Lightning Source LLC
Chambersburg PA
CBHW020615260626
47157CB00003B/1018